NO JUSTICE

NO JUSTICE

NO JUSTICE

No Justice Series: Book 1

NOLON KING
DAVID WRIGHT

STERLING & STONE

To YOU, the reader.
Thank you for your support.
Thank you for the wonderful emails.
Thank you for the thoughtful reviews.
Thank you for reading and loving our stories.

Chapter 1 - Mallory Black

MALLORY BLACK STARED at the endless rows of brightly colored Kewl Chik dolls — with their endless array of accessories, makeup, and hairstyles — trying her damnedest to remember the name of the specific doll her daughter had requested for her tenth birthday.

Was it Ali?

Kati?

Jessika?

Which one did Ashley ask for?

The cartoonish looking dolls technically had different styles, unique outfits, and wildly varying hair colors ranging from blonde to black to neon green and blue, but they all looked the same after a while. Mal couldn't remember which ones Ashley already had. At least twelve. She played with them, carried them around, even used them to wake Mal on occasion, but hell if she could remember any of them now.

She should've written it down, but Mal rarely had to write things. She had an almost photographic memory, which made her a great detective. But something as simple as a doll? She was coming up blank.

"Damn it," she said, louder than she meant to.

"They don't have the one you want?" said a man behind her.

Mal jumped, startled, not realizing someone had approached so quietly.

She expected to see someone in a Toys-R-Us shirt offering assistance. Instead, there was a young, slightly tanned man, handsome in casual business attire, with short brown curly hair and piercing blue eyes.

"I don't know. I can't remember the damned doll my daughter wants for her birthday."

He moved his basket of toys from one hand to the other. "Yeah, whatever happened to seven Barbies to choose from?"

She laughed. "Big Barbie fan, were you?"

"No, but my sister was. I was Team *Star Wars* all the way. So, how old is she turning?"

"Ten going on thirty. Yours?"

He showed her his perfect row of pearly whites. "Oh, I don't have one. Buying for my niece. She's turning ten, too. They grow up so fast, don't they?"

Mal nodded, looking into his basket to eye the selection. She saw a familiar looking purple-haired doll wearing a black dress and purple thigh-high boots. Her name was Ariel.

Ariel!

A lightbulb went off in her head.

"I think that's the one! Where did you get it?"

The man led her to the end of the aisle, and a peg with two remaining Ariels. She grabbed the second to last one.

"Thank you! You just saved my daughter's birthday. Well, assuming this is even the right one!"

"Glad I could help. But don't blame me if I'm wrong."

Mal laughed, then shifted her feet through an uncomfortable silence. That awkward moment where the guy was trying to conjure small talk and extend the conversation while working the courage to ask her out. Mal always showed her wedding bands — an excellent prop to wiggle out of exactly this sticky situation. The awkward guy didn't have to know that her marriage was more or less on the rocks, or that she and Ray weren't living together.

Usually, after showing the rings, one of three things would happen. The guy would sheepishly excuse himself with an apology, he'd find a witty way to persist, or he'd ignore all subtlety, dig in obnoxiously, and annoy the hell out of her.

Mal wondered which way this would go.

Then her phone rang.

Her partner, Mike Cortez, waiting in the car.

She looked at the handsome, slightly awkward man. "It's work. I've gotta take this."

The man smiled.

Mal answered the phone.

"Hey, we need to go."

"What's up?"

"Old couple found dead in their home two blocks away. Deputies waiting for us."

"What the hell?" Mal rounded the corner and saw a single checkout lane with the world's longest line.

Mal dropped her basket and ran from the store, hoping she'd be able to come back later, and that there would be at least one Ariel left.

Chapter 2 - Jasper Parish

JASPER PARISH NEEDED to hang up.

He was on the phone with Larry, one of the Crisis Hotline's regular callers for more than a year. Larry always had the same problems: nobody loves him, nobody even likes him, his mother is domineering, and he can't seem to keep a job for more than a week. Jasper felt bad for the schlub at first. While Jasper was thirty-six now, his awkward youth just paces behind him. If he hadn't found basketball, and the discipline that came with regular practice, he might never have pulled his life together, become a cop, or invested wisely enough to retire early and choose when and where to work.

But guys like Larry were too soft for sports, let alone an officer's life. He'd crumble five minutes into the Academy, then beg for his domineering mommy to take him back into her clutches. Still, Jasper could sympathize — at first.

But after hearing the same complaints for six months straight, Jasper could see why no one liked Larry. It wasn't that he was fat, ugly, or a loser, all of which were presumably true. It was because the man didn't even *try* to fix his life. You gave him advice, and he gave you excuses of why nothing would ever work *for him*. As if he were the one person in the world for whom the equation of work plus effort didn't equal results.

It was exhausting, and Jasper was practically seen as a saint for taking calls from a man who had burned out two crisis workers before Jasper started taking his calls six months ago.

He let Larry drone on about his overbearing mother and the latest drama, without really listening. Instead, Jasper stared at the clock on his cubicle desk and its slowly disappearing minutes.

He had to make another call, one far more important than this one. A call he *couldn't* miss.

He had twenty-five minutes left, but could easily see Larry going on and on for at least another thirty. And working a crisis hotline meant you could never hang up on someone, no matter how much they were annoying you.

You're right, Larry, your life does suck. You should kill yourself. Let me send you some YouTube tutorials so you won't screw that up!

As fun as that would be for Jasper to say, he couldn't quite do it. You never knew what might push people over the edge, and finally make them take their own life. Jasper had talked to countless people attempting to end their lives over things far more trivial than being hung up on by a crisis counselor.

As annoying as Larry was, Jasper didn't want him dead.

After another five minutes of listening to him blather on about his mother, Jasper finally had enough.

"Hey, Larry. I understand what you're going through. And like I said, *you* give your mother the power you think she has over you. You can take that power back by standing up for yourself. Right?"

"Right," Larry agreed, clearly disappointed.

"Larry," Jasper seized the moment, "I've got to ask you a favor if you don't mind."

Guys like Larry never minded. They *liked* doing favors. It gave them some of that recognition their regular lives failed to give them.

"There's a situation at home that requires my attention. Sort of an emergency. But I'll be back in about an hour. Can I call you then?"

Larry paused, probably trying to decide if he was being given the short shrift.

"I wouldn't ask you normally, Larry. But you can understand where I'm coming from, what with family stuff. Right?"

"Yeah, no problem," Larry said, his voice a bit more ebullient.

"Great. Thanks, man. I appreciate it."

"Sure thing."

Larry hung up, and then Jasper put in a quick call to Marcy, who oversaw the hotline's seven-person team. "Hey, I'm sorry, something's come up, and I need to cut out. Is that okay? I'll be back in about forty minutes or so."

"Yeah, is everything okay?"

"It should be if I take care of it."

He didn't bother explaining what 'it' was, figuring Marcy would understand. And she did.

"Thanks."

Jasper hung up then signed out of his computer, grabbed his backpack off the ground under his desk, and quickly left, waving at a few of the other counselors on calls, looking up at him as he eased by their cubicles.

Jordyn was waiting in the parking lot, leaning against his car, arms folded, her black duster hanging over purple leggings that *exactly* matched the purple streaks in her jet-black hair.

"Sheesh, what took you so long?" his daughter asked.

"Larry."

She rolled her eyes as seventeen-year-old girls were particularly masterful at doing. "That loser? What did he want? To whine about his mommy some more?"

Jasper unlocked the car, opened his door, and climbed inside. Jordyn joined him, plopping down in the passenger seat, putting her black boots up on the dashboard.

"I really shouldn't tell you stuff about these people. Especially if you're gonna make fun of them."

"Sorry. But come on, if you didn't tell me, who would you tell? You need *someone* to unleash all that crazy on, or else it stays stuck in your head."

Jasper backed out of his spot. "Fair point."

"So, why'd you call me?"

"I need to know ... are you sure?"

"About the cop's kid? Yeah. Why?"

"I'm calling her."

"What?"

"We need to warn her."

"You *sure* you wanna do that? It's not like we can change what's going to happen."

And it was true. Jasper had tried to intervene on five separate occasions, tried to stop her visions from coming true. He'd failed *every time*.

"Maybe we can't stop it," Jasper said, meeting Jordyn's gaze. "But shouldn't we try? Wouldn't you want to know if *your* kid was in danger?"

"I'm not having kids. Kids gross me out."

"You know what I mean. If you did have a kid, you'd want to know if someone was going to kidnap her, wouldn't you?"

"I guess," Jordyn sighed. "But I still think it's dangerous for us to be calling the cops about anything."

"It's not like I'm using *my* phone. I have burners. I'll warn her then ditch it."

"You don't think she's gonna be curious as to *how* you know what's going to happen to her daughter? Won't she think you are part of it?"

"It won't matter. It's not like I'm gonna tell her my name. I call, warn her, then hang up."

Jordyn said nothing.

"Come on; I raised you better than that. I know you're not nearly as cold as you're pretending to be."

"Am too." She tried to scowl, but was mostly grinning.

Jasper laughed. "See, I knew it. You can act cool around your friends, but you can't fool your father."

"Whatever," she said, crossing her hands over her chest and staring out the window. "So, where are we going?"

"I wanted to put distance between work and where we make the call. Triangulation and all."

"Ah, right," she nodded.

Though Jordyn was still a sweetheart acting tough on the outside, she was a cool daughter. How many teenage girls voluntarily hung out with their dad? Or had visions that showed them things that were going to happen?

"So, I suppose you have to *work* late tonight?"

"Yeah," he said, ignoring the way she twisted the word *work*. "Got another job."

"I'm not stupid, Dad."

"What do you mean?"

"You can tell me if you're seeing someone. It's not like Mom would've minded. Hell, she'd want you to be dating. It's been six years."

"I'm not seeing anyone. I have a job."

She looked at him skeptically.

Of course, he couldn't tell her the truth.

Not yet.

She was too young to know the things he did to make the world a safer place. And maybe too sensitive to know that he used her visions to select his targets.

"All of your clients just happen to have cases you need to work on at night?"

"You go where the work is, no matter the time."

"I still don't get why you're working all the time. It's not like we need the money."

This was Jordyn's way of reminding him that her visions had also allowed them to invest wisely in the market. They weren't stupid rich, but they sure as hell didn't need to punch a clock.

"I like being able to help people."

She didn't need to know that he hadn't taken a new case in nearly six months, or what he was really doing late at night. While he still had a license as a private investigator, and still technically worked for the law firm that had employed him when he moved here, Jasper was on a sabbatical, one he didn't plan to ever return from. His investments were paying off even better than he'd hoped. Soon, he'd never have to work again.

Then, he could devote all of his time to his Purpose.

"So why work at the call center? You hate it. And they don't pay shit."

He lifted a finger. "That's a dollar in the swear jar when we get home."

She laughed. "Seriously, though, you don't need to work anymore. I'll be out and on my own soon, and you'll wish you spent more time with your adorable, funny, perfect daughter."

She laughed, but there was truth in her jest.

And how could he justify the night job, and the call

center gig, over spending time with her, especially when he didn't *need* to work?

But his Purpose wasn't just work. It was a calling, and he couldn't expect Jordyn to understand when he couldn't even tell her what he did once the sun went down.

"Okay," he said, not sure if he meant it. "I'll slow things down at work."

She smiled. "Thank you."

He stopped at a park which he knew had no security cameras and looked at his cell, hesitating. His earlier try had gone to voicemail.

And Jasper didn't want to leave anything on record.

The last thing he needed was a direct line back to him, which could then lead to Jordyn. Deputies would appear at work or home, asking, "How did you know about the kidnapping?"

And what could he say?

Jasper didn't know the name of the man who was going to do it. He didn't know exactly when it would happen, other than *later today*. Nor did he have anything credible to offer as proof.

They'd either think he was a crackpot or, if the kidnapping occurred as predicted, they'd think him complicit.

But that was better than them knowing about Jordyn's gift.

It was Jasper's job to keep that gift a secret from those who would exploit it.

There were secret government entities devoted to developing Jordyn's gift. If anyone discovered that she could glimpse into the future, they'd take her, lock her in some underground black site lab, and pick her apart until they could replicate her ability for themselves. Then turn it into a weapon.

Until now, he'd operated in the shadows.

And while his phone wasn't traceable, and he'd put distance between himself and his work and home, he'd have to leave his voice if she didn't answer.

And his voice was a path they could trace to him.

He wished he'd thought to look into a voice changer. But Jordyn's vision had come last night, with no time to plan or do things the right way.

He had two choices: allow the kidnapping, or risk his daughter's welfare to save the child.

Jasper looked at Jordyn, leaning against the car, training her phone's camera on a crane, walking stealthily as a giant white bird ambled toward something in the bushes. Jordyn was into photography, and often gave her favorite pictures some clever name that sounded cooler than what was actually happening. A stork stalking an insect might be called, "Stealthy Long Legs Slithering Sneakily."

He encouraged her photography bug, but the years had given Jordyn a number of hobbies, none lasting more than a few months, so he didn't encourage it enough to purchase expensive equipment.

Jordyn looked back at Jasper. "You gonna stand there all day, or you gonna call?"

He nodded, then dialed Mallory Black.

Voicemail again.

He hung up. "Shit."

Jasper looked at his watch: *2:05 P.M.*

He had the distinct feeling that he was running out of time.

His heart raced as he weighed options against a ticking clock. No matter how many times he tried telling himself that he had more than one choice, he always came back to the same one: *Leave a message.*

He dialed.

The message played.

Then the beep.

He took a deep breath, then said the thing he'd been working himself up to say since this morning.

"Hello, Mallory Black. You don't know me and have no reason to trust what I'm about to tell you, but your daughter is in danger. She's going to be kidnapped today. I can't tell you how I know. But I do. And you must act quickly if you expect to save her."

He hung up, his heart racing.

Jordyn approached, hands stuffed deep into her dusters pockets. "Well? Did you do it?"

"Yeah."

Jordyn raised her phone and snapped a photo of Jasper.

"What are you going to call that?"

"Far-Sighted Father Fucking Up."

"Swear jar," he said, hoping she wasn't right.

Chapter 3 - Mallory Black

MAL AND MIKE pulled up to the house on Bleaker, to see the usual spectacle when something bad happened on a suburban street. Patrol cars kissed the curb, an ambulance waited, and practically every neighbor stood outside, some on their lawns, others clustered together, trying to eye the crime scene and speculating about what might be happening.

Mal scanned the neighbors looking for anyone out of place, like someone returning to the crime scene to watch things unfold.

Not seeing anyone too unusual, she followed Mike to the rear of the house where they met the officer who was called out after a neighbor reported seeing a broken window in the back yard.

The deputy, a patrolman named Steve Billings, briefed them.

"Neighbor saw the broken bedroom window, and some blood outside the window, then called it in. The Horowitz's were supposed to be on vacation as of yesterday, so a broken window is obviously suspicious. My partner and I arrived on scene, looked in the window and saw nothing, then went around to the sliding glass doors looking into the kitchen. That's where we saw the bodies. We went inside to see if we could administer help, but it was too late. Then we called it in."

"Thank you." Mike slipped on his gloves and shoe covers to keep the scene uncontaminated for the evidence technicians who would be following behind them taking photographs and collecting evidence.

Mal did the same, then followed Mike inside.

The elderly couple was dead on the kitchen floor, dressed in their pajamas, breakfast on the table, half-eaten.

The woman appeared to have six to eight stab wounds in her chest. Her husband's face had been hit with something blunt, probably the blood-soaked cast iron skillet lying on the ground beside him.

As Mal bent to observe the spatter patterns, she remembered the blood outside the bedroom window.

She went back outside, removed the shoe coverings and slipped them in her jacket, and examined the broken window.

This was how the killer entered the house. He broke the window and probably cut himself going in or out. She could go back inside and see if there was blood in there, but at the moment that didn't matter.

She looked around on the grass beneath the window. St. Augustine grass was dry, like it usually was in October as colder air came to claim Northern Florida.

And there she saw it, drops of blood leading away from the window.

Mal followed the trail. Just a few drops every few feet, not a gushing wake, but surely enough to work with.

The drops formed an intermittent trail, snaking around

the home's side and into the front yard before dying in the middle of the street.

Mal looked up and down the road, past the patrol cars and police tape, toward the congregating neighbors. There were people in front of several houses, older folks who made up a large part of this area, a few stay-at-home moms with their kids, and a handful of adults in their thirties who worked from home, or maybe were unemployed.

An old woman with thick-framed glasses stood next door to Mal's right, waving, likely wanting to get her attention, and the inside scoop.

Mal ignored her, looking up and down the street, seeing who stood in front of what yard, then eyed the houses where no one was standing. Some belonged to people who weren't home. It was the middle of the day, after all.

But one house, three doors down and across the street, caught Mal's attention. It had three cars in the driveway. With three cars, surely *someone* was home. And yet, no one was outside.

It was an older house with an unkempt yard and every shade drawn.

Mal wondered if any of the bystanders belonged to the home. Or were the residents inside and ignoring the commotion?

Mal approached an old lady next door.

"Hello, Ma'am."

"Hello, officer. What happened?"

"We're investigating now. I was hoping you could help me."

The woman leaned forward, conspiratorially, and in a thick Boston accent said, "How can I help?"

"That house there," Mal pointed toward the trio of vehicles, "do you see the owners anywhere?"

The old lady looked up and down the street. "No. They're probably inside."

"And did you see them today, at all?"

"No. I was on the Skype with my grandkids earlier."

"What can you tell me about them?"

"Oh, nothing but trouble, those folks."

"Yeah? Why is that?"

The old lady lowered her voice. "All three of 'em are trailer trash. The only one that works is the father, but he's a trucker and almost never home. Mom and her son just sit in the house and get drunk all day, it seems. And they're always fighting."

"How old is her son?"

"Thirty-one and still living at home! Get a job!"

The woman waved her hands as if to shoo the son away, her face filled with revulsion.

Mal smiled. "What else can you tell me about him?"

"What's there to tell? He's a loser. Always drunk, been locked up a few times for petty theft, possession, and who knows what else? A real piece of work from what I hear. Hasn't had a job in years. Cops have been to their place at least twenty times for noise disturbances. They ought to kick him out."

"Thank you," Mal said.

"Did that loser have anything to do with this?"

"I don't know yet, but I appreciate your help."

Mal walked away from the woman, returned to Mike, then radioed in for a bloodhound.

MAL AND MIKE stayed behind the bloodhound and his officer.

The canine sniffed at the trail, following the blood right back to the three vehicles and the house behind them.

"Wow, you so called this," Mike said as they approached the front door.

Mal knocked.

A fat woman answered. In her 50s, wearing sweats, a T-shirt that looked more like a muumuu, and her hair in a ponytail. A long cigarette hung sideways from her mouth.

She had the worn expression of someone used to opening the door to sheriff's deputies. "Yeah?"

Mike took lead — he was always more charming with the ladies.

"Hello, ma'am, we're investigating a break-in across the street, and our dog here is on the trail of something. Would you mind if we came inside looked around?"

The woman, whose name was Eunice Brandon, and whose son was named, no shit, Benny Brandon, let out a small sigh then opened the door.

Instead of asking any questions, she returned to her kitchen and whatever she had on the stove.

Mal looked at Mike, who shrugged.

Mal told the bloodhound and his handler to hang tight at the front door.

Inside they were immediately overwhelmed by the acrid stench from years of cigarette smoke, caking the walls and ceiling in yellow. The home was dark and messy, with threadbare, stained carpet, holes in the walls, and furniture that a thrift shop wouldn't touch.

The living room was in the back, where Benny Brandon's 6' 7" and 400 pounds were stuffed into a sagging recliner watching TV, hands shoved into his jacket pocket. The TV, a giant 55-inch flat screen, was cranked close to 100, blasting a wrestling match with thumping music, angry men in a faux argument, and eager crowds waiting to see some man-on-man in spandex action, even if the shit was faker than Jerry Springer.

Mal and Mike entered the living room. Benny stared at the screen, engrossed.

Mal made a point of passing in front of the television on her way to look out the back door, as if she were searching for something.

Usually, when you went poking around someone's house, they would demand to know what you were looking for. Or at least they'd acknowledge you. When you walked in front of the TV, a person would crane their neck to look around you.

But Benny's droopy eyes stared straight ahead.

He might've thought he was playing cool, but he looked like a jackal.

Mal had to be careful, especially given his size. Benny might be a fat pile of shit, but that didn't mean he wasn't dangerous.

His hands were still buried in his pockets.

Mal finally spoke. "Hey, Benny."

"Hey," he said, not looking at her, as if it were customary for the sheriff's department to pass through his living room.

"We're looking into a break-in across the street and talking to neighbors. Seen anything suspicious today?"

"Nah. Been watchin' TV."

"Ah, okay," Mal said.

She returned to the front porch and asked the handler to come inside.

The bloodhound began sniffing at the carpet, moving forward.

Neither Eunice nor Benny seemed to notice.

The hound led them to the bathroom, then jumped into the shower, sniffing at the drain and barking.

Mal looked at Mike and whispered, "I'm thinking he came home and washed the blood in the shower."

Mike nodded.

So did the handler.

Mal thanked the deputy, then asked him to wait outside and returned to the living room. Benny was still sitting there like an imbecile, glued to his wrestling match, left hand out of his pocket and sitting on his lap, but the right still concealed. He was definitely hiding it.

Mal tried to imagine how he got his entire fat frame through the window, and couldn't quite work it out, but if she could get a look at his right hand, she'd probably find the wound that proved he was there.

"Well, I can't find what we're looking for. Thanks for your time, Benny."

She approached him, working out which of her hands would get him offering his right. She extended her left, and immediately realized her error.

Shit!

She shook Benny's left hand, a large and sweaty paw, thanked him again, then started to leave.

She slowed her pace, trying to think of a reason to turn back. Then, with a glance at the TV, she asked, "Is this one of those pay-per-view matches?"

"Nah. It's from the weekend. I DVR'd it."

His eyes were nervous. The last thing Mal wanted was for this to get ugly inside his house. He could have a gun in the cushion.

"And isn't that short guy the one on those pizza commercials?" she asked, vaguely remembering him from TV.

"Yeah, that's him. His name is Bobo Bomber Clinton."

"Bobo Bomber?" Mal asked, laughing.

"That's his nickname because he likes to do a diving

elbow drop on his opponents. Little guys like that don't got power moves, so they go aerial."

Mal was surprised how cogently he spoke about the sport. She engaged him further, asking questions about different wrestling styles and who his favorite wrestler was, along with a bunch of other stuff that no girl had probably ever asked Benny before.

He was animated as he spoke, with a light in his eyes that surprised her.

How the hell can he be going on like this? Did he forget that he just murdered two old people?

A smarter suspect wouldn't be nearly as into the conversation. They'd be worrying where this was all going, or when the other shoe might be dropping. But not Benny Brandon.

She glanced over at Mike. He was smiling in either admiration or mockery. She'd probably hear no end of wrestling conversation for the next three months.

After the conversation died, Mal reached out her hand, this time the right one, and thanked Benny again.

His right hand came out, heavily bandaged.

"Oh," she said, shaking, "what happened to your hand?"

His nervous eyes flitted away from hers. "I cut it earlier."

"Ah, hate when that happens."

Mal turned to leave, then spun around one final time. "Oh, I almost forgot. Can I talk to you outside for a moment?" She gave a sideways glance to the kitchen as if she wanted to ask Benny something in private, away from his mother. Dumb fuck probably thought she wanted to ask him out.

"Uh, sure," he said, following Mal outside.

Once outside, Mike prepared himself behind Benny, just in case force was necessary.

Mal pointed to the Horowitz home. "How well do you know the Horowitz's?"

Benny looked down, shuffling his feet. "Not too well."

"Would you mind coming with us to the station where we can discuss it further?"

He looked at her, confused. "Is that necessary?"

She nodded, holding her friendly smile. "Yeah, Benny, I'm afraid so."

~

BENNY SAT in the interview room across from Mal, fidgeting in his seat. They hadn't cuffed him nor read him his rights yet. Just some friendly questioning. Mal even made a point of leaving the door open behind her.

From behind the two-way mirror, Mike was watching, maybe along with her boss, Sheriff Gloria Bell.

One of Mal's favorite parts of the job was questioning suspects, getting them to lower their guard and confess to the crime. Reading people was one of her strengths, and something she was proud of. She figured Benny for a pushover. A troubled kid, even though in his thirties, with several drug arrests, some disturbing the peace, and a few fights with his parents to litter his rap sheet.

But he wasn't evil.

Then again, neither were most people she sat across from in an interview room.

Their situation was often a combination of a crappy childhood and parents who didn't give a shit, usually from broken homes with abusive family members. They were junkies more often than not, with a recent uptick in opiate and heroin abuse. A poor upbringing plus a lack of lucky breaks and too many poor choices could make otherwise good people fall into some terrible things.

She figured that was the situation with Benny.

It was this sympathy, this ability to appreciate the suspect's plight, to make them see her as someone who understood them, that got most people talking.

Mal put her hands on the table, palms down.

"Listen, Benny, I like you, so I'm gonna shoot straight. Can I do that?"

He met her eyes.

His lip was trembling.

He was swallowing a lot. She wasn't sure if it was a nervous tic or if he was experiencing some sort of withdrawal.

"Yeah."

"We've got people who saw you go in their house earlier. Saw you climbing in the window and cutting yourself."

His face looked on the verge of collapsing.

"Now you seem like a nice guy, Benny. I saw your rap sheet, and it looks like you've just had a lot of bad breaks. Am I right?"

He nodded. "Yes, ma'am."

"You never meant any harm. You were just trying to get by. And it's not easy these days, I know. I see a lot of heinous shit, let me tell you. Plenty of good people forced to do terrible things."

Mal nodded as she spoke.

Benny mirrored her.

"I'm thinking you didn't mean to kill them. That something went wrong. Am I right?"

He looked down at the table, his face twisted in anguish, fighting tears.

"It's okay, Benny. I'm here. You can tell me what happened. I'll help you work things out."

He met her eyes, then broke down crying.

She waited.

Finally, he said, "They weren't supposed to be there. They were supposed to be on vacation."

He continued, telling her that he only wanted money for Oxycontin. He never meant to hurt them, but they'd caught him breaking in. They'd recognized him and were going to call the police.

"I'm so sorry," he bawled. "They were nice people. They didn't deserve this."

Mal listened. The camera recorded Benny's confession.

Times like this, when the killer showed actual remorse, Mal felt terrible. It would've been easier interviewing a stone-cold killer than someone like Benny — someone who never really had a chance. Someone who started from Go with shitty parents, no support system, and a learning disability that got him bullied in school.

Guys like Benny didn't go on to become *productive members of society.* They ended up on the fringes, doing whatever they could to cope or get by. Perhaps the cruelest twist was that Benny was confessing because of Mal's kindness and mercy, or her pretending to be kind and merciful to extract that confession.

It was hard not to wonder how his life, or the lives of any number of people she'd interviewed over the year, might have turned out differently had they experienced a genuine kindness or mercy earlier in their lives—before it was too late.

Still, no matter how bad Benny's life had been, and regardless of his blame, there was never any excuse for murder.

He chose each of his wrong decisions.

Plenty of people had it worse than Benny and managed not to murder anyone.

She flashed back on the Horowitz's bodies, then looked at the hands that had committed those crimes.

Anyone capable of that didn't deserve to be free, and it was her job to put Benny behind bars.

~

MIKE MET with Mal in the hallway after the interview. "That's some good work in there, partner."

"Thanks."

"But don't think I'm letting that wrestling thing go. Hmm, what would your wrestling name be? Mad Dog Mal?"

She lifted her left hand and extended her middle finger.

Mal felt a buzz in her pocket.

She didn't recognize the number, but saw that it had called earlier and that whoever it was hadn't bothered to leave a message. She let the number go to voicemail.

"I hate this phone," she said, dropping it in her pocket.

"What's going on?"

"Remember how I got that new iPhone and the new number?"

"Yeah. I told you to get an Android."

"Yeah, screw that. Anyway, I keep getting bill collectors looking for whoever had the number before me, some bitch named Allison."

"Bitch?" Mike laughed.

"Yeah, she has like twenty different creditors looking for her ass."

"Yeah, fuck her, then."

Mal remembered what she was doing three hours ago before they got the call about the Horowitz's.

"Shit. I forgot about the doll. Can you start the paperwork while I run back to the toy store for Ashley's gift? They only had two left."

"Yeah, no problem, Mad Dog."

Mal flipped him off with a smile that Mike couldn't see.

Chapter 4 - Ashley Black

"DID you invite Dante to your birthday party?"

"*Noooo,*" Ashley said, turning to wrinkle her nose at Rebecca. They were halfway home, and her best friend was getting annoying. "Why would I invite him?"

"Because you like him, idiot."

"Do not," Ashley said, feeling her face getting hot.

"Oh my God, you are such a liar!" Rebecca said, laughing.

"Shut up." Ashley punched her lightly in the arm.

"Besides, he doesn't even like me. He likes Brooke."

"No, he doesn't. He told Carrie Vartan that he can't stand Brooke."

"Really?" Ashley said. "I've seen them hanging out like *allll* the time."

"I'm just tellin' you what I heard. Whatever. So, is your mom doing cake or cupcakes?"

"I think she's getting cupcakes from that new place."

"Cool. My mom took us there last week. It's *so* pretty."

Ashley had been looking forward to this weekend for

months, ever since her mom said she could have her birthday at the Algonquin.

Ashley's friend, Brianna, had a birthday there last year, and it was the most amazing place, with fancy food and a room where you could dance. It was also going to be the biggest party that Ashley had ever had. She was allowed to invite fifteen people — five more than the ten she had at her seventh birthday.

"Will your dad be there?" Rebecca asked.

"Yes."

"That's cool. My dad had to work and couldn't come to my birthday last year."

"That stinks."

"It's okay. He felt guilty. That's why I got my iPhone."

Ashley laughed. "Well, as much as I'd like an iPhone, I want my dad to come more."

"Divorce sucks."

"They're not divorced!" Ashley argued. "I hate it when you say that."

"Sorry," Rebecca said, looking at her shoes. "I'm sure they'll get back together."

Ashley wanted to walk the rest of the way home alone. She didn't like when Rebecca wanted to talk about the "D" word. Her parents had separated two years ago, then divorced last year, right before her birthday.

But Ashley's parents weren't like Rebecca's.

For one, they rarely fought, and Rebecca's fought all the time.

For two, they were still friends. They talked on the phone almost every night. You didn't do that if you hated the other person. Friends could still work out their problems — whatever they were.

Ashley had asked both of them why they broke up five

months ago, and they both always said the same thing, as if rehearsed.

We just need some time to figure things out.

Ashley turned to Rebecca. "Yeah, they just need to work things out." After a long pause, she added, "Being an adult is confusing. I think after this weekend, I'm going to stay ten forever."

Neither of them spoke for a while, walking along the busy road beside the park. They were about three blocks from their street, but neither was in a hurry. Ashley's mom wouldn't be home until around six, and Rebecca wasn't in a rush to deal with her mom, who'd been crabby all week.

Ashley took in the oaks and maples lining the street, leaves changing color, though not yet autumn's prettier oranges, yellows, and reds. A cool breeze blew through her long blonde hair. Ashley inhaled, smiling. She loved the first cool days of fall because they reminded her of happier times, dressing up for Halloween and trick-or-treating with her parents, Thanksgiving, then Christmas with her family.

She couldn't help but be happy when the weather started to change.

She wondered how different this year's holidays were going to be.

"Hey," Rebecca said, pointing to a car, slowing on the next street. "You know him?"

Ashley looked up and saw a black sedan. It looked like the undercover cars that the sheriff's department sometimes used. A dome light sat on the dash, though it wasn't turned on.

It slowed to a stop fifteen feet away.

The tinted window rolled down revealing a good-looking young man in a deputy's uniform and hat.

"Ashley?" he said with a kind smile.

"Yeah." Her stomach was a nest of angry hornets,

wondering if something awful had happened to her mother.

"I'm Deputy Michaels. Your mom sent me to pick you up."

"What's wrong?" Ashley stepped closer to the car, with Rebecca right behind her.

"Your teacher didn't tell you?"

"Tell me what?"

"Oh, man. Your mom was supposed to call the school and tell you to wait for me."

"Why? What's wrong?"

"I can't say too much right now, but you might be in danger."

"Danger? What's going on?"

"Your mom will have to tell you."

"Where is she?"

"She can't leave right now. That's why she wanted me to come get you."

"I dunno." Yes, he was a cop, but Ashley didn't know him. And technically, that made him a stranger.

The officer held up a finger, said "Hold on a second," then leaned over and picked something up.

A second later he was holding up a doll. A Kewl Chik. Ariel. The one she'd been begging her mother for.

"She told me to give you this, an early birthday gift."

Ashley smiled and ran to the car.

Deputy Michaels smiled and handed her the box.

Rebecca followed, keeping some distance. "Come on, Ash, let's go home."

She looked at the deputy with his kind eyes and friendly smile. "How far away is my mom?"

"About ten minutes, if we drive."

She looked into the car, saw the radio just like the one

in her mom's car, and a bulky black laptop just like the one her mom always carried.

He also had a Creek County Sheriff's Office badge on his uniform.

Still, Ashley couldn't be sure he was who he said he was.

"Can I see your ID?"

"Sure thing, kid." He smiled then reached into his pocket, pulled out a wallet, which had both his name, Andrew Michaels, and a Sheriff's Department ID, just like her mom's.

"Can you give my friend a ride home?"

Deputy Michaels smiled and said, "Sure. Hop in the back."

Chapter 5 - Mallory Black

MAL WAS DRIVING to the toy store when her phone rang again.

She looked at the number — the same collection agency that had called her at least a dozen times already.

Before the woman could get out two words, Mal said, "What's your name?"

"Excuse me?"

"I asked for your name. You keep calling my number, even though I've told you all dozens of times that this is a new number, and that I'm not Allison. And I've asked that you change your contact info so I stop getting her calls, but nobody listens. So I'd like your name and a number I can reach you at, so the next time one of you calls, I know whose ass to chew out."

The woman gave her name, then apologized and promised to remove Mal's number from Allison's contact info.

"Thank you," Mal said, then hung up, knowing damned well that she'd be having this same conversation again in a few days, if not tomorrow.

She swung into the toy store's parking lot and was about to get out of the car when she remembered her waiting voicemail, from the number she didn't recognize. Her annoying calls were usually out of state.

But that number had been local.

She wondered if maybe it was one of the parents responding to the birthday invites she and Ashley had sent out last week.

Mal pressed *Play*, and a man's voice filled her ear:

"Hello, Mallory Black. You don't know me and have no reason to trust what I'm about to tell you, but your daughter is in danger. She's going to be kidnapped today. I can't tell you how I know. But I do. And you must act quickly if you expect to save her."

Her heart racing, Mal looked at the time on the phone.

Ashley should be walking in the door any minute.

She called home, but it went to voicemail.

"Ashley, hon, are you there? I need you to call me the second you get this."

She waited, expecting her daughter to pick up any second, perhaps out of breath from running inside.

But there was no response.

Mal stared at the phone, unsure of whom to call.

This has to be a joke, some sick prank or something.

Has to be.

She looked up Rebecca's number and dialed.

Come on, come on.

"Hello?"

Thank God!

"Rebecca, it's Mrs. Black. Is Ashley with you?"

"No, a sheriff's deputy picked us up on the way home from school. He just dropped me off. He's bringing her to you now."

"A sheriff's deputy? Who?"

"Um … Deputy Michaels."

Deputy Michaels? There isn't any deputy named Michaels on the force.

"Deputy Michaels? Are you sure?"

"Yeah."

"And you're *sure* he was with Creek County Sheriff's Department? He wasn't a police officer out of Butler? Was his uniform green or blue?"

Green was Creek County. Cops in Butler wore blue.

"Green. He said he worked with you, and that you asked him to pick her up, that something big was going down."

Mal couldn't breathe.

Her heart felt like it would explode.

It was all she could do to keep talking.

She asked Rebecca to tell her *exactly* what had happened, step-by-step.

Rebecca got to the part of the "officer" pulling up, and Mal asked if he was driving a sheriff's car.

"No, it was one of those black cars, with a little light thingee on the dashboard."

"And you all just got in the car with him?"

"Yeah, he showed us his ID. What's wrong, Mrs. Black?"

"What did he look like?"

"Um, I dunno. Handsome. Brown hair, blue eyes. He had a nice smile."

"Did you happen to get a picture of him?"

"Why would I do that?"

"I don't know! Shit. Did he say *where* he was taking Ashley?"

"He said he was bringing her to you."

"Yeah, I got that, but did he say *where?*"

"No," Rebecca said, her voice rising as if realizing what had happened and now near tears.

"I have to go. If you hear from Ashley, have her call me. *You* call me. Do anything you can to find out where she is, okay?"

"Okay, Mrs. Black."

Mal hung up.

Her mind was dust in a storm.

This couldn't be happening.

There had to be some explanation.

Mal thought of the voicemail. A warning sent more than an hour ago.

The warning she ignored because she thought it was a marketer.

No, no, no.

She called her boss.

Gloria answered.

"Sheriff, it's Mal. Did you have anyone pick my daughter up?"

"Um, no. Why?"

"I think Ashley's been kidnapped."

Two Years Later

Chapter 6 - Paul Dodd

PAUL DODD STOOD in Target's greeting card section trying to decide between the *Happy 10th Birthday* card with the puppy covered in frosting, which would make Jessi laugh, or the princess from that Disney movie she liked.

He reached up and scratched under his baseball cap, debating the merits of both cards.

He went with the dog, because animals covered in frosting was always a win. Besides, Jessi could use a pick-me-up, and the envelope came in a nice, almost comforting orange.

He headed to the girl's clothing department but had no luck finding something that felt right. Outfits for Jessi's age range were either too revealing or didn't seem like her style.

Since it was October, Paul went to the rear of the store where there was a bigger selection. And there he found the perfect princess costume. White and puffy, with pink and purple frills. The same dress worn by the girl in the movie. No, it wasn't something you'd wear every day, but it was her tenth birthday, a special occasion, and he was certain she'd love the dress.

Paul held it up, trying to decide if the new dress was the right size, when he thought again about the card with the dog covered in frosting.

If I get the dress, I ought to get the card that matches.

He gingerly set the dress in the front of his cart, then went back to the front of the store, found the slot to return the dog card and its orange envelope, then traded it for the princess card. It was pretty and girly. Jessi would love it.

Paul took his items to the checkout, got in line, patiently waiting as the older-than-dirt cashier rang up enough bags of large dog food to outlast the apocalypse. The woman in front of him was disgustingly obese, wearing jean shorts, with ugly tattoos running the length of every limb. She was also wearing flip-flops, and the edges of her feet were dry, like cracked earth baking under the sun.

He backed up, a couple of inches, certain the woman also stank.

Paul watched the old lady struggle to lift the bag and locate the barcode. Then he looked at the thoughtless pig of a woman, wondering how someone could be so cruel as to get into the oldest cashier's line and pile ten bags, which probably weighed fifty pounds each, onto the conveyor. There were four other lanes open, each with a younger person who could've handled the bags without any problem.

"I only need the one," the old lady said, after finally scanning the first bag's code.

The pig in front of Paul said, "Oh," then proceeded to put the bags back into her cart, before rummaging through a crap-filled purse. "Hold on. I've got a coupon for that."

You've got to be kidding me.

She finally found her coupons and handed them to the old lady, who raised it to her eyes, squinting to read the fine print.

"I'm sorry, ma'am, but these coupons expired last year."

"Oh, come on," the pig said. "I come in here all the time, and nobody ever gives me a problem."

"Sorry. I can't ring up expired coupons."

"I want to see your manager."

The old lady sighed, reached behind her register, and flicked a button that turned on the red light to indicate that she needed assistance.

The pig looked back at Paul, not to apologize for the delay caused by her unreasonable demand, or for her self-ishness, but rather to remark, "Can you believe this shit?"

Everything about this woman disgusted Paul.

"No," he said, matter-of-factly. "I can't."

The woman smiled, not sensing his disdain. If she could see through Paul's shades, there would be no mistaking his eyes. She thought she had a comrade. Hell, she was probably turned on. Paul was used to women flirting, even hogs like this one. He found it amusing that woman approached him. It was as if God were playing some cruel joke, never sending the right ones his way.

The manager came over, heard the woman's complaints, as the cashier stood helplessly by, probably wishing she'd saved for retirement.

The manager also refused the coupon.

And the woman threw a fit.

Unable to take any more, Paul said, "Excuse me, how much is the coupon for?"

"Fifty cents off two bags."

All this over five bucks?

He reached into his pocket, handed the cashier a Five, and said, "Here. Apply this to her bill."

Everyone was looking at Paul. He immediately wished he hadn't done anything. He hated attention, and had surely angered the swine.

But the pig wasn't mad. Instead, she was all smiles, as if he'd bought her a drink. "Thank you. It's good to see that there are still some gentlemen left in this world."

She said that as if it was some kind of burn on the Target employees refusing her coupon.

After the hog was gone, the old lady thanked Paul for his patience.

"No, it's you who should be thanked for yours." And, since the front end manager was still standing by, he added, "I don't know what this lady makes, but you ought to give her a raise for dealing with people like that."

The manager laughed.

Paul paid for his stuff with cash and then left.

Outside, the boar came toward him in a big SUV.

She rolled down her window. "Thanks, honey."

"No problem."

She looked him up and down. "Wanna get a drink some time?"

Paul couldn't stifle his laugh. He was amazed at how badly she was misreading the situation.

Well, now she wasn't.

Her eyebrows arched. "What's so funny?"

"Sorry, ma'am. But no thank you."

He pushed his cart, eager to put distance between them.

"Asshole!" she yelled, pulling away.

Paul laughed.

❧

He brought his bags inside the house, went to the pantry and grabbed a loaf of bread, then got two slices and set them on a 10-inch pink plate with yellow flowers. He made a PB&J, slicing the sandwich into four diagonals, then folded a paper towel neatly into a fan and placed two lemon cookies onto the plate. He grabbed a tall plastic tumbler from the cabinet and poured cold milk into it.

He placed the meal and the drink onto a pink tray, grabbed a bright pink Gerbera daisy from a vase and laid it on the tray. He smiled, wondering if Jessi appreciated these little touches in his presentation.

He opened the door leading down to the basement and carried the tray downstairs. Holding it with one hand, he dug into his pocket, grabbed his keys, unlocked the padlock, then the door itself, and pushed it open.

"Guess who's home ..." Paul's voice was a song, entering the bedroom that he'd spent ample resources turning into a little girl's paradise.

The walls were pink, lined with posters of familiar characters and adorable animals. The four-poster sleigh bed was something any girl would love, and it had over 1,000 five-star reviews to prove it. The shelf above the bed was lined with stuffed animals looking down with big eyes and giant smiles. There was a toy box across the room, filled with dolls, books, art supplies, and other stuff to keep Jessi busy while Paul was at work. There was also a full bathroom with a tub. Plants hung above concealed one of the room's many secret cameras.

Jessi sat on the bed, under the blanket, knees to her chin, not saying a word or looking at Paul.

"I made you dinner."

She continued avoiding him, not saying thanks or showing the slightest bit of gratitude.

He resisted the urge to get angry, reminding himself

that Jessi was still living under the illusion that she would see her father again, and was madder with every day that passed, holding more of Paul's excuses as to why he couldn't come get her.

"I want to see my dad."

"Soon. But right now, people are watching him. If he comes now, the police will put him in jail."

"But you're a police officer, aren't you? Can't you tell them not to?"

"I'm afraid it doesn't work that way, honey. It's complicated. You don't want to get your dad in trouble, do you?"

"No," she said, her bottom lip jutting out.

Paul hated to see Jessi upset and hoped she wouldn't stay mad once she realized the truth. He wanted to win her over.

Paul found himself looking at her big blue eyes, her long blonde hair, and her bright pink lips. She was beautiful, could easily have been a child model.

He wished he could freeze her in this moment forever.

Wished he could keep her from growing up. Keep her in this room as a pretty little princess forever, *his* pretty little princess.

But that wasn't an option. You couldn't stop time, and all girls, no matter how sweet and innocent, grew into women — lying evil bitches, every one of them.

But maybe, Paul thought, he might keep this one past her tenth birthday. They could have so much fun.

As she continued to sulk, Paul wished that he'd bought the other card, the one with the dog and the frosting.

Chapter 7 - Mallory Black

MALLORY SAT at the table in the back of McKinley's Pub staring at her whiskey shot, trying to remember how many she'd had.

She'd lost count after seven.

Whatever the number, it wasn't enough to forget.

Tomorrow Ashley would have been twelve.

But instead of celebrating her birthday, Mal was drinking alone to the looming two year anniversary of her death.

They found her body a week after she would have turned ten. Time of death estimated was right around her birthday.

Killed on the anniversary of her birth.

What kind of sick fuck does something like that?

She downed the shot, then raised her glass to signal the waitress, a redhead in her thirties named Judy who'd been working at McKinley's for at least the year and a half that Mal had been drowning her sorrows.

Judy came over and grabbed the glass. "You want anything else to eat?"

Mal looked at her phone — 10:15 PM — then at the bowl of pretzels she'd been more or less ignoring since getting there two hours ago. "No thanks."

Judy looked like she might try and convince her, but then simply smiled and left.

Mal had been coming here long enough that Judy, as well as the other people employees, knew who she was: The Ex-Deputy Who Lost Her Kid Then Won the Lottery the Following Year.

To the staff's credit, they didn't pester Mal about her daughter, nor did they ever hit her up for money. That was the mark of a good establishment — filled with people who were perfectly happy to leave you the fuck alone. And if you happened to get in a fight with an aggressive asshole every once in a while, they'd look the other way. Provided you paid for whatever you broke.

McKinley's was a faux-Irish sports bar, catering to working class stiffs, college sports fans, and, if you came late enough, desperate people looking to score. It was loud and reeked of fried foods and alcohol. The perfect place to lose yourself in a drink or ten.

It was also the sort of place she wasn't likely to run into anyone she used to know. Most cops hung out at real bars on the other side of town, or in the trendier sports bars along the beachside in Pine Harbour. McKinley's was in Butler, the county's oldest city — a small burg with a rich historic district replete with boutique shops, bed and breakfasts, and some of the county's best inland restaurants.

But the bar was on the wrong side of the tracks, literally, in a ten square mile blight full of federal housing, high unemployment, and one of Florida's highest crime rates.

Mal could easily have moved to a new house untainted by terrible memories, in a town where she wasn't known. But for reasons she didn't understand, leaving felt like abandoning her daughter. Mal had even left Ashley's room exactly as it was the day she vanished, just in case.

As if she might someday walk through the door.

As if they'd never found her body naked in a drainage ditch.

As if the dental records hadn't matched.

As if she didn't bury her daughter in the pouring rain.

As if the past could ever be different.

Leaving was like cowardice to Mal, even though she had legitimate reasons to go. She was a multi-millionaire. She should move to a proper gated community, or at least to a place where people didn't know who she was. Where people might not think to rob her. It hadn't happened yet, but these were desperate times and people got robbed for less than a Benjamin.

But instead of leaving, Mal bought a new state-of-the-art security system and dyed her blonde hair a dark brown.

And she was always packing.

Let a fucker try and rob her.

Mal refused to run.

Judy set another shot on the table, then said, "Want some company?"

Mal looked at her, uncertain if Judy was asking out of kindness or flirting with her. It didn't seem like flirting, but Mal was so drunk, she couldn't be certain of anything. And she supposed Judy had seen Mal leave with enough men and women to know she was plenty promiscuous.

"No thanks. Just doing some thinking."

"Okay. Lemme know if you change your mind, about either the company or the food."

Mal nodded, said, "Thanks," then took her shot with a swallow.

Mal wasn't gay, nor even bisexual, though maybe the

dabbling meant that she was. Who knew? Judy was attractive, and would surely be pleasant company to leave with.

Mal wanted to be alone, but she didn't want to be lonely. Which was why she'd come here. If she got drunk enough, she could leave with someone, and maybe forget her pain for at least a little while.

But sleeping with staff that she'd have to see again seemed like a certain mistake.

Her phone buzzed.

A phone call from her old partner, Mike.

She let her voicemail answer, same as for every other call today: her ex-boss, her sister, her ex-husband, Ray.

She couldn't listen to them.

Not tonight.

Not when she wanted to wallow.

Mal also ignored a call from a reporter, no doubt wanting a quote on the missing child, Jessi Price. Whenever a kid went missing in the tri-county area, some reporter wanted a quote about the effectiveness of parenting, laws, or whoever was currently being blamed for bad shit happening to good people.

An obnoxious braying laughter yanked Mal from her misery.

The guffaw was coming from one of two men in their late twenties or early thirties, playing pool with a pair of girls. Maybe college freshmen. One man was tall and handsome. He looked like a former football player, wearing a red cap backward. The other was a seedy-looking dude, too skinny, resembling every low rent drug dealer Mal had ever arrested during her years in violent crimes.

The girls, a blonde and a brunette, were pretty. Mal could tell they came from money. The only question was whether they were slumming it tonight, or if these men were their usual type. If so, they wouldn't maintain their youthful looks or their parents' money for long. These guys were vampires and would suck up both, getting the girls addicted to drugs until their parents buried or disowned them.

Mal shook her head, watching the girls giggling at every stupid thing the assholes said.

Whenever Mal saw girls like this, she wondered if she could've ensured her daughter didn't wind up the same way. Ashley was pretty, creative, and whip-smart. But even at nine, her need for attention would've put her in the crosshairs of men like this.

Mal liked to tell herself that Ashley would've been too smart to fall in with such a crowd. But as a product of a broken marriage and — if Mal was honest with herself — a shitty mom who spent more time working than being present, it was a practical recipe for creating a needy girl with a lack of confidence, the exact kind of girl that assholes preyed on.

Mal liked to think that things would have been different, particularly after she won the lottery. But she didn't play the lottery back when she was still working, so she might never have won if Ashley had lived. She might still have been working long hours, missing important things, and never being there for Ashley in the way a more present mother would have been.

The alcohol wasn't enough. Mal needed something more.

She stood, went to the restroom, dug into her purse, and found the small plastic pouch with two pills tucked inside.

She popped them in her mouth, washed them down with a handful of water from the sink, then closed her eyes, waiting for the opiates to kick in.

She'd started taking pain pills after hurting her back a

half-year ago. But they had the unexpected side of *making her happy*.

Mal had worked as a detective long enough to know the dangers of drugs. Not only from people she busted but from fellow cops. And opiates were among the scariest — they got their hooks in you, then they owned your ass.

But Mal never realized how intoxicating they could be, until her first.

It was as if she'd never known true bliss. Someone had put a dampener on her pleasure receptors, and the pills ripped it off to inject pure, unfiltered joy into her brain.

Finding that kind of happiness after her life had been anything but, was life-altering.

Soon Mal was taking the pills several times a day, even though she never again reached the same high.

Now, she needed them just to get through the day.

They made her stable more than happy. Sure, the euphoria was still there, and incredible before it faded. But the feeling never lasted long.

Mal left the restroom and returned to her table.

A new drink was waiting.

She sat, swallowed, and enjoyed her buzz.

Leaned back, closed her eyes, and fell into the moment.

One of the young girls stumbled past Mal, leaving the restroom looking obliterated, before making her way back to the pool table.

She told her friend that they needed to go. The brunette thanked the guys for a fun night, then started to help the blonde toward the exit.

Jock and Dealer traded a glance then started laughing hysterically. Dealer said something to Jock that Mal couldn't hear. Then Jock said, "Hells yeah!"

They followed the girls into the parking lot.

Mal sighed. She knew exactly what was going to happen.

The guys would try to talk the girls into going back to their place for some date rape. Mal was feeling a nice buzz and didn't want to fuck that up.

But nobody else seemed to give a shit about the drunk girls leaving the bar with a matching set of losers.

She stood, grabbed her purse, and headed outside.

McKinley's lot was small, meaning that at busy times you had to take your chances parking on the residential streets behind the bar. For the first few blocks, you were fine. People in those homes mostly took care of them, and crime wasn't too bad. But a few streets further back, in the asshole of Butler as the deputies called it, the reality was much worse. You only wanted to park that far from the bar if you felt like having your rims stolen or your car broken into, or maybe if you enjoyed harassment from people with nothing better to do than start shit in the streets.

The guys were laughing, following the girls down one of the side streets.

Jock was trying to sway the girls to his pad.

Mal laughed. She hadn't heard anyone call their place a "pad" in years. These guys were total douchebags.

The blonde giggled as Jock grabbed her, pushed her up against a car, and kissed her.

The brunette whined in a voice that said that this wasn't how she wanted to spend the night. "Come on, Sammy. Let's go."

Jock raised his finger to silence her, while sloppily making out with the blonde.

Dealer started chatting up the brunette, but she clearly wasn't into him.

"Come on," the brunette pleaded again.

Sammy pulled away from Jock and hugged her friend. "I love you so much, Evie."

She started to walk with Evie.

But Jock yanked Sammy back.

Evie tugged at her friend and yelled, "We've got to go home!"

"What the fuck?" Jock blurted, throwing his arms out like he was about to brawl with a dude who spilled beer on him. "We're having fun. Why you wanna ruin it?"

"Because fun time is over, Brad. We've gotta go."

She started to walk, but Dealer blocked her.

She tried to lead Sammy around him, but he only slid over, further clogging her passage.

She stopped. "Please, let us go."

Mal couldn't hear what Dealer said this time, but it must've been bad. Evie yelled, "Help!"

Jock hit her in the back of the head and sent her to the ground.

Mal ran toward them with balled fists.

Sammy screamed, probably not understanding that Mal was there to protect them. Evie was on the ground, trying to stand.

Jock turned around, eyes wide.

Mal kicked his crotch and sent the asshole to his knees.

"Stay down!" Mal yelled.

Dealer was already running. Mal gave chase but surrendered a half-block away after realizing that she couldn't catch him in pumps, and that she'd left Jock alone with the girls.

She returned to the girls but didn't see Jock.

"Where'd he go?" Mal asked.

Evie looked dazed.

Sammy was bent over puking her guts out.

Mal looked up and down the street, pissed that she'd left Jock to chase Dealer.

Suddenly, footsteps behind her.

He must've been hiding behind a parked car.

He charged her, sending Mal back into a van, hard.

She tried to bring her knee up into his groin, or his gut, but Jock quickly backed away. Then he swung, hitting Mal in the jaw and sending her down to the ground.

Mal's purse fell beside her, gun spilling onto the street.

He didn't notice. His wide, crazy eyes were all over her.

He screamed, punching her in her forehead.

Mal cried out, then socked him in the knee cap.

Jock screamed as he doubled over, "You cunt!"

He was hurt, but she didn't break a thing.

He started toward her, his meaty hands open.

Mal ducked, grabbed her gun from the ground, and screamed, "Down on the ground, fucker!"

Jock's eyes went wide.

He stared as if deciding whether he should fight or listen.

Mal prayed that he listened. She would enjoy beating the shit out of him, but she didn't want to explain a shooting.

A siren blurted behind her, flashing blue and red.

A man's voice shouted, "Drop the gun!"

The perfect shitty ending to a perfectly shitty evening.

MAL WAS SITTING in the back of the Butler City police car, as the three officers on duty spoke to the two girls and Jock.

Why she was in the back of a car while Jock still wasn't cuffed was beyond her. Didn't the girls tell the cop what was happening?

Mal stared daggers into the backs of the police officers, all men whom she didn't know. Butler's police department paid shit, so the department had constant churn. The good ones went on to Creek County Sheriff's Office, while the bad ones either burned out or rose through the Butler ranks.

She told the questioning officer that she was a former sheriff's deputy, but he more or less ignored her, as if *she* were the trouble maker.

Granted, she'd been involved in three fights this year at the bar: one time when a guy got too grabby, another when two men assaulted a server, and a third when some asshole biker's girlfriend thought Mal was hitting on her guy, which she wasn't.

Mal had somehow avoided getting into too much trouble or being sued out of her millions. Mostly thanks to her lawyer, Art Spaulding. But she did have to pay almost two hundred grand to the grabby guy, just to keep the shit storm away.

She probably had a reputation, and that was likely why she was in the back of a patrol car instead of the fucker on the verge of date raping a drunk girl.

Mal watched as the officer cuffed Jock and led him to the back of the other car. She clapped, and yelled, "About damned time!" so loudly that Jock looked over at her, pure rage still claiming his face.

She flipped him off, hoping he'd try and rush her. Give the cops a reason to taze his stupid ass.

The door next to her opened, and a familiar figure stepped forward.

"Mikey!" Mal said, "Tell these fuckers I'm not the bad guy."

Mike made a face, waving at her alcohol-laced breath. "Wow, Mad Dog, how much did you drink tonight?"

She smiled, then slurred, "Not enough to find you attractive, if that's what you're asking."

Mike was like a brother. And if you couldn't be a drunken ass in front of your brother, who could you be a drunken ass in front of?

"Come on. I'm gonna take you home."

"Oh, am I free to go?" Mal said, glaring at the cop who had put her in the back seat in the first place.

Mike grabbed her elbow. "They were putting you back here so you didn't attract attention."

He nodded down the street toward a growing horde of onlookers, cell phones in hand, recording the show to post on social media later.

Mal stumbled on her way out of the car.

Mike caught her — she would've fallen face first onto the road if he hadn't.

"Come on," he said, looping an arm around Mal and leading her toward his car. "Don't give these clowns anything they can sell to the media."

Mal wanted to turn around and flip off the looky-loos.

Thankfully, better sense prevailed.

Chapter 8 - Jasper Parish

STANDING JUST INSIDE THE ENTRANCE, Jasper could hardly believe his eyes.

Jeff Stone's home looked like something out of an episode of *Hoarders*, packed from floor to ceiling with shit. The crap most people had the common sense to toss — old newspapers, magazines, used food containers, a metric ton of grocery bags filled with God only knew what, boxes upon boxes, many not even open.

There were also several plastic totes, the kind people usually used to clean a mess, standing five high in several stacks with no particular order. The place reeked of sorrow, insanity, and urine.

"What the hell?" Jasper was afraid to take another step into the monster's place. "Please tell me you know where his collection is."

Jordyn lowered her headband to cover her nose and shrugged.

"You've gotta be shitting me. How the hell can we find anything in this mess?"

"Maybe we skip the whole 'proving the guy is guilty'

phase of our investigation, and get right to the punishment?"

They'd done this dance before. Jasper glared at his daughter. "Nice try. You take the living room. I'll take the bedroom."

"*Really?*"

"Really."

Jasper didn't know if it was Jordyn's laziness that prevented her due diligence, or if she was just that cock-sure of her visions' veracity, but she was always trying to skip the first part of their process.

She would ask why they needed evidence, and he'd argue that they weren't cold blooded murderers. They had a burden of proof before dispensing justice.

"Come on, Dad. You can tell he's guilty. No innocent person keeps a house like this. This is Crazy Town!"

"He's guilty of being a crazy slob. It's our job to see if he's guilty of anything else."

Jordyn sniggered.

Jasper ignored her, heading to the bedroom.

He turned the knob, bracing himself for whatever he might find behind the door. Would there be dead animals? Or literal shit?

The door opened, just barely, caught on a pile of clothes.

"How's the bedroom?" Jordyn called from her search near the couch.

"Immaculate."

She stood, eyebrows arched, and looked over, "Really?"

"No, more of the same." He sighed.

She frowned and returned to her search.

Jasper entered the bedroom, eyes probing, searching for the stash.

Serial killers like Jeff Stone almost always kept a keepsake from their victim. Even if that something could be evidence linking them to the crime, bagged then presented during a trial to lock them up. But they couldn't help themselves.

Of the three serial killers that Jasper had taken down, each had kept trophies. One kept locks of hair. Another, photos. Yet another kept jewelry. The stash was never in plain sight, nor in a big red box marked *Trophies*.

Stone's five victims shared three similarities: they were all brunettes, they were all prostitutes, and they were all found missing their left ring finger. The third item never made the news. The cops kept some things to themselves as a way to weed out the solid tips from the crackpots.

But Jordyn had seen it in her vision, along with where Jeff lived.

Jasper wished her visions were more useful, but it wasn't like she had any control over her gift — or curse.

He stepped over more clothes, wondering how many were dirty versus clean. How many had ever been worn? Some were still on the hanger.

Oh, who am I kidding? They're all dirty, by virtue of being in this hellhole.

"Holy shit!" Jordyn shouted.

Jasper's hand found the pistol in his pocket.

He ran, hoping that Jeff hadn't come home early. He wasn't due from work until after six, which gave them at least another four hours.

But Jeff wasn't home.

Jordyn was standing in front of two of the five-high stacks of plastic totes, lids removed from the top of each one.

Jasper moved closer to see what she was staring at.

One of the boxes was lined with old VHS tapes with

violently sexual titles, most handwritten on the spine. The other box was full of DVDs in plastic cases.

"Swear jar," Jasper said.

Jordyn rolled her eyes, then looked back at the collection of recorded media. "Maybe there's evidence here?"

"Even if there is, I don't have the stomach to pop any of these in for a look."

"I will."

"No," Jasper said sharply.

"You'll let me help you do this thing we do, but you don't want me to watch porn? Sheesh, hypocritical much, Dad? I'm nineteen. I've seen things, you know."

"You haven't seen anything like this. And trust me, dear, some things you can't unsee."

"Suit yourself," she said, snapping the lids back into place, then unstacking the other boxes to investigate their contents.

Jasper looked to the left and noticed that the kitchen wasn't nearly as messy as the rest of the place. It wasn't immaculate, or sanitary enough to prepare food without the risk of illness, but it was relatively clean.

Maybe *too clean*.

He stepped into the kitchen, scanning for anything that looked like it might make a good hiding spot. The pantry was orderly, like the cupboards. Even the kitchen sink was only half-filled with dirty dishes, rather than overflowing.

Well, at least we found something our guy cares about more than murder.

Jasper couldn't shake how oddly unsullied the kitchen was compared to the horror show in the rest of the house. He'd never seen anything like it. Granted, he hadn't seen many hoarders' homes up close and personal, but it was usually all or nothing. Once you let most of the house go, you let all of it go.

Why the kitchen?

It was the one room in the house that wasn't just clean; it had a sense of style. A few small paintings on the wall gave the kitchen some color. There was a doily on the table with a bowl of relatively fresh fruit. There was also a vase filled with flowers on the window sill over the sink, looking out onto the front yard.

Jasper's eyes zeroed in on the fridge and photos of a brunette that looked like they were taken maybe a decade earlier, with a younger version of Jeff in a few of the pics.

A girlfriend?

The first victim?

Jasper wondered if she was the reason behind the clean kitchen, some sort of homage? Or was this kitchen a part of his post-killing ritual?

Something clicked.

The freezer!

Body parts are meat, and where do you keep meat?

Jasper opened the freezer.

It was relatively in order, though most of the food was crusted with a mound of frost that would take a jack-hammer to get through.

In the back of the freezer, behind a box of Eggos, Jasper found a sealed plastic purple bowl — the only thing not covered in frost.

He opened the bowl.

"Got it!"

Jordyn rushed into the kitchen, eager to see the trophies.

Jasper showed her the bowl of frozen gray fingers and her eyes lit like she was opening a box full of puppies.

"You are *really* weird."

"Well, I am your daughter."

"Fair enough." He closed the bowl and returned it to the freezer.

"Well, you've got your proof, *Detective Parish*. So, what's the punishment gonna be?"

∼

JASPER PACED in front of the large man tied to his kitchen chair, waiting for him to open his eyes. The minute Jeff had walked through his front door, Jasper had knocked him out with a chloroform rag.

Now he walked circles, waiting for the chloroform to wear off.

Jordyn was sitting on a kitchen chair opposite the man, tapping her boot on the ground as she waited.

"Sheesh, can't you just get started?"

"No, I want him awake, so he knows why it's happening."

Jordyn had only been on a few of Jasper's kills, and this was the first one she came inside for. He still wasn't sure he wanted her to watch him murder a man. That wasn't the sort of thing your kids should see you do, even if they knew about it.

Jeff woke, murmuring confusion through the rag.

He looked up and saw Jasper, now without his mask, and Jordyn, still in hers. His eyes went wide.

He mumbled something, probably wanting to know who they were and why the hell they were in his house.

But Jasper didn't give a shit about what Jeff had to say. And he wouldn't be talking much longer.

Jasper grabbed a chair and sat in it backward next to Jeff, just inches away.

"So, Jeff, I've been trying to figure out the best way to punish you."

He muttered some more, shaking in his chair, trying to break free. The duct tape was thick. He wasn't going anywhere.

"At first I thought I ought to cut your fingers off. That seemed fitting. But then—" Jasper stood, went to the living room, dragged a plastic tote into the kitchen, then popped off the top. "—Well, then I found these."

Jeff's eyes were wider than ever, sweat dripping off his fat face.

"Tell me, Jeffrey, what sorts of stuff do you have on these tapes? Were you a big *X-Files* fan? I remember taping episodes back in the day. But that seems like a lot of tape for one show. Maybe you had a bunch of favorites, but little time to watch them, what with your hectic cleaning schedule?"

Jasper waved his hand around the dump. "That it?"

Jeff murmured something. Jasper still didn't care.

"Then I had another thought. I bet this is some real nasty shit. The kinda crap they don't show on TV. The kind that perverts trade. I mean why else would you still have boxes of video tapes, Jeffrey? You know you can go to Walgreens and get this shit on DVD, right? Oh, wait, you can't, because those employees would take one look at what's on these tapes and call the cops, wouldn't they? Even minimum wage workers know a monster when they see one."

Jeff squirmed, screaming into his gag.

If he wasn't careful, he'd choke on his spit.

"So, what kinda shit are you into, Jeffrey? Scat? Women squishing animals? Oh, wait, I got it. You're into snuff, aren't you?"

Tears streamed from his Jeff's eyes as he looked help-lessly around the room. Jasper snapped in front of his face.

"Eyes over here, man. There's no escape. And she's not gonna help you. She thinks you're disgusting."

Jeff looked over to where Jordyn was sitting, then back at Jasper, saying something inaudible, lost in the gag.

He picked up a cassette and smacked Jeff in the face. "So, am I right? Is it snuff on these tapes?"

Jeff nodded.

"Jesus. I was hoping it was just a bit of sick porn, not actual snuff."

Jeff tried to say something, but still, Jasper couldn't hear him.

"So, I got to thinking, what would be the ideal punishment for a man who goes around killing prostitutes? I considered hiring someone to kill you. Fair play, right? But then I'd have to worry about accidentally hiring a cop. Why is it that so many people hiring hitmen wind up asking an undercover officer? You'd think people would wise up by now."

Jeff yelled, likely begging for mercy.

Jasper still didn't care.

"Then I had another idea. Since these videos seem to be such a hobby of yours, why not use them for your punishment?"

Jasper grabbed a cassette from the box, broke the end off, and began to unspool the long black tape.

"Did you know this stuff is toxic? Not only are there a bunch of chemicals coating the tape that can get into your lungs and stuff, but the tape itself is flammable."

Jasper unspooled the tape faster, then stood to wrap Jeff like a mummy.

The man shook violently in his chair, but he was no match for the binding.

Jasper grabbed another tape and unspooled that around Jeff, too.

Then, because he didn't have all night, he picked up the entire box and dumped the contents on Jeff. Tapes clanged as they hit him, then bounced off of his body to crack on the kitchen floor.

Jasper pulled out a lighter, flipped the lid, and turned the metal wheel.

A flame shot up. Jasper smiled, holding it in front of Jeff.

Jeff screamed, shaking his head violently back and forth.

He was probably promising never to hurt anyone again, never watch snuff again, or maybe turn himself into the police.

But again, Jasper didn't care.

He lowered the flame to the wad of tape piled on Jeff's crotch.

It took a moment, but the tape began to melt, the flame's red edges finally starting to spread.

Jasper looked at the flame, shaking his head. "Hmm, not nearly as flammable as I imagined. That fire looks like it's gonna burn itself out."

Jasper reached into his jacket pocket and pulled out his can of lighter fluid. "This should help things along."

Jeff's eyes bulged as he shook his head harder and faster, bellowing into the rag.

Jasper sprayed fluid onto the burning tape.

Chapter 9 - Mallory Black

THEY DROVE in silence on the way to Mal's house.

She just wanted to get home, take a few more pills, and leave the night behind her. She was hoping Mike would stay quiet, but with only about five minutes left, he finally spoke.

"Why?"

"Why what?"

"Why don't you just move? Why stay here? If I won the lottery, you'd never see my ass again. I'd be in Hawaii or better."

"Nobody knows what they'll do until after they win. Hell, most people spend all the money and go broke again. I'm not gonna be that stupid."

"I'll give you that, but I still wouldn't hang out in this shit town. Come on, Mal. You can go *anywhere*: New York, Paris, Italy, Toronto, or hell, you can probably buy a freaking island. *Why* do you stay here?"

"I don't know," she lied, then changed the subject, asking about her former co-workers. "How's Lou?"

"Crotchety as always."

"Gloria?"

"Still a pain in the ass."

"Who they got you with now?"

"Reynolds."

"Skippy Reynolds from narcotics? That asshole?"

Skip's real name was Stan, but the guys teased the hell out of him because of a story he once told about his ex-wife whom he said utilized a jar of peanut butter to get a dog to lick her nether regions. It didn't matter that *he* never used the peanut butter. His nickname was Skippy, anyway.

Skip was a loud-mouth muscle head — way too reckless a partner for Mike. Hell, Mike could barely keep up with Mal, and she was way more regulation than Skippy.

"Yeah, Skippy."

"How is he?"

"He's not you." After a full beat, he added, "Thank God."

She laughed. "Well, we can't all be Skippy."

It'd been a long time since Mal had been around other cops, or enjoyed busting the balls of her fellow deputies. As juvenile as some of them could be, she missed their company.

As if sensing her thoughts, Mike said, "You can always come back and be my partner again."

Slightly slurred: "Watch out, I might take you up on that."

"As much as I'd love to see you back, you'd be crazy to come. I mean who the hell wins the lottery and keeps working? Hell, Gina and the kids might not ever see me again if that was my ticket!"

Mal laughed. "I think Gina and her brothers would hunt your ass down."

"Yeah, you're right. But I definitely wouldn't go back to

work. And I suspect if you came back, people wouldn't know how to treat you."

"Because of me being rich and shit?" Mal said, still laughing.

"That, but also ... well, you know."

She wasn't sure if Mike was referring to Ashley's death or the panic attack six months later, which everyone politely referred to as "the incident" — an *incident* that nearly cost people their lives because of Mal's inaction, and made her unable to trust herself enough to continue the job. Either way, she didn't want to discuss it. Ashley was still dead, and her panic attacks hadn't returned since she started taking the pills.

After a full minute of silence, Mal asked, "What's happening with the Jessi Price case?"

"What?"

"The missing girl. What's going on with her? Any leads?"

"We like the dad. Parents were in the middle of a nasty custody battle, and Dad picked the girl up from school. That was the last anyone saw either of them."

"The Feds involved?"

"They're coordinating search efforts, watching airports and stuff in case the father tries taking his kid back to England."

"Doesn't anyone think the timing is funny? Two years almost to the day. *And* she's turning ten on Saturday, just like Ashley was."

"We considered that. But we like the dad."

"Nobody's looking into anything else? Cell phone pings? Talking to sex offenders and searching their homes?"

"Gloria doesn't want to cause a panic or waste resources."

"She ought to turn this thing over to the FBI. But *noooo*, wouldn't want to fuck up her re-election bid."

"She's a good sheriff. Better than Barry was."

Mal rolled her eyes. "*That's* not saying much." Claude Barry was a racist, crooked asshole who nearly bankrupted the county with all the discrimination and wrongful death lawsuits under his watch.

They pulled up to her house.

Mike didn't say anything else, but she didn't want to let the matter go.

"I'm just saying, *someone* ought to be following other leads."

"I know this is close to home, so I won't take offense, but you've gotta trust that we're doing all we can to find her. This isn't our first missing child case. We've had ten in the past year, all solved, and every one of them a relative or family friend. You know how these things go. The girl and dad will get busted in Georgia getting gas or something routine."

"I know. I just feel so helpless sitting on the sidelines."

"Then come back," he offered, this time sounding more serious.

Their eyes met. Mike looked as if this was something he'd given plenty of thought.

"You forgot, people will be uncomfortable with me being rich and shit."

"I'm serious, Mal. We miss you. Hell, *I* miss you, and you drove me fucking nuts."

"Not like it was that long of a drive."

"Come on; you miss it. Why else would you hang out at dive bars waiting for trouble?"

Mal wished she wasn't drunk and extra lonely. Because as stupid as the idea sounded, a part of her wanted to jump at the offer.

She smiled. "Thanks, but I can't."

"I'm sure Gloria would take you back in a heartbeat. Believe me, everyone's forgotten all about the *incident*. Hell, everyone was on your side. They understood. Nobody thought you should've been forced out."

"First, no one's forgotten the incident. And second, not everyone was on my side. IA was looking for a reason to get rid of me ever since I betrayed Barry and helped Gloria get elected. I gave them everything they needed to get me out of there. But it wasn't even just them. Gloria didn't have my back, either."

"You're right." Mike nodded. "She should've stood up for you. Especially since you helped get her elected."

"It's not even that. I didn't help her because I expected favoritism. I believed she was the right person for the job. I'm just disappointed how quickly she turned into a politician, like the rest of them. Gloria hung me out to dry. So as much as I'd love to work with you again, Mike, I refuse to put myself in that position."

He sighed. "You're right."

Mal was quiet for a long moment, watching fat rain drops beading on the window. Tears welled up in her eyes.

"Are you okay?" Mike asked.

A part of her wanted to tell him about the pictures of Ashley, left on her doorstep from the killer last year. But she hadn't reported it then and couldn't do it now. Doing so would ruin everything.

She met Mike's sad brown eyes. She wondered if he was missing her and their friendship, or was maybe feeling the pain she felt for *The Anniversary*. Or some odd combination of both.

"Yeah, I'm okay. Just ... well, you know."

"Yeah."

He took her hand and squeezed it. "You want some company?"

A part of her did want company. To hang out, drink some more, maybe talk about the old days, talk about Ashley. Get drunk(er) and cry.

But that would ruin the evening's *other* plans.

"No, I'm sure Gina is waiting up."

"I can call. Let her know I won't be home because my alcoholic ex-partner decided to beat the hell out of some other drunk asshole. She'd probably come over and congratulate you."

Mal smiled. "No, it's okay. But thank you."

She withdrew her hand, opened the door, and climbed out of his car.

She went inside the cold, dark house, closed the door, and let out a bottomless sigh.

She wiped fresh tears from the corners of her eyes, then went to the bathroom, opened the medicine chest, and withdrew her bottle of pills. She palmed two, smacked them in her mouth, then chased them with water.

Normally, she'd take the pills before drifting off to sleep. It was the only way to silence, or at least minimize, the reminders and regrets that haunted her night time.

But there would be no relaxing tonight.

She had to be ready for her daughter's killer.

If he returned with another gift, it would be the last thing he ever did.

She grabbed the gun from her nightstand, turned off the safety, and headed upstairs to the third story loft.

She sat in a rocking chair in front of the circular window, looking out at the rainy night and the creaking oaks blowing in the breeze. She remembered how many times she'd brought Ashley up here to watch the lightning.

She'd been afraid of storms as a toddler until Mal

brought her pink teddy bear — a bear named Pinky that she used to sleep with in her crib — to the loft and turned the storm into an adventure.

"Pinky" would tell Ashley stories about the lightning, and how it was bears wrestling in the sky or some other nonsense that always earned a raspy giggle.

Mal stood, went downstairs to the second story, entered Ashley's room, and saw Pinky lying face up on the bed, waiting for the friend who would never play with her again.

Mal grabbed Pinky and brought her upstairs to sit, waiting for Ashley's killer and the gift he might bring.

Chapter 10 - Mallory Black

MALLORY WOKE to warm sunlight on her face, gun on the floor.

Shit!

She looked out the window to see if there was anything on her porch, but couldn't quite see the entire porch past the awning.

She grabbed her gun, jumped up, then scrambled down the stairs, making a beeline to her front door.

No, no, no!

She couldn't believe she fell asleep.

Mal was twenty feet from her front door and fully expected to open it wide to another package. She would die knowing that the killer had the nerve to return and she'd somehow slept through it.

Mal had been waiting a full year for this moment, and she let it slip through her stupid, drunken, drugged out fingers.

She reached the door, seized the knob, and swung the door open.

She looked down at the concrete porch.

Nothing there except some leaves gathered against the wall on either side of the door.

But there wasn't any gift.

Mal approached her sidewalk, looking around to see if maybe he'd left it somewhere else.

But everything seemed to be in place.

She glanced at the mailbox and felt a chill.

She ran to it, flinging the door down so hard she nearly ripped it from its hinges.

But the mailbox was empty.

She saw two women, a lesbian couple from down the street, pushing a stroller with their adopted two-year-old daughter, Olivia. Mal didn't know them well, outside of a lone conversation when they moved in a few months ago.

They were looking at her in alarm.

Mal realized how she must look — a disheveled mess, standing in front of the mailbox with a crazed expression, holding a gun.

One of the women, a redhead named Felicia, asked, "Is everything okay?"

Mal's face felt flush as she stammered, "Yeah, um, false alarm."

She closed her mailbox, smiled awkwardly, and went back inside.

A sudden realization: *she'd never unlocked the front door.*

She paused in the doorway, trying to remember coming home. Had she forgotten to lock the door? She *never* forgot to lock her doors or set the alarm.

But then again, last night was fuzzy.

She looked at her door jamb for any signs of tampering. Seeing nothing, she stepped back inside, closing the door softly behind her, moving in slow motion, trying to remember last night's steps.

She locked the door, turned around, and looked at the

hallway leading to the dining room. Seeing her surroundings might trigger a missing memory.

Her heart froze.

There was a gift box on her dining room table. It wasn't wrapped, but decorated in pink with white unicorns and cupcakes, a bright blue bow atop it. Not a wrapping bow, but the one Ashley was wearing when she vanished.

She swallowed, her eyes tearing up.

He came in here?

He was in my house?

She stared at the box, her heart pounding.

She couldn't move.

Could barely breathe.

The box was about a foot wide, and maybe two feet high.

Her mind was dizzy, imagining what he might have put inside. Last year, he'd sent photos of Mal's daughter in an unfamiliar pink bedroom. They were close-ups, Ashley's eyes haunting for their lack of life.

Mal never brought the photos to the police or told them that the killer had left them on her porch because they hadn't managed to do anything with a full year and the FBI's help. Mal took matters into her own hands instead, trying to track down everything from the paper to the printer that had spit out the photos, but she'd come up with nothing. Just like the department.

Mal also didn't want the police to consider that the killer might come back a year later. She wanted to be alone, waiting to dispense a justice that the bastard would never get in their custody.

If he broke in, she could legally shoot him.

But she failed. And fell asleep. If she'd told the police, at least they would have him in custody.

But now Mal had nothing.

The killer was still free.

And she wanted to vomit.

Mal stared at the box.

Then another thought: *What if he's still in here?*

Gun in hand, Mal checked the bottom floor, then the top, hoping the killer was crazy enough to hang around.

But her home was empty.

Mal remembered her security system.

After the killer brought her a gift last year, she installed cameras all over her yard and in every room. Recordings were stored locally and to the cloud. There wasn't a way inside that he wouldn't have been seen.

She raced to her office, sat at the huge L-shaped desk which occupied a wall and a half, then turned on her computer and scrubbed through the security footage.

She found the spot in the recordings where Mike had dropped her off. Saw herself stumbling to her door, then coming inside. She'd locked the door for sure, which was a small relief.

Mal scrolled through her movements until she saw herself fall asleep in the loft chair, still holding her gun.

She slowed the speed to 5X, watching every frame, waiting to see someone other than herself.

At 3:11 AM, a figure appeared in her front yard, box in hand.

She slowed the recording to regular speed and watched as the man — she assumed he was male given his height and movement — approached her home.

He was wearing jeans, a hoodie, and a black ski mask. He stepped onto the porch, looked up at the camera hidden above her door in a light fixture, and waved.

He knows the camera is there.

What else does he know?

A chill filled her.

A second camera, hidden in the bottom of a bird feeder in her tree, captured footage of the man at her doorstep. She couldn't see how he opened it, whether he picked the lock, or had a bump key, but it didn't take him long to enter.

She watched as the interior cameras recorded him entering her house. He wasn't slow or cautious as one might be when breaking and entering into a dark and unfamiliar home. He moved with confidence, as though he knew the lay of the land and was sure that he wouldn't run into anyone.

How many times has he been in my house?

Did he know I was asleep?

He set the box on Mal's table, and paused as if deliberating the best placement. He moved it a few times, then stood back to admire his work.

Then he headed to the second floor.

Mal could hear the camera's audio picking up the creaking stairs.

She leaned forward in her chair watching, her heart still racing.

Where is he going?

She watched him pass every room in her hallway, heading straight to the third story loft.

She held her breath; eyes still fixed on the footage.

He opened the door and stepped toward her sleeping body.

He was right here!

She watched the man, staring down at her as she slept in the chair.

What the hell is he doing?

The clock lost three full three minutes as he silently stood there.

And then, he finally moved.

The man bent down, pulled the gun from Mal's hand, held it to the back of her head, whispered, "Bang," then put it on the ground, turned, and looked up at the camera on his way out of the room.

Mal watched in horror as the man descended the stairs then walked out the door and into her yard before vanishing into the night past her fence.

The air felt suddenly icy.

The room foreign.

Her home unsafe.

Mal stood, ran to her bathroom, then fell beside the toilet and puked.

Once her stomach was empty, she stood on wobbly legs then went to the sink and washed her face.

She caught her eyes in the mirror, and anger claimed her.

Do not let this fucker do this to you.

Fight like a cop.

She stared into the mirror, no longer seeing her reflection. Instead, she saw a clarity that had been missing for too damned long.

Everything clicked.

Mal went into her home office to don a pair of gloves and protect the crime scene's integrity, then she went downstairs, grabbed her camera, and took several shots of the table and box from every possible angle. You never knew which details might be needed.

She set down the camera, took a deep breath, then went to the box and lifted the lid.

There was only a thumb drive inside.

Mal wanted to bring it to the nearest computer, plug it in, and see what was on it. But doing so could result in a number of other issues — a Trojan horse to compromise her computer, a virus to crash it, or maybe a self-destructing message. She needed to properly document whatever was on the drive, in case it became evidence or could lead to an arrest.

Staring into the box, Mal knew she could no longer handle this alone.

She picked up her phone and called Mike.

"I'd like to report a signal 21."

Chapter 11 - Jasper Parish

JASPER WOKE up in a cold sweat, his heart racing, and a crushing sense of doom weighing down on him like a lead blanket. It was still dark outside, and he'd slept two, maybe three hours at most.

He always woke up like this after a kill, worried, nervous that he'd left some clue behind and that the cops were seconds from breaking down his door. It was a cycle, and he knew he should do something to fight it, but what could one do to counter anxiety? Jasper didn't drink or do drugs and wasn't about to start taking any pharmaceuticals. It wasn't that he doubted their efficacy. He'd taken a few in the past and they worked *too well*.

They placated the fiery part of him that demanded justice for the victimized, for those whom the justice system didn't work, and for those who had lost their lives.

Sometimes he thought it would be easier to stop caring. To take some pills, or shots, and tune out the world and its terrible news. That's how most people got through the day — sticking their heads in the sand, pretending that the system wasn't broken, that the good guys could protect you from the bad guys. But Jasper knew all too well the dangers of sticking your head in the sand. And temporary ease wasn't worth the price of lapsed vigilance.

So he'd deal with the anxiety. It was his cross to bear. Still, it didn't make the mornings after any easier, especially with a crushing migraine.

He got out of bed and headed into the apartment's small living room. Jordyn was already awake, stretched out on the couch, arm propped on the penguin pillow he gave her when she was seven, watching the morning news while tapping away on her phone.

The living room was way too bright.

He hit the light switch, plunging the room into darkness, save for the soft blue light bleeding from the TV.

"Can you turn that down?"

"Got another headache, Daddy?" Jordyn bounded up from the couch and went into the kitchen. "Want me to make you some coffee or breakfast?"

"Why are you up so early? Didn't you sleep?"

She smiled. "Who needs sleep?"

Jordyn was bubbly and energetic, as she always was after a kill, full of childish enthusiasm without adult fears or guilt to slow her.

"No, no, I just need to decompress before my workout," he said, moving past her to the cabinet where he kept his medicine. He grabbed a couple of extra-strength Ibuprofens, then went to the fridge and grabbed a Coke to wash them down. Then he headed to his recliner beside the couch, sat, closed his eyes and waited for relief.

He could hear Jordyn starting the coffee maker. He wasn't sure if it was for him, even though he declined, or if she was making iced coffee, which she practically lived on.

He heard her sit on the couch. Seconds later, the TV's volume fell to a whisper.

"Working out after barely any sleep?"

"My aging cells don't take the day off, so neither can I. Anything on the news?"

"Not a peep."

"They probably haven't found him yet."

"Don't worry. We didn't leave any evidence."

They'd had this conversation a dozen times or more.

"Wishful thinking doesn't make it so, Jordyn."

"It's not wishful thinking. We're careful. We have systems — systems *you* built to minimize mistakes."

"Minimize, not eliminate. You can never account for every variable."

"Okay, fine. You win. We dropped the ball. We missed something big, and it's only a matter of time before the police come to get us. Is that what you want to hear?"

Jasper didn't respond.

"But hey, look at the bright side. We'll be in jail. There's no shortage of people who deserve justice there!"

"They're already in jail."

"Yeah, but maybe they ought to be dead. And who better to make things right than us? Maybe we'll get time off for good behavior, appreciation for killing the worst of the worst."

"Stop."

"What?"

"Trying to manipulate my mood."

"When you stop all this unnecessary worrying, I'll stop trying to talk sense into you."

"It's not me I'm worried about. I couldn't live with myself if this thing we do were to hurt you."

Jordyn was quiet.

After thirty seconds, he opened his eyes to see if she was still there.

She was staring at him. "You don't need to worry about me. I have *gifts*, remember?"

"Yeah, well you don't see *everything* coming our way."

Jordyn looked down at her hands.

Another long moment of silence.

She wiped tears from the corner of her eyes. "We're in this together, Daddy. Nothing is going to happen to either of us. I promise."

"Oh, you *promise?*" He smiled. "Shit, I didn't know I was dealing with a super powerful entity who could make promises like that!"

She picked up her penguin pillow and tossed it at him. Then she raised her arms as if she were about to summon a storm. "Didn't you hear, I've got *all* the gifts."

The coffee maker beeped. "You want coffee or not?"

"Nah, just make yourself two iced coffees."

"Like I wasn't going to."

Jordyn bounded into the kitchen. Jasper couldn't help but feel a bit better. He often wondered if he was wrong to drag his daughter into this life. But it wasn't as if he had an option. She more or less forced her way in, and he couldn't say no. Plus, she was great at balancing him out, easing his anxieties when they threatened to undo him.

He watched her pour coffee into the giant tumblers. She still had a little girl's slightly crooked smile. Jasper thought for the millionth time about how quickly she'd grown. He and Carissa took her home from the hospital just yesterday. He'd been a cop for two years and was prepared for any situation, but still remembered feeling scared and woefully unprepared for a baby. He remembered asking Carissa, "Isn't anybody going to come home with us to tell us what to do?"

She'd laughed, told him not to worry. They'd figure it all out together.

And they did. Until her passing.

He looked at Jordyn and wished that Carissa was still here to see what a wonderful young woman their baby girl had become.

Jordyn put one of the two tumblers in the fridge, then headed back into the living room with the other one. She froze halfway there, practically paralyzed, eyes rolled back in their sockets, arms shaking, as one of her visions took over.

Jasper jumped up and stood behind Jordyn, putting one hand on her back, another on her stomach, to make sure she didn't fall. He'd learned over the years not to try and shake her out of a vision, or say anything. He simply stood nearby to calm her once she came to, or to catch her if she blacked out and fell, which had happened twice.

Jasper looked at the TV and saw a small blonde-haired girl's photo on the screen. Jessi Price. And under her name: *MISSING*.

She'd been missing for several days, and yet Jasper was only now hearing about it. He wondered why. Surely the girl's disappearance had been on the news before now.

Jordyn stopped shaking, turned to Jasper, and met her father's eyes.

"I saw her. He has her."

"Who?"

"The same man that took the cop's kid."

A chill raked his spine. "Is she still alive? What else did you get? A name? A location? Do you know what he looks like?"

"Yes, she's still alive. I got a bit of what he looks like, but not enough for a sketch artist. He's tall. White. Brown curly hair. But beyond that, nothing."

"Shit."

"But I *did* get something useful."

"What?"

"I saw through his eyes as he was riding a bus. He looked at his phone to check the time. It was 6:45 in the morning, right as it stopped in front of Rooster's."

There was only one Rooster's Wing House — twenty minutes from Jasper's apartment.

He looked at the clock on the cable box: *5:15*.

"Was it today? When he looked at the phone did you notice the day?"

She closed her eyes, trying to remember.

He waited anxiously, watching Jordyn's eyes flutter under their lids. While her gift was valuable, the missing details could be maddening. Jasper wasn't sure how her psychic visions worked. At certain times it seemed like she was tapping into some collective unconscious, and at other times, into someone's mind. As fantastical as that seemed, Jasper could see how it could work. After all, human senses were limited. There were all sorts of things that occurred outside of most people's ability to perceive them. Some people could hear things that others couldn't. Some could see colors. And some people, like Jordyn, could see things remotely. But that didn't explain how she could see things that had yet to happen.

Jasper presumed there was some quantum mechanical explanation, something to do with time not existing as we experience it, that everything happens in one instance, and it's only our perception that changes.

It made no sense to Jasper, but he tried not to think too much about it. He didn't want to risk ruining it. Like when Wile E. Coyote chases Roadrunner off a cliff, overshoots a turn, and is somehow able to run in midair. There's always that moment where the character is somehow defying gravity because he's unaware of it. The jig is up once he looks down. Only then does he plummet into the canyon below. Jasper wished he could understand what was happening to Jordyn, or learn to control it so they could get better information. But he refused to look down.

Jordyn grinned. "I saw the day. It's tomorrow."

Jasper smiled. "Thank you."

"One other thing: He has a bandage on his left hand. It might make finding him easier."

Jasper pulled his daughter to him, and gave her a big kiss on the cheek. "You're the best!"

He went back to his room, got dressed, and returned to the living room waiting for Jordyn to get ready.

She looked up from the couch. "So, I guess you're not working out?"

"It'll have to wait."

❧

JASPER SAT on one of the two sheltered bus benches in front of Rooster's, watching each bus drive by, noting numbers in his journal. So far, two buses had passed, the number 90 and 51. It was fifteen minutes before the killer's bus would pass, assuming it kept the same time and route each day.

Jordyn was sitting beside him on the bench, knees under her chin, arms wrapped around her legs as she watched the passing cars.

She punched him in the arm. "Punch buggy blue."

He looked up and saw a blue VW Beetle drive by.

"Come on, you know I hate this game," he said.

"Still being Mr. Cranky Pants?"

"I'm not cranky. Just tired."

A disheveled looking older man was staring at them from one bench over. He was wearing gray pants, frayed along the cuffs, and a cream-colored dress shirt that had also seen better days. His unkempt, dirty-blond hair looked like it had gone through a car wash. Jasper couldn't tell if the guy was homeless or waiting for the bus. Nor could he tell if he was ogling Jordyn, had no social skills, or was insane. Hell, when a person rode the bus, they could be that special Florida blend of all three.

Jordyn seemed oblivious to the man's gawking. As long as she wasn't bothered, Jasper would try to ignore the man rather than engage. He didn't have time for Crazy today.

"Why do you think he's riding a bus?" Jordyn asked.

"What do you mean?"

"Well, we saw him driving in a van once, and another time in a car. We couldn't get a make on either, but we can assume he has access to vehicles. So why take a bus?"

"I dunno. Maybe he uses the time to read up on the latest Murderers self-help book? Maybe get some work done? You didn't see anything else?"

"He had a laptop bag. But he wasn't working on anything when I peeked in."

"Hmm, I dunno."

Jasper glanced over to see the guy on the other bench still staring at them. He sat up as if itching to say something. Jordyn noticed her father's distraction and looked over at the man, then back at Jasper.

"What's *his* deal?"

"Hell if I know."

Jordyn turned to him, smiled, and waved.

Jasper knocked her hand down. "Don't do that."

Jordyn laughed.

The man kept staring, the way a psychopath might stare at you before coming over to ventilate your body with a knife.

Jasper whispered, "There's obviously something wrong with him."

He wasn't worried about their safety, as much an interruption. He glanced at his watch: *7:01 AM*. A few more minutes.

"Do you think he's on the bus now?" Jordyn asked. "Think we should get on?"

"As much as I'd love to, I think we wait. Just to make sure there's not more than one bus that comes around the same time."

"Good point."

At 7:04 bus number 115 squealed to a stop, lurching forward as the doors hissed open. The bus route was fixed to the front.

Jasper recorded the route and number. He peered through the windows hoping to spot the killer among the passengers. But Jasper couldn't see anything through the tint and the large ad painted on the side, windows included, for one of the city's notorious ambulance chasers.

Jordyn read the advertisement. "Are you serious? Attorney Ronald J. Law? That can't be his real name."

"I'm pretty sure he made it up."

"Only a tool would make up a name like that."

"Well, he *is* a lawyer."

The creepy and possibly homeless man left his bench and headed toward the bus, still staring at them, mostly Jasper, with a weird expression.

Jasper met the man's stare, part of him wishing that they didn't have more important business to deal with. Jasper might've asked him what his problem was. Then again, he might have said nothing. The guy could be mentally ill, and Jasper didn't want to get in a fight with a guy who legitimately couldn't help it.

He'd dealt with a number of mentally ill people on the job, and it was hard to stay mad when you saw what paved their road. Some were born to junkie parents, some were a product of abuse, and others were soldiers returning to a home neither equipped or caring enough to take care of their needs. He was sympathetic to their pain and thought that only a bully would try to engage them in violence.

The bus rolled away. While Jasper couldn't be certain, he was reasonably sure that the man kept his eyes on them until he was out of sight.

Alone again, Jasper and Jordyn waited for the next bus.

It was another twenty minutes before the next arrival. He wrote the number, then: *20 minutes after.*

He circled the 115 multiple times. "I think this is our bus."

"So, what do we do?"

"We go home, find the route, and get on the bus at an earlier stop tomorrow."

"And then what?"

"We take this bastard down."

Jordyn smiled.

Chapter 12 - Mallory Black

MAL STEPPED into her former police precinct with a mix of homesickness and alienation. Thankfully, Harriet Brown was the receptionist on duty. She'd been there for fifteen years, long before Mal.

"Mallory! Oh, my God!" Harriet smiled from her side of the bulletproof glass.

She buzzed open the door and came outside for a hug. Harriet was a big woman, and her hug was like a bear's. "How are you doing, honey?"

"Okay," Mal said. "You?"

"Good."

"Charles? Kenny?"

"Charles is still Charles. Kenny just graduated from Florida State."

"That's great."

Harriet was about to launch into small talk, and as much as Mal hated cutting her short, she'd be here all day if she didn't.

"Is the chief in?"

Harriet's brow furrowed. She looked like she was about

to ask for more information, but stopped herself. She could go on and on about personal matters, but she was a good employee who knew when it was time for business. And she could probably tell that something was wrong.

"Yeah, hold on a sec."

Harriet went back inside the door, then disappeared.

Mal watched a family sitting in the lobby, a heavyset woman with two toddlers, maybe twins, a boy and a girl. The girl was crying on her mother's shoulder while the boy sat in his chair, staring at Mal.

Mal smiled at the boy.

He didn't smile back.

His eyes and nose were red.

She wondered if they were there to report a crime or were visiting someone in lock-up. They didn't have much, judging from their clothing, but at least their mother was comforting them. Mal had seen way too many families come into the station where the parents would ignore or yell at the children for bugging them. Mal often wondered why people like that even bred. They certainly didn't deserve any offspring.

Seconds later, Harriet returned and buzzed Mal in through the employee's entrance.

Mal stepped past the threshold and into a wall of memories. She nodded, waving at both familiar faces and new ones, passing six neat rows of cubicles into the Sheriff's office in the back.

Gloria Bell was standing outside of her office. She greeted Mal with a hug.

Gloria looked pretty much the same as when Mal had last seen her, though a bit worse for wear. She'd been sheriff for nearly three years, and as both the first female and black sheriff in Creek County, Gloria had broken many barriers. But it wasn't her only battle. Shattering ceilings and walls was an ongoing endeavor. After a while, the stress appeared on her face and the weight yanked on her shoulders. Gloria had been an excellent cop, one who told it like it was and didn't suffer fools. Mal wondered how Gloria managed to navigate the tricky waters of dealing with the public, and county and city commissioners, while still getting actual police work done.

"Mike told me you have something?"

As if on cue, Mike popped out from behind his cubicle wall to join them.

"Yeah. Ashley's killer sent me something," Mal said.

Then she pulled out the flash drive and showed them.

MAL AND MIKE sat opposite Gloria behind her desk as they waited for the station's resident tech guru, Aanya Batra, to safely extract and duplicate what was on the hard drive. As they waited, Mal came clean about how the killer had reached out to her a year before with the photos.

She withdrew the year-old envelope from her jacket and slid them across the desk to Gloria.

"Why didn't you say anything?" Gloria opened the envelope. Tears filled the corners of her eyes as she shuffled through photos from Ashley's final days.

"It had been a year since her murder. I didn't want this to become a big story."

"Isn't this around the time that you did that TV interview with Presley Jennings?"

"Yeah, I did that as a favor, and believe me, I regret it every day. It was right before the anniversary. Maybe that interview is what drove the killer to send the photos. He saw me break down and wanted to fuck with me more."

"Jesus," Mike said, now looking through the photos. "You could've told us, Mal."

"I wanted to handle it myself."

"Yourself?" Gloria asked, eyebrows arched.

"I was hoping he'd come back this year. I was waiting for him last night. But … I had too much to drink and fell asleep."

Mike shook his head, likely wishing she'd told him of her plans so he could have been there.

Mal pulled a second thumb drive from her coat — copies of the surveillance video. "I got video of him coming into my house, standing over me, and putting the gun against my head as I slept passed out."

"Shit," Mike leaned forward in his chair. "Did you get a good look at him?"

"He was wearing a hoodie and mask. But maybe you all can get something, I dunno."

Gloria shook her head. "You should've come to us earlier."

"Well, I didn't. But I'm here now. And maybe you can get something off the flash drive. I also have the box he delivered it in, though I doubt you'll find any prints."

Gloria looked at Mal for a long moment. Then, "What were you going to do if you caught him breaking into your house?"

Mal met her eyes. She wasn't sure who was asking the question. Was it Gloria her friend, asking out of concern? Gloria the sheriff, asking without really wanting to know the answer? Or Gloria the politician, asking so she could find the best way to spin the situation?

"I was going to arrest him," Mal lied.

Gloria looked into her eyes for a long, uncomfortable moment. Mal wasn't sure what she saw. Gloria's bullshit detector was one of the best, and Mal hated lying to her.

But what was she going to do? Tell the truth? That she planned to murder the bastard the second he stepped foot in her house and she verified that he was the monster she'd been hunting? That wouldn't go over well.

A knock on the door.

"Come in," Gloria said.

Aanya held up a laptop. "You were right not to plug this into your computer. There was a RAT installed."

"A RAT?" Mike repeated.

"A Remote Access Trojan, a back door allowing the user to take over your computer, spy on you with your webcam, pretty much anything they want. Anyway, the only other thing on the flash was a video file. I haven't watched it yet. I brought it right over."

Aanya handed the computer to Gloria. She placed it sideways so everyone could see the screen then looked up at Mal.

"You sure you want to watch this?"

Mal nodded, heart in her throat.

Mike leaned back and closed the door so nobody could walk by and see whatever they were about to watch.

Gloria pressed *Play*.

Chapter 13 - Mallory Black

MAL WATCHED the computer screen as the video began to play.

"Is it on?" Mike asked.

The screen was still dark, and the scrub bar along the bottom was crawling. Suddenly, an orange glow illuminated a small, narrow hallway.

A man's voice crackled to life on the speakers, singing *Happy Birthday* as he continued down the hall to a doorway. The camera panned to a birthday cake with white frosting, pink flowers, and ten lit candles.

The camera briefly showed a padlock on the door before the video cut to it slowly opening.

The man continued to sing as he entered the bedroom.

"Rise and shine, birthday girl."

The camera moved closer to the bed and a girl sleeping beneath the blanket.

Mal held her breath as the shape beneath the blanket moved, then revealed itself.

Ashley!

Ashley looked at the man, his cake, and the camera, confused, and scared. "What's happening?"

"It's your birthday, sweetie."

"Am I going to see Mommy today?"

"Yes, yes you are," the bastard lied. "Do you want to say something to Mommy? I'm sending her this video."

Ashley smiled. Her eyes were rimmed with dark circles, but she seemed otherwise okay. "Hi, Mommy! Uncle—" a shrill scream cut out whatever name she said, as if edited in from some horror movie like a censor's beep. Mal wondered if the scream was Ashley's death cry. "—said I'm going to see you for my birthday. I can't wait to see you again. I miss you so much!"

"Anything else, Ashley?"

Hearing the man say her baby girl's name felt like someone defiling her grave. Mal wanted to reach through the computer and strangle the fiend.

"I love you, Mommy."

The video cut to black.

Mal leaned forward even more, watching the black screen, waiting for something, anything, as tears streamed down her face.

"Is there more?"

Gloria pressed play again and the video started.

Mal stared at the screen, her throat tight, a cold chill squeezing her spine.

Her heart was pounding.

Her face was flush, hot.

And her hands, folded in her lap, were trembling.

Her throat tightened further as if a building knot of seething rage was making it impossible to breathe.

She tried to swallow, but couldn't.

So Mal screamed, unleashing countless pent up emotions.

She wanted to lash out. Wanted to break stuff. Wanted to smash the laptop into a million little bits. Wanted to find the killer and do the same to him.

But she couldn't break the computer because it might be their only lead to finding Ashley's murderer. So Mal had only her scream.

She got up and fled the office, fast as she could before Gloria or Mike tried to wrap an arm around her for comfort.

But that's not what she wanted.

Mal wanted revenge.

Needed the fucker dead.

MAL SAT in the parking lot, trying to calm herself. She wanted to leave but knew she couldn't. She had to compose herself, go back inside, talk to Gloria and Mike, and see what else they could do to catch this guy.

She reached into her purse, found the pills, and took one, swallowing it dry. Just something to take the edge off.

She closed her eyes, waiting for the pill to calm her.

Rain began to fall, pelting the roof of her car with a calming sound.

She thought about taking another pill, but a knock on her window arrested the thought.

She opened her eyes.

It was Gloria, smoking an e-cigarette.

Rain fell harder.

"Can I come in?" she asked.

Mal nodded.

Gloria ran around to the passenger side, opened the door, and took a seat beside Mal. "I'm sorry."

Mal stared out her window, watching rain drizzle on

the glass, not wanting to meet Gloria's eyes and break down into tears.

"No, I'm sorry. I should've stayed up last night. Shouldn't have gotten drunk. What the hell was I thinking?"

"Maybe you were drinking because you were scared of what you might do?"

Mal wasn't sure what Gloria was getting at, if anything, but she supposed it made sense. "I wasn't going to kill him if that's what you mean."

"I'm not sure *I* would've been that strong. Then again, I never had a kid, so I suppose I can't know what I'd feel."

Gloria had tried to have kids twice. Both miscarried, killing part of her and all of her marriage.

They sat in silence until Mal finally broke it. "You're right. I should've come to you guys. I was just afraid that if he saw cops hanging around, he'd get spooked." At least this was partly true. "But maybe his boldness would've blinded him. Maybe we could've caught him."

"Maybe," Gloria said, taking a drag.

Mal laughed morbidly, "Well, there's always next year. Wonder what *gift* he'll bring then."

Mal couldn't stop thinking about seeing Ashley on the video. It was likely the last video of her little girl still alive. She'd watched countless videos of Ashley since her death, and in every one Mal wished she could somehow freeze the moment, go back in time, and warn herself. Tell herself to pick up Ashley from school.

She thought of the phone call from the mystery man who did exactly that. They could never trace the call or get any information on who made it. There were two theories. One was that it was the killer himself making the call, probably after he'd already kidnapped the girl, just to fuck with Mal and/or the police. Mal had acted, called the school, but was too late to do anything.

The other, less popular, theory was that it was someone maybe working with the killer. He might've grown a conscience or gotten scared off from kidnapping and killing a cop's daughter.

"It wasn't him," Mal said.

"What?"

"The man who called to warn me. It wasn't his voice on this recording. It's two different people."

"You remember his voice?" Gloria asked.

"Oh, yeah. I hear it in my head all the time, wondering why the hell I didn't answer sooner."

"So, you think we should look into that caller again? Maybe put something out there to try and appeal to his desire to help?"

"Maybe." After a long moment of trying to figure out how to bring up the Jessi Price case, Mal laid it bare. "I saw your press conference on Jessi Price, and how her father was a person of interest. I don't think it's him."

"What?" Gloria said, brows raised.

"I think it's Ashley's killer."

Before Gloria could object, Mal continued, "Both girls vanish around the same time, two years apart. And both girls were taken just before their tenth birthday."

"We looked into it, but didn't come up with any leads."

Mal didn't want to throw Mike under the bus by saying how much she already knew about the investigation, nor could she let it go.

"Did you interview the registered sex offenders?"

"We talked to a few. But no, not all of them."

"Why not?"

"I'm not going through the details of an active investigation with you, Mallory. But believe me, we're doing everything we can."

"*Everything?*"

Gloria glared at her. "Is there something you'd like to say?"

"I'd like to help."

"That's a bad idea."

"Why?"

"Really? I need to spell it out for you? First, you don't work here any—"

"Bring me on as a consultant."

"Second, this would be a conflict of interest having you investigate a case which could be connected to your daughter's murder."

"So, you admit they're connected?"

Gloria stared at Mal, then finally said, "I'm leaving, Mallory. We'll be in touch if we get anything in regards to your break-in."

"Jessi Price is going to die in four days if you don't catch this man."

The Sheriff met her eyes. "Then maybe you shouldn't have gotten drunk off your ass last night. Maybe *you* would've caught him. Why don't you get your own house in order before telling others what to do?"

Gloria opened the door, stepped out into the rain, and slammed it shut.

Mal's fists tightened as she watched Gloria head back into the station.

She screamed, punching the steering wheel with both fists.

Hard.

Chapter 14 - Paul Dodd

PAUL SAT on the toilet of his tiny work bathroom looking at the telephone, checking to see if there was any news on Mallory Black.

He wondered if she was even awake, given how much she reeked of alcohol. If she was, had she seen the flash drive? Had she watched her security footage to see him creeping through her house and putting the gun to her head?

Paul couldn't wait to get home and check one of his computers to see if she'd installed the drive, which would have, in turn, uploaded a RAT onto her computer and granting him total control. He didn't *think* she'd be that dumb, but you never knew. She had yet to discover that he'd hacked into her security system and could watch her whenever he wanted.

Most people weren't especially tech savvy, which surprised him given the frequency of hacking and related stories in the news. You'd think some of these people would brush up on their security and knowledge, or maybe change the factory settings on their home's routers and devices. He found it entertainingly ironic that as more people turned to high tech security solutions, they failed to implement the most basic common sense in securing these devices designed to safeguard their lives. But most people were stupid, and that made it much easier for people like Paul to operate in shadows.

He didn't see anything new regarding Mallory. She probably wouldn't go to the cops. She'd probably be too embarrassed. She'd see the footage, freak out, then get drunk and/or high again. Such a waste of life.

He'd felt such a rush standing over her, with the power to extinguish the whore's existence. She was long past her prime, now little more than a wretched drug addict. If anyone deserved to be put out of their misery, it was her.

But he didn't want to grant Mallory Black such mercy.

He wanted to make her suffer, and he wasn't even sure why.

Paul usually knew why he did the things he did, as fucked up as they might make him. He at least understood *why* he was fucked up, why he was attracted to little girls, and why he needed to end their lives before they became bitches who did nothing but ruin all that they touched.

But he couldn't understand his obsession with Mallory. It was the first adult he'd ever obsessed over, and it wasn't sexual. People obviously found her attractive, particularly given the number of men and women she'd slept with, but Paul found her repulsive, like most of the loose women of this era. Maybe the obsession with Mallory was a way of reliving his moments with her daughter, Ashley. At least that made sense.

He thought about Ashley and began to get hard, his heart racing, lust and desire swirling like a vortex, demanding that he exorcise them.

Paul grabbed his cock with one hand and flipped through his phone's directory with the other until he found the encrypted folder.

He looked at his pictures of Jessi, lying in bed, asleep and drugged. He'd removed her shirt, but he hadn't yet touched her because he didn't want to spoil her birthday.

He stroked himself faster, flipping through his directory until he found what he was looking for — video he took of his night with Ashley, when he'd undressed her and finally made love to her.

The phone shaking in his hand, he barely managed to press *Play*.

He didn't last thirty seconds.

Shit.

He stood, wiped himself off, cleaned the wall with paper towels and Windex, then washed his hands, sorted himself out in the mirror, and returned to his desk for lunch.

AFTER EATING a turkey sandwich at his desk, Paul closed his eyes and rubbed his temples, trying to ease his swelling headache before his break ended and chaos ensued.

He'd already taken two Tylenol and was thinking about swallowing a third when Tracy Adams from next door stepped into his room.

"How's it going?" she asked, smiling. Tracy was in her late twenties with long blonde hair, blue eyes, and a cute smile. She was easily the most attractive of his coworkers, and sometimes he wondered if she had a crush on him, even though the girl was engaged.

"Okay," he said, then noticed that she was looking at the open Tylenol bottle on his desk. "Woke up with a killer headache. You wouldn't happen to have some earplugs?"

She laughed. "No, fresh out, but I bet that Mr. Ridley might have something stronger than Tylenol."

Paul laughed. "I bet he would. Too bad I'm on duty."

She laughed, a bit too much. Then there was an uncomfortable silence where she was looking at him like she wanted to say something but had forgotten, or was trying to muster the courage.

"I was wondering if that offer for coffee was still on?"

He paused. "By that offer do you mean when I asked you two years ago if you'd like to go for coffee?"

"Yeah," she said, laughing. "That offer still good?"

"Um, sure."

Paul was going to ask about her fiancé, then realized that she wasn't wearing her engagement ring.

Hmm, I wonder when that happened?

"Great. Tom and I broke up a couple of months ago."

"Sorry to hear that."

"Don't be. He was a jerk. My sister says I was born with a jerk magnet or something."

He laughed.

Her face went red. "Not that I'm saying you're a jerk."

"No, of course not," Paul smiled. "At least I don't think so. But then again, would a jerk *know* he's a jerk?"

"Fair point. But I've been working next to you for a while. I think I'd know if you're a jerk by now."

"True."

Suddenly noise in the hallways outside as Mrs. Everly returned from Library Time with both of their classes.

"Well," he said, grabbing his bottle of Tylenol, "looks like I better take another."

"Maybe I should, too."

They both laughed as the kindergarteners filed noisily back into their seats.

Rosita Sanchez and Billy Evans both ran up to him pointing to one another, accusing each other of pushing in line.

"She cut in front of me. I was in front of her, then she cut in front of me," Billy exclaimed, eyebrows arched, wildly waving his hands as he talked.

"Did you push her?" Paul asked.

"I was trying to put her back in her place."

He looked up and saw Tracy suppressing a laugh.

"You can't push girls," Paul said.

"Can I push boys then?"

"You can't push anyone, Billy. Now tell her you're sorry."

"Fine," he said, pouting, "I'm sorry."

"It's okay, Billy!" Rosita smiled, then hugged and patted him on the back.

Paul smiled as they returned to their desks.

"She's so adorable," Tracy said. "Okay, I guess I better head back to my classroom before the little monsters tear it apart. So, for that other thing, how about Wednesday night?"

While he liked the prospect of a date with her, as it had been forever since he'd been with an adult, he didn't want anything to ruin him for Jessi.

"Sounds great," Paul said, smiling. "But can we make it next week? I just remembered that I promised a friend of mine that I'd help him with this thing he's got."

A vague as hell excuse. Pursed lips and nodding suggested that Tracy thought she was being blown off. Paul added, "He's going through a divorce and needs a friend to lean on."

She seemed to relax. Tracy was fragile. Easier to

manipulate, but more difficult to get away from — he'd seriously have to consider meeting her after hours. He had a good thing going at the school and was flying under the radar. Sleeping with the teacher next door could screw all of that up.

"Okay, next week," she said, smiling on her way out the door.

Chapter 15 - Mallory Black

MAL SAT at her kitchen table staring at the empty gift box while eating her chicken sandwich and gulping a Diet Coke.

She had her iPad open on the table, standing at an angle, but had yet to turn it on. She'd usually browse the local news websites on her iPad or Facebook, even though she never posted anything. It was her one way of keeping up with people and far easier than calling them. She'd more or less shut herself off from everyone after Ashley's death, and even more so after winning the lottery. She found it utterly distasteful, though not at all surprising, how many people hadn't reached out to her after Ashley's death, yet thought nothing of calling her more than a year later after hearing about her winnings.

People sucked.

She considered turning the iPad on but didn't want any distractions while trying to figure out what had been bothering her all morning.

She was missing something regarding the killer, something she should've picked up on. And it was driving her nuts.

She ran through last night and the morning as she ate, methodically going over everything, hoping to find what she was missing.

Her phone, sitting beside the iPad, startled her with a ring.

She picked it up, looked at the caller ID, and saw it was Mike. She wondered if Gloria had relayed their conversation. Mike was one of her most trusted detectives, but they weren't exactly close.

Mal answered, "Miss me?"

"You know it. Just wanted to give you a heads-up that Gloria sent out a detail to watch over your house the next couple of days."

"Are you fucking kidding me?"

Mal stood, went to the front window, and ripped the curtains open.

She could see two figures sitting behind lightly tinted windows in an unmarked patrol car across the street.

She wasn't sure who was inside, nor did she care.

She flipped them off, then closed the curtains.

"Tell her to call them off."

"Yeah, I don't think that's gonna happen. She seems to think you're in danger. And ... I'm inclined to agree."

"Oh, come on, Mike. I can handle myself."

"Like last night?"

"Come on. If he wanted me dead, he would've killed me, don't you think?"

"Maybe, but you never know. Maybe he's waiting to come back. Maybe he's planning to kidnap you, too."

"Let him try."

"I'm serious, Mal. You need to be careful. He got in your house once. You need to take some precautions."

"Like what? Get a proper security system? Maybe head to a hotel and hide out for a while? Fuck that, Mike. I'm not leaving my house because of this bastard. If he wants me, let him fucking well come and get me."

"I'm serious, Mal."

"Tell her to call them off."

"I'll see what I can do."

She hung up, knowing that Mike wouldn't say shit. He was too worried about her welfare. Any other time, she might appreciate the sentiment, but right now she was annoyed by the deputies sitting in front of her house, and watching her every move.

Then it hit her.

Watching my every move.

She remembered reading a story in the news a few years back about a weakness in webcam systems. She hadn't thought about it until now, but it made perfect sense.

She went to her iPad, clicked on the browser, and searched for her particular model of security camera and "hackable."

Several hacker forums popped up.

She skimmed a few, looking to confirm her fears. On the fourth article, she found it. There were two ways someone could hack into her security camera feed: capture her wifi signal as most of the cameras didn't encrypt the streaming video, or brute force her password on the camera's website.

He'd likely done one or the other. Hell, maybe both.

Pure rage flared again.

She felt vulnerable and watched, under some sick bastard's microscope. Fire in her veins burned even hotter.

She glanced up at the camera, the one that had

captured the bastard breaking into her house not even twelve hours ago.

Is he watching me now?

Recording my every move?

She glared at the camera, wanting to threaten him, to let him know that she knew exactly what he was doing. She wanted to rip the camera from its mount and scream into it, "Come and get me, you pussy!"

But then she quickly moved her gaze to the table, pretending to read her iPad, while trying to calm herself and conjure the best possible solution.

It was never smart to let the criminal know how much you knew. Playing ignorant was far more likely to grant her an advantage.

Mal pretended that she wasn't being watched, remembering how steadily he'd moved through her house, through the front door, into the dining room, and straight up the stairs without pause.

He hadn't been treading carefully, peeking inside bedroom and bathroom doors. He'd moved deliberately, like someone familiar with her house — like someone who had been inside many times before.

Mal felt practically frozen.

She was shaking, biting her cheeks to keep from screaming.

She closed her eyes, slowly counting backward from ten, a method she learned in a brief flirtation with meditation back before surrendering all illusion of control.

Surprisingly, it worked, clearing enough of the anger for Mal to take her next steps. She could talk to Aanya, assuming she could suggest the best means to handle this situation. If he'd hacked into the camera, then *maybe* he was setting up something nearby to capture the stream, something he'd need to pick up. If he was logging into her camera's website, then maybe they kept IP logs, and she could track the killer that way.

This was all assuming a lot, that the murderer was indeed watching her through her cameras, and that there would be a way to trace that use back to him. But for the first time since waking up, Mal felt a ray of hope piercing the clouds.

She took one last drink of her Diet Coke and smiled.

I'm finally going to find you.

Chapter 16 - Jasper Parish

JASPER SPRINTED toward the park bench, his gray tee soaked through as he struggled to catch his breath.

Jordyn sat on the bench, reading something on her phone, probably one of her young adult vampire books or something.

"You really should join me sometime," he said.

"Yeah, running isn't my thing."

"Youth is definitely wasted on the young."

She rolled her eyes. "Are we ready to go home yet?"

"No, just taking a short break. Got another two laps."

"*Two more?* Sheesh. You preparing for a marathon?"

"Gotta make up for missing my morning run. You in a rush or something?"

"No."

"Good," he said, slapping her on the back before returning to the path that wound through the wooded seaside park.

Jasper wasn't sure why she even came with him to the park given her aversion to exercise. He supposed part of it was making up for lack of father-daughter time growing up. For most of her life, Jasper was always working and rarely had time for his family, something he never thought much about until it was too late. Until cancer took Carissa when Jordyn was eleven, leaving him to raise their girl on his own.

He looked back at his daughter one last time before disappearing into the woods. Her eyes were fixed on the phone. Maybe she'd finally made a friend.

He wondered if she was happy.

She'd been a happy, bubbly little girl, a social butterfly with tons of friends whom she played with all the time. Then her mom died, and everything changed.

Jordyn became withdrawn, spending most of her time alone, reading books in her bedroom.

At first, Jasper let it go, figuring it was a natural reaction to her mother's passing and a phase she'd grow out of. But things only got worse in high school. He still didn't think much of it, figuring she'd changed as kids tended to do. But one night in tenth grade, while all her old friends were at the homecoming dance, Jordyn broke down crying and confessed that "nobody liked her." No boys would even look at her, much less ask her to the dance.

Jasper hugged her, tears running down his cheeks, wished he could take that pain away, wished he could make other kids like her, make boys see her as the wonderful young woman she was growing into.

But being a parent was an exercise in helplessness and futility. Jasper knew there was only so much he could do for his kid, and he was ill-equipped to help her through this rough patch. He'd barely made it through his own awkward adolescence. As an introvert, he'd had few friends, and never needed them. One or two was fine. He spent most of his time reading, studying, or working to improve himself. Who had time for distractions?

But Jordyn wasn't wired like Jasper.

She needed friends, and for some reason he didn't understand, she couldn't connect with anyone anymore.

Things got way worse before they got better.

Three and a half years ago, after getting wounded in the line of duty, Jasper retired and moved out of South Florida, heading north to Pine Harbour for a fresh start.

Jordyn, now free from a past that weighed heavily on her shoulders, was back to being the bubbly, happy girl he once knew. But she had yet to make friends, get a job, or do any of the things a child required to find their independence.

A figure stepped out onto the path in front of Jasper, jarring his trip down memory lane. He was startled, fists clenched, until he recognized the old black man wearing a gray pea coat, jeans, and a matching hat.

"Jesus, Barnes, you scared the hell outta me!"

Lenny Barnes used to coach a youth basketball team in South Florida, where he more or less raised Jasper after his father died of a heart attack when Jasper was just eight. He taught kids how to play basketball, and gave them the self-discipline that kept many — though never enough — out of jail.

He was also the one who convinced Jasper to become a cop. And the reason Jasper moved to Pine Harbour, insisting that it was a good place to raise his daughter.

"How's it going?" Barnes asked, adjusting his charcoal fedora.

"Okay, I guess. What's up?" he asked, trying not to let his nerves show.

Something was up if Barnes had tracked him down in the park.

"How'd it go last night?"

"Good."

"You sure? You don't look so good."

"It went fine. His place was a mess, though. Like *Hoarders* disgusting. Why, did you hear something? Is it in the news yet?"

"Not yet, no."

"So, what brings you to the park? You wanna join me for a run?"

Barnes laughed. "Boy, if I were twenty years younger, I'd show you a thing or two."

"Twenty years and maybe forty pounds ago, old man," Jasper joked.

"Yeah, yeah, whatever," Barnes said with a wave. "No, nothing's up. I just wanted to check in and see if everything's okay."

"Yeah. It's okay." Jasper couldn't shake the sense that the old man was fishing. "What is it, Lenny?"

"Just wanted to check in after you called me last night."

"Called you? I didn't call you last night."

"Yeah, you did. Like three in the morning. And you sounded out of it."

Jasper looked at Lenny in confusion. His old friend loved to bust balls, but he wasn't the type to joke like this. "What did I say?"

"You said something about Jordyn almost puking last night. Please tell me you didn't bring her on one of your jobs."

Crap.

He hadn't told Barnes that Jordyn had been joining him for the past few months.

"What else did I say?"

"Hell if I know. You mumbled some shit then hung up." He paused. "So, why did you bring her?"

"I don't know. She wanted to come."

"Man, this isn't 'take your child to work' day. It's bad

enough she knows what you're doing, but now you involve her? Why would you risk her future like this?"

Jasper looked at the ground, unsure of what to say. He wasn't about to tell Barnes that this wasn't the first time he'd brought Jordyn on a job. "You believe in what I'm doing, right? I mean, it was pretty much your idea."

"You know I do."

"Well, so does Jordyn. And did you forget that she was already involved? *She's* the one with the visions. She's like dispatch, telling me where to find the bad guys."

Barnes rolled his eyes. "Visions are one thing. But now you're bringing her to a crime scene? Dispatch doesn't go to crime scenes, do they? You're making her an accessory to murder."

Footsteps came up fast behind them.

Jasper flinched, his heart rate spiking. As long as he was doing the things he kept doing, part of him was always ready for the cops to roll up on him from nowhere.

But it was just two women in their early thirties out for an afternoon jog.

Jasper nodded, exhaling with a deeply relieved sigh.

Barnes doffed his hat and gave the women his most charming smile.

The women said "hello," then passed them.

Barnes's eyes bored into Jasper's as he whispered, "I don't like this. Next thing you know you'll be putting a knife in her hand."

Jasper said nothing, ashamed of himself.

Barnes's eyes widened. "You didn't do that, did you?"

"No, of course not!"

"So, why'd you bring her?"

"I don't know."

"Well, *that's* a good reason to throw her life in the garbage!"

"She put two and two together. Figured out why I was asking her about the people she was having visions of, then saw that they were showing up dead or missing. She's not stupid. Jordyn asked, and I told her the truth. Then she asked if she could help. What could I say?"

"You could've said no, fool!"

"It's not easy to refuse her. And besides, how can I say no if our mission is just? To say no is to imply that what we're doing is wrong."

"Bullshit. Every mission has its soldiers and support roles. She's support, not a soldier."

"She'll be fine."

"Yeah, you can guarantee that, can you? Listen, Jasper, you're a soldier. You know the risks and have decided they're worth it. *You* can help those who can't help themselves. You have the talents, and she has an incredible gift to assist you. But she's your daughter. And practically a kid. She's trying to please you. Be part of something with you. But she doesn't *really* understand the risks. It only takes one screw-up, Jasper. Are you ready to risk her entire life over one mistake?"

"I don't make mistakes. I'm *very* thorough."

Barnes dismissed him with a snort. "Bullshit. You can't be *very* thorough when you've got Jordyn with you. No matter your level of supposed perfection, or how separate you think you're keeping things, it's impossible to juggle everything you need to do and account for her."

"So, what do you want me to do, tell her no?"

"Yes! That's exactly what I want you to do. Be her father, not her friend."

"She won't be happy."

"Show me a teenager who is."

"Get your house in order, son," Barnes said, then turned around and headed back down the path.

Jasper watched his old friend walk away, considering his words and wondering if Barnes might be right.

He wasn't sure why the hell he ever said yes to Jordyn. It didn't make sense. He *was* putting her life in danger. They could never account for every variable — the bad guy escaping, a neighbor spotting them, law enforcement showing up. There were too many risks, and having Jordyn along increased the odds that something would go wrong.

It somehow felt *right* with her by his side.

He was also passing on valuable skills to his daughter: he taught her how to get the drop on people, how to break into homes, how to fight, and how to kill them. In many ways, it was like a father teaching his kid to hunt. They just happened to be hunting bad guys. And make no mistake, these people deserved to be hunted. Every one of them deserved to die.

But Jordyn had yet to kill anyone.

That was a line he wasn't ready for her to cross.

But she could at least know *how* in case she ever had to.

That couldn't be a bad thing.

But Lenny was right. If they got caught, they'd both end up in jail. Maybe even get the death penalty.

And that thought was a knife through his heart.

What the hell have I done?

Even if they didn't get caught, how could Jordyn ever have a normal life after being a part of this? He'd already given up on ever having a normal life for himself, and that was *his* decision, but she didn't have to take this path. She could still have a life … he hoped.

But how? How do you go from killing people with your father to getting a job, getting married, having kids, and raising a family?

How could this not ruin her forever?

Jasper wished he'd never involved her.

Wished he'd never asked her about her visions.

Wished he'd never brought her along.

He stood on the path for a long time feeling the weight of his shame like a smothering blanket. Lenny, as usual, was right.

Jasper needed to find a way to get his house in order.

He looked at the path ahead.

His body was aching, with two laps to go.

Jasper gritted his teeth and got back to work.

Chapter 17 - Mallory Black

MAL BOUGHT a new laptop and a brand-new phone — she couldn't be sure if the killer had tampered with or cloned her old one.

She had to start fresh.

On the way to her car, Mal spotted the two deputies waiting in a parked across from her in the unmarked sedan.

One of the officers, Bill Wilson, had been on the force for five years or so. He was a good cop, even if he was a chronic smart ass. The other officer was a young guy who looked greener than Mal's last salad.

She approached them.

Wilson rolled down the driver's side window. "Hey, Mal."

"Listen," she said, "I don't need an escort everywhere I go."

"Just doing our jobs."

"Yeah, you and Hitler Youth."

Wilson laughed. "Still busting balls, eh?"

She relaxed a bit, and wondered if she had overreacted. "I don't know why she put you on my house, but whatever. Thanks, I guess."

Wilson smiled. "Was that so hard?"

She flipped him off, went to her car and stowed the new computer beneath the passenger seat, then drove to the library.

~

SHE FOUND A DESK IN BACK, opened her computer, set it up, and logged into the website for her security camera. She entered her account details and found the last ten IP addresses to log in. There was the library's IP, her own, then another, logged in four times during the last week.

"Gotcha," she said, copying and pasting the number then sending it to her phone.

She did a reverse lookup of the IP address and found that it was in town, but she didn't have an address. She'd need to reach out to her contact at the cable company.

Mal went into her old phone, which she kept active so as not to alert the killer if he was keeping tabs, and copied all of her contact info.

She found the number for Diana Trembly, who worked at the cable company, and dialed.

"Mal! How are you?"

"Not so good. Was hoping you could help me."

Mal filled her in with just enough to get Diana overlooking the rules. Mal had worked with her enough in the past to build trust. Additionally, she'd helped Diana with a slight stalker issue, so the woman was more than happy to help by sharing customer information, even if she shouldn't have.

She gave Mal an address on the other side of town — Cuppees, a local coffee shop.

Shit.

"No way to tell who it was, though, right?"

"Not unless you got a time and can get security footage or something. Even then, if your guy was in the parking lot, you might not have much to go on, unless they've got CCTV out there, too."

"Thanks, Diana. I appreciate it."

"Good luck."

Mal hung up wishing she'd landed an easier lead.

But at least she had something.

MAL WENT INTO CUPPEES, asked for the manager, and was greeted by Nadine, a short, stocky woman with a severe crew cut, lots of tattoos, and large dark framed glasses. Mal wasn't sure why, but the woman was borderline hostile from word one.

Maybe she'd busted Nadine at some point, but didn't remember her.

Mal explained the relevant parts of her situation.

Nadine said, "You're not a cop now, right?"

"No."

"Sorry," she said, looking anything but sorry, "can't help you then."

"So, if I were a cop, you *could* help me?"

"Yes, we're happy to work with the authorities."

Mal smiled, said, "Hold on right there," and went outside.

She knocked on the unmarked car and waited for Wilson to roll down his window.

"Wanna be useful?"

THEY SAT in the back of Cuppees, watching Nadine reluctantly scroll through video for the only day with a recording to match the log-in time.

The shop was small but busy. There were at least two dozen people using the wifi. Most were women, which Mal ruled out.

They found a handful of men using either a tablet or laptop.

"Can you get me names on those?"

Nadine ignored Mal and turned to Wilson. "Are you asking, or is she?"

Wilson, not missing a beat, said, "Can you get the info or not?"

"Give me a day."

"A day?" Mal asked.

Nadine, still not looking at her, said, "Yeah, I need to match records to the time and pull the sales, assuming they used a credit card."

Mal said, "Can we also get pictures of these men?"

Nadine looked at Wilson. He nodded.

"Yes, I'll get them both to you by tomorrow."

"Thank you," Mal said, giving Nadine the most artificial smile in her arsenal. The one she used when trying not to call someone a fucking asshole.

Wilson laughed on his way out of Cuppees. "What'd you do to piss *her* off?"

"Hell if I know. She was a bitch from the get go."

"You know I have to call this in to Gloria, right?"

"I wish you wouldn't."

"What's going on?"

Mal explained how she was pretty certain that her investigation would lead to Ashley's killer. How the man had very likely logged into her security camera footage to spy on her.

"I wouldn't have said anything if you didn't involve me, but now that the Coffee Nazi is sending me this info, it's official police business. I've gotta pass it onto whoever's working the case."

"Fine," Mal sighed, walking away.

She got in her car and stared at the steering wheel, wishing for more answers. She hated waiting. And police work often required waiting on other people who may or may not provide what she needed. Most cops chased other leads while waiting, but Mal didn't have anything else to go on. This case was dark, and every trail cold.

She could try talking to registered sex offenders in the area just to see if something rattled loose, but since she was no longer a cop, no one had to talk. She was a citizen conducting an inquiry without any leverage.

She thought back on Mike suggesting that she ask for her job back.

Times like this, Mal wished she'd stayed on. Gloria wouldn't let her near a case involving a break-in at her house or her daughter's murder, but at least she could conduct her own investigation. People would see the badge and be more likely to help.

Mal's old cell phone buzzed.

She picked it up, looked at the name on the Caller ID. Presley Jennings, a reporter for Channel 4 who did the anniversary feature on Mal last week, the one where she broke down on camera.

Mal hated that interview. Hated breaking down. Hated that the station used that footage. She'd thought Presley was better than other reporters. Thought she could trust her given their past off-the-record dealings when Mal was still a detective. She'd called and asked why they used the footage, and Presley said it wasn't her call. Still, Mal felt burned. And it only reinforced Mike's constant refrain, "Never trust a reporter."

Mal let the call go to voicemail, waited a minute, then played it.

"Hey, Mal. It's Presley Jennings. I was reaching out hoping you could talk to me about a story I'm working on. I'm on a tight deadline, so I'd love it if you have a few minutes to spare."

Mal thought about calling her back, then decided against it. She put the phone on the seat beside her and backed out of the library's lot.

She watched the officers follow in her rearview mirror.

Chapter 18 - Mallory Black

MAL SAT in her living room watching the news and getting progressively drunker.

She turned on Channel 4 to see if there were any updates on Jessi Price, but according to the news anchors, there was nothing new. People were still being urged to call if they'd seen either Jessi or her father. After less than two minutes, the anchors moved on to a reporter standing in front of the county commission building discussing a vote regarding a land use change.

Two minutes, then on with the show.

That was one of the sad things about missing children. A lot of times they barely got coverage, unless they were white and/or came from a relatively well-off neighborhood. Once they did get coverage, it only lasted until the killer was caught, while talking heads tried to analyze a sick bastard or find someone to blame. The killer was the star of the show, and the child vanished from the headlines. The world went on as if the kid had never existed.

Mal tried to forget that her daughter's killer might be watching her. She'd been careful not to let him see her new phone or laptop. The new computer stayed in her trunk. The phone was in her bathroom, tucked in the vanity drawer. She had to maintain things as they were. She'd briefly considered changing her password so he couldn't spy on her, but decided against it for now. Maybe she could use his perceived advantage against him, lure the fucker into a trap.

Yeah, if I don't pass out again.

She took another drink, got up, went to the window, and opened the blinds a bit to see who was out there now.

Wilson and the rookie went home for the night, replaced by another pair of officers sitting in an unmarked car. She couldn't tell who they were from this distance, nor did she care.

Mal closed the blinds and went back to the couch.

Her cell phone rang: Gloria Bell.

She didn't answer.

Instead, she fished out her new phone, dialed Gloria's number, and walked outside to make the call.

"Hello?" Gloria answered, confused.

"It's Mal. I got a second phone. Can't trust that the other one isn't bugged or something."

"Um, okay. So, I talked to Wilson, and he told me about today. What're you doing?"

"Following up on leads to find the fucker who broke into my house."

"What leads?"

Mal told Gloria about the other IP address logging into her security site.

"You want to conduct an investigation, fine. But you can't be using our resources to do so."

"What are you saying? You're not going to share whatever info you get with me?"

"No, we're investigating the matter, and we will handle it. I don't need you getting yourself into any more shit."

"Yeah, well my case didn't exactly seem like a priority."

"I said we're working on it."

"And what about Jessi Price?"

"We're also working on that."

"Yeah? Then why isn't the news talking about the latest developments?"

"There *are* no new developments."

Mal laughed. "I can't decide if you believe that or if this is political."

"*What?*"

"Well, you're up for re-election, and a second missing child doesn't look good, does it? Better to play it off like the dad took her."

Mal could hear Gloria breathing out through her nostrils.

"I don't know if you're drunk or if you honestly believe that, but for both our cases, I'm hoping it's the former. I'm going to go before you piss me off and make me forget my manners."

Gloria hung up.

Mal stared at the phone, seething.

She dropped her phone in the sink, headed back into the living room, plopped on the couch, unscrewed the bottle of Jack, and took a deep swig. She looked at the pill bottle on the coffee table. She'd resisted its siren song so far, wanting to be alert if her enemy returned. But hell if she couldn't use *something* to ease her mind.

She got her new phone and called Mike.

He answered, sounding exhausted, or like he'd just woken up.

"That bitch!" Mal yelled into the phone.

"What? Who is this?"

"It's Mal. I got a new phone. Long story. Did I wake you?"

"It's okay. Hold on a sec."

She heard him get up, telling his wife that it was Mal on the phone, then heard him shuffle away from the bed, likely heading to his office down the hall. After a long moment, she heard him sit.

"Okay, who's a bitch now?"

"Gloria."

She filled him on her day and the call she just had with her old boss, then said, "Can you believe that shit?"

"Did she *say* she's not working on your case?"

"No. But she sure as shit doesn't want me working on it."

"I hate to say this, but you really should let us handle this, Mal. We will find this guy."

"Before Friday? How? She doesn't even think the cases are linked! Hell, she's too damned afraid to admit what's happening here."

"What you *think* is happening."

"Really, Mike? Did they force you to drink the Kool-Aid or are you chugging it all on your own?"

"I'm not saying that they're *not* connected. But right now, we can only follow the leads we have. You trust me, don't you?"

"Yeah, I trust you. But I don't trust *her*. And I think she's pushing the investigation somewhere it shouldn't be going."

"I like the father for it, too. I think you're too close to this to see clearly."

"Yeah?" Mal said, itching for a fight. If she couldn't yell at Gloria, she'd yell at Mike. "And I think you've got your head so far up your ass that you all can't see what you need to be seeing."

"You're drunk, Mal. Go to bed before—"

"Before I say something I'll regret? Jesus, do you two get together and script these things out?"

"What?"

"Never mind," Mal said.

She hung up, clutching the phone, wishing it was Mike's neck.

How the hell can nobody see what's so fucking obvious?

Mal tried removing herself from the equation, to see if maybe she *was* too close. She didn't think so. Yes, there wasn't much linking the Price case to her daughter's. And really, there wasn't any evidence to go on, or any leads they were ignoring. But she still couldn't shake the idea that they weren't considering every angle, doing more interviews, or putting a fire under that fucking coffee shop Nazi to get shit quicker.

If Mal were working this case, she'd exhaust every lead no matter how likely. She'd pour in the hours, do everything possible to find Jessi Price before Friday, chase every lead, no matter how unlikely it was to bear fruit.

Because that's what a good cop did.

"Fuck these people," she said, picking up her old phone and finding Presley's number. She copied the contact into her new phone.

She stared at the reporter's name, finger hovering over the *CALL* button.

She set the phone down, went into the living room, grabbed her pills and the bottle of Jack, and went back into the bathroom.

She took two pills, washed them down, and set both bottles on the sink.

Then she dialed.

Chapter 19 - Jessi Price

JESSI PRICE COULDN'T SLEEP.

She sat in the bed in Officer Bob's secret room, staring at the ceiling, lit only by the glow of the pink night light.

She wished she'd never gotten in the car.

Officer Bob had told Jessi that he'd been sent by her father and that she had to keep it a secret from her mom because if they got caught, her dad would go to jail. He said that her mom was a very bad person and that she was trying to hurt Jessi's dad. He was going to help her reunite with him.

Her parents had been arguing a lot on the phone. She hadn't seen her dad in more than six months, and missed him terribly. That was why she got in the car. She missed her daddy more than she missed her cat, Mable, who died last year.

She had thought the police officer was telling the truth when he said he wanted to help Jessi and her father.

But the more she thought about it now, he probably wasn't even a cop.

What was he?

Who was he?

Was his name even Bob?

And why did he take her?

Why was he hiding her in this room, if her dad wasn't coming?

She wanted to ask him, but there was something scary about the man. Even though he'd been perfectly nice until now, there were times when they were eating, and she'd catch him staring at her in a weird way. She always looked away, never asked why he was looking at her like that. Doing so was rude, and she wasn't ever supposed to be rude to adults. Besides, the question might anger him.

Officer Bob had never let her outside, or even upstairs in the main house. He said that she had to hide here, that he was risking his job to help her father. He also said that she had to follow his rules — stay quiet, be good, and listen to what he told her to do.

Officer Bob said that those were her father's instructions.

And Jessi wanted to believe him.

But in the dark of the night, in this strange bed in this room that wasn't hers, she no longer could.

Jessi realized with a sudden certainty, the only way she would ever see either of her parents again was to break this man's rules.

Wednesday Oct. 18

Chapter 20 - Paul Dodd

PAUL ARRANGED the two plates of eggs, toast, and sausages on the tray, adding a decorative flourish — an orange slice and parsley — to each breakfast. He wrapped a fork into a pink linen for her, then a fork and knife in a white linen for him, and smiled. The presentation would be worthy of an Instagram photo if he chose to dabble in such mindless trivialities.

He glanced at the clock. It was five fifteen. He'd wanted to wake up a bit earlier today so he could have breakfast with Jessi. She hadn't eaten at all yesterday. He should be there to make sure she got something in her stomach.

He carried the tray to The Room, opened the door, turned on the light, and saw Jessi still asleep, covered in blankets.

"Good morning, sweetheart. Officer Bob made a yummy breakfast!"

The girl didn't move.

He sat the plate on the dresser, then went to shake her gently.

He reached out, touching her shoulder under the blankets.

Jessi didn't move.

His heart began to race, a panic swelling in the pit of his stomach.

Oh, God. She's dead.

Then she moaned and moved beneath the covers.

He sighed with relief and pulled the blanket aside.

She turned away, burying her face in the pillow.

"Come on, sleepy head. I'm going to eat breakfast with you."

She turned, looking at him, confusion knitting her brow. "Where's Daddy?"

"He's not here yet. But he will be. This weekend."

"I need to pee." She got up, went to the bathroom, and closed the door behind her. She probably would have locked it if she could.

Paul waited, listening as she pissed, wondering if today would be a turning point, that she'd eat something and maybe find a better mood. There was nothing worse than having someone who so obviously didn't want to be there, who fought you every step of the way. That made it difficult to enjoy the moment when they finally made love. It reminded Paul of the angry women he dated back before he gave up on ever having a real relationship.

The door opened.

"Did you wash your hands?"

She looked at Paul and shook her head.

He pointed to the bathroom.

She turned, went back inside, washed her hands, then came back out and headed to the bed. She started to crawl back under the covers.

"Nope. First, we eat."

She looked back at him, groggily, eyes with dark circles

around them. He wondered if she'd been up all night crying.

He carried the tray to her bed, set it down, then took a seat at the corner.

Jessi sat up, looking at the plate, then at him suspiciously. "What is it?"

"Eggs and sausage."

"I don't like eggs."

"Have you ever had them?"

"No."

"You've *never* had eggs?" he laughed. "How could you have never had eggs?"

"I dunno."

"Then how do you know you don't like them?"

"I dunno," she said, her stomach growling.

He picked up a fork, dipped it into the eggs on her plate, stabbed it through, and lifted the fork to her mouth. "Open up."

She shook her head, lips pursed.

"Come on, at least try them. If you don't like them after you try them, then you don't have to eat them."

"I don't want to."

He set her fork on her plate. "Do you like sausage?"

She looked at the plate nervously.

"It's good." He said picked up his fork and knife, cut a piece of sausage, then raised it to his mouth.

He made an *mmm* sound as he swallowed the warm, peppery meat. "You never had sausage?"

She looked at it like she couldn't remember. "Do you have ketchup?"

He chuckled. "Ah, ketchup. I should've thought to bring that. Ketchup makes everything great, even eggs! Do you want ketchup?"

She nodded, and he'd swear something close to a smile tugged her mouth at the corners.

He stood, crossed the room to her door, closed and locked it from the outside, then headed into the kitchen. He smiled as he thought of her almost smiling. Maybe ketchup would be the thing to bond them.

He laughed at the idea of something so silly making such a difference, but he should've known better. On the days he had lunch duty, his kids slathered their food in ketchup. And those little moppets would put it on *everything* — French fries, meatloaf, potatoes, pizza, corn bread, pretty much anything you put on their plate that wasn't sweet, was worthy of ketchup.

He grabbed the bottle from the fridge and headed back into the room, hopeful for the first time since bringing Jessi home.

He sat down on the edge of the bed and held up the bottle. "Ta-da!"

She looked up at him, with a nervous half-smile.

He opened the cap and plopped a dollop onto her plate. "That enough?"

She looked at it, then back up at him. "A little more?"

He added a second dollop, then added some on his plate.

She wiped the eggs off of her fork, stabbed a piece of sausage, dipped it in the ketchup, then took a bite.

"Here, let me cut that for you," he said, going to grab his knife.

But it wasn't on the plate.

He looked at her plate, then up at her. "You see my knife?"

"I don't know. Maybe it fell under the bed when you got up."

He looked at the ground but saw nothing. The blanket was draped there, so the knife might have been covered.

He got on all fours, then looked under the bed. It was too dark to see far, so he reached under the bed, feeling around.

"Hmm," he said, rising, "I can't—"

And then she stabbed him.

Chapter 21 - Jessi Price

JESSI PLUNGED the knife at the man, aiming for his neck.

But he raised his hand, catching the blade as she stabbed.

He *screamed*.

Blood gushed from one hand as he grabbed the knife with another.

She saw the open door behind him.

A voice in her head yelled, *Run!*

She was afraid to do it, just as she'd been afraid to stab him.

But she couldn't stay in the room. Because now he was really angry.

She jumped out of bed and raced toward the door.

She was almost halfway out when he grabbed her by the hair.

She stopped.

Then he swung her backward with a loud scream.

She slammed into the wall.

"You ungrateful little bitch!"

She looked up to see him standing over her, blood dripping from his hand, all over his face and the front of his shirt.

His eyes were red and wide, his teeth like a dog's.

He wound back to strike her.

"I'm sorry, mister," she said, raising her hands. "Please, don't—"

He grabbed Jessi's arms, yanked her up off the ground, and dragged her toward the bathroom door.

Oh no, what is he gonna do?

He's going to kill me.

I hurt him, and now he's about hurt me.

She tried to kick and pull away, but the man was too strong.

He shoved her into the bathroom.

She fell hard to the tile floor.

Instead of coming into the bathroom with her, he slammed the door.

She sat on the ground, crying, staring at the door, waiting to see if he'd come in.

She heard the door lock.

The lights went out, and she remembered that the switch was outside the bathroom.

"See how you like being in a dark room all day!"

He stomped out of the room, then slammed her dungeon door.

She got up, went to the bathroom door to see if it would open.

But of course, it wouldn't.

She was trapped in the darkness.

Jessi fell to the ground and sobbed.

Chapter 22 - Paul Dodd

PAUL SLAMMED the door then locked it, growling as he stared down at his gashed palm.

How the hell am I supposed to explain that to people at work?

He couldn't believe the little bitch had stabbed him, and after he was trying to do something nice by getting her ketchup. She'd seemed so sweet when he'd first laid eyes on her. Not the kind of girl who would do something like this.

But maybe her change was starting early. The same change that had turned his sister into a bitch who ruined his life. The same change that turned all little girls into devious fucking little cunts. Why couldn't they stay nice and innocent forever? Was it some cruel trick by God? Some biological thing that determined women were better off by becoming horrible bitches? Whatever it was, Paul didn't like it. Not one fucking bit.

With each girl, he hoped it would be different. That they would be the one to appreciate him for who he was, that they'd see his actions as a kindness, that he was trying to preserve them in a world out to poison them.

But not a single one had seen the light.

That's why none lasted longer than a couple of days after their tenth birthday. Jessi Price wouldn't suffer the same fate. He wouldn't wait an hour after the clock struck midnight to finish her off.

He cleaned his wound in the bathroom, noting that the cut wasn't as bad as he'd feared. It looked awful with the blood flowing, but holding a bandage on it, Paul saw that he'd be fine. He washed his wound a final time, dressed it, then wrapped himself in a bandage.

That gave him an idea. So delicious that it caused him to smile.

No, he wouldn't kill her right away.

He'd keep this one longer, prolonging the pain.

He quickly showered, found a change of clothes, then grabbed his computer bag and headed out to his car.

He got in, keyed the ignition, and ... nothing.

"What the fuck?"

He tried again.

Nothing.

"Damn it!" Paul hit the steering wheel with his banged up hand.

He screamed, realizing the error as pain shot through his hand and arm.

"Fuck!" he banged again, this time with his good fist.

He grabbed his phone and found the number for a local cab service.

No response.

"What the fuck?" He got out of his car and glared at the broken Infiniti.

He looked up and down his street for any sign of someone leaving for work, but nobody was out. Paul didn't know any of his neighbors well enough to ask for a ride. And it wasn't a good idea to start asking for favors, and possibly invite unwanted attention into his affairs.

"Fuck it," he said, gripping his bag and walking down the block. He was less than a mile from a bus stop for a route that went by his work. He'd used it once before when his battery died. He wasn't a fan of buses, particularly the dregs of humanity that rode them, but it was his only solution if he expected to arrive at work on time.

He grabbed the phone from his pocket, called the front desk, left a message saying he might be a few minutes late, and asked if they could pull a sub to watch his class until he got there.

As he walked to the bus stop, Paul wondered what the hell he'd done to warrant such a shitty morning.

Chapter 23 - Jasper Parish

JASPER AND JORDYN drove to the beginning of the bus's route early in the morning, timing it so they'd be on the bus passing Rooster's at around the same time as the killer.

Jasper took a seat in the back, while Jordyn claimed one a row ahead.

The bus was half-full with the saddest lot that Jasper had ever seen — the tired, the poor, the huddled masses all on their way to jobs they hated, or night shift workers heading home from their graveyard misery.

Nobody talking.

Nobody chatting.

Nobody smiling.

It was too early for pleasantries.

Jordyn was listening to loud music through her ear buds while reading a book on her phone. Each time the bus stopped, she looked up, scanning incoming riders for the white man with a bandaged hand.

Jasper watched and waited from behind dark shades and a faded Miami Marlins cap. He was dressed in old jeans, a ratty shirt, and a black leather jacket, looking more like a tired, possibly homeless man than a vigilante hunting for a child killer.

They were one stop from Roosters, and still no one fit the bill. As the bus pulled to a stop and nobody boarded, Jasper wondered if they'd timed the schedule wrong. Or maybe Jordyn was off on the date or time.

Maybe he should get off, wait for the next bus.

Outside, someone was sprinting in the early morning darkness, trying to catch the bus before it pulled away from the stop.

"Driver," Jasper called out. "Someone's coming!"

The driver looked back in his rearview, seemingly annoyed, likely eager to get on with his day.

He stopped and waited for the straggler.

The man boarded the bus: tall, good-looking, white with curly brown hair and a bandaged left hand.

Jasper pretended to look out the window, using the reflective glass to watch the man walk the aisle toward them.

He took a seat in the middle, seeming to keep his distance from the unwashed masses.

He sat and rifled through his computer bag, looking flustered as he did. Jasper wondered if he was looking for something lost, or checking to make sure he left the house with everything he intended to. Seemingly satisfied, he zipped the bag closed, then leaned back and sighed.

They passed Roosters, and just as Jordyn had seen, he checked his phone.

Jordyn glanced back at Jasper, smiling.

Jasper smiled back.

I've got you now.

～

THE BUS HAD BEEN DRIVING for fifteen minutes, stopping every half mile or so for pick-ups and drop-offs. Jasper ignored them all, holding his focus on the man.

He thought not only of the fact that this man had killed the cop's kid, but also about Jessi Price. Assuming the kidnapped girl was still alive — hardly a safe assumption, particularly given his hand — Jasper had to figure out the best way to save her.

He had two options: follow the man to his job, wait for the end of his workday, then follow him home and strike.

But that was risky.

If the man figured out he was being followed, he'd probably run. Jasper was in excellent shape but wasn't willing to put the little girl's life into a test of his ability to chase down this killer.

That meant the equally dangerous second option.

The bus stopped alongside a busy street corner surrounded by several storefronts and restaurants.

The man stood.

This is his stop.

Jasper had to act.

The killer was among four people standing to disembark, one in the front, the others in the back. He was second in a line of three waiting for the back door to hiss open.

Jasper got out of his seat, casually so as not to attract attention.

Jordyn stood, too.

The back door hissed open.

The three people in line began to step off the bus.

Jasper moved toward the doorway but was blocked when a tiny old black woman in a waitress's uniform got up and clogged the aisle.

Come on!

She was frail and moving at a snail's pace, her entire body practically trembling toward the exit.

The killer was already off the bus.

Jasper stared helplessly at the back of the woman, taking forever to shuffle five feet.

The killer clipped along the sidewalk. He'd be gone before long, disappearing into one of the storefronts, down a side street, or crossing the road off to who-knew-where. Soon, his one sure shot at getting close to the killer would be lost.

Jasper couldn't push the old lady, so he vaulted past her, running up to the front, footsteps pounding, scaring several passengers. He smiled sheepishly at a few, ignored the driver's judgmental glare, and bounded off the bus onto the sidewalk, eyes scanning for the killer.

He spotted the man, already some forty feet down the sidewalk.

Jasper had to catch up, but couldn't walk so fast that the man heard him coming, then turned and saw a giant black man behind him. That would guarantee he spooked the guy.

Jasper didn't wait for Jordyn — still stuck behind the old lady. He walked briskly, trying to close the distance between himself and the killer.

They were the only two people on this part of the sidewalk. It was still dark out, so sneaking up on him wouldn't be easy. It was easier to follow people in broad daylight under the presumption of safety.

Right now, he had to tread carefully.

Jasper followed the man along the main street, wondering if he'd already made him. Maybe he was altering his route because he was going straight rather than turning into any of the parking lots for the shops or restaurants.

Where the hell is this guy going?

Jasper looked around. He'd only been in the city for a couple of years, and while he knew the area reasonably well, he didn't know its every nook and cranny. Nor did he know where the guy was going.

Jasper spied a pair of buses ahead, leaving a side street, one after another. He was near an elementary school.

Don't tell me this guy works at the school.

Please.

Jasper walked faster, but it was hard without outright running because the killer was practically sprinting himself.

The man turned onto the street where the buses had come from, and where a third bus was now pulling out.

Out of sight, Jasper risked running, hoping that the man wasn't testing him, waiting behind some bushes. It was game over if so, and Jasper didn't know what he'd do then.

Jasper ran as fast as he could.

He assumed Jordyn was following, but couldn't check. She knew how to find him if she got lost.

He reached the corner and saw two things at once: the killer walking about fifty feet ahead, and the school about a block away. If Jasper didn't speed up, and the killer *was* heading to the school, there was a definite chance that Jasper wouldn't reach him in time.

Fortunately, they were on a residential sidewalk, and though it was still dark outside, traffic was heavier — people walking their children to school, kids riding their bikes, and people walking their dogs. Jasper could blend right in, pick up his pace without attracting the killer.

The killer reached the school gates.

No!

He was about to disappear inside when a pair of women and their kids stopped him to chat.

Yes!

Jasper walked faster, timing the bump just right, praying he was a wallet in the back pocket kind of guy, in addition to being a pedophile. If not, there was a slight chance Jasper could find it in his coat, but an equal chance he'd get busted patting him down. And a black dude trying to pickpocket a white teacher in this part of town wouldn't go over well.

Jasper focused on the group ahead, determining his best approach — how best to distract everyone from noticing what he was about to do. He took a deep breath, trying to slow time, if only perceptually.

Ten feet away.

Jasper held the phone to his ear, pretending to be lost in conversation.

He heard the killer laughing at something one of the kids said.

It sliced Jasper across the gut. If these people only knew the monster before them. He wanted to end the man right here and now.

The killer looked up, straight at Jasper.

Jasper pretended not to notice.

Pretended not to see any of them as he bumped into the killer.

Jasper dropped his phone in front of the killer, then pressed against the man's back, hard with one hand, while finding his wallet with the other.

It was a delicate balance of distraction and theft that Jasper had practiced for years.

"Hey!" the killer yelled.

Jasper already had his wallet and was carefully shifting into his own back pocket, as he met the killer's eyes.

Time froze.

Even though it wasn't Jasper's psychic vision, he felt as if *he'd* been spying on the man rather than his daughter.

It seemed like the killer had looked right back, and could see Jasper for who he truly was.

There were two ways to play this. One was to be overly apologetic and hope to slink away without the killer realizing what had happened.

If the killer was even somewhat street smart, there was an excellent chance that he'd see this attempt for what it was. He'd reach back and feel his pocket; then the jig would be up.

Jasper went with option two — anger.

"What's your problem, man?" He shoved the killer hard in his chest.

The killer was stunned. He stumbled back into the women but didn't fall.

Their eyes locked.

Jasper saw what he was looking for, a glimpse into the man's soul — to the killer hiding behind the meek mask, the savage beast that wanted to come out and fight right now in front of the school.

But he couldn't do that, could he?

Not if he worked here.

Not if he was a teacher.

He *had* to stand down.

Jasper bent to grab his phone off the ground, mumbling, "Ain't never seen people so damned rude in my life."

One of the women said something, defending the killer, but Jasper ignored her.

He grabbed his phone, turned, and began to walk away, not too fast, lest he surrender the ruse. Lest the killer find his pocket empty and give chase.

It was a long slow walk, and he didn't dare turn around.

The killer's eyes burned the back of Jasper's skull until he finally turned the corner.

Jasper ran, beating a path back to the main boulevard, then across the street, to a grocery store parking lot.

Inside the store's restroom, Jasper opened a stall, sat inside, and dared to seize his reward.

He opened the killer's wallet and smiled.

Jasper had the killer's name and address.

I've got you.

Chapter 24 - Mallory Black

MAL WOKE up in Ashley's bed to a terrible pounding.

She thought it was her head, then realized that someone must be trying to break down her front door.

She grabbed her gun from Ashley's nightstand, leaped out of bed, unlocked her daughter's bedroom door, then ran to the stairs, focusing her gun on the front door through her descent.

Her head was throbbing and thoughts foggy. She had to be careful not to shoot if it was only some aggressive solicitor.

As she approached the door, a woman's voice yelled, "Open up. I know you're in there."

Gloria Bell.

Shit. What did I say last night?

She vaguely remembered being pissed, getting drunk, and calling the reporter. Vaguely remembered talking to her, but hell if she could remember a word. She could've said anything in the state she was in.

"Hold on," Mal called out before running back

upstairs, setting her gun on the nightstand, and retrieving her phone.

She pulled up Channel 4's website and saw the problem, right under the header **BREAKING NEWS**.

Former Cop Says Jessi Price Case May Be Tied to Ashley Black's. Mother Says Jessi Price Case May Be Connected, Sheriff Not Doing Job.

Mal didn't have to read the story or watch the accompanying video to know this was *very* bad.

What the hell did I do?

Her stomach scraped the floor.

Gloria kept pounding. "You better not be crawling out the window!"

Shit.

She put her phone down, then went downstairs to face the music.

She opened the door and light waged a full frontal assault on her senses.

"What the fuck were you thinking?" Gloria yelled, storming into Mal's house without waiting for an invite.

Mal closed the door behind her ex-boss, and turned to her, saying nothing. Best to let Gloria vent, then deal with the aftermath.

"Why the hell would you do this?"

Gloria was standing with her hands on her hips, eyes wet, glaring at Mal, awaiting her answer.

Mal wasn't sure what to say, or what she said last night. She didn't know how badly she laid into the sheriff or the department. Everything was a hazy mess, and she hated not remembering, not knowing how many people she hurled under the bus. She wondered if she'd said anything about Mike. Mal could never forgive herself. It was one thing to go after the sheriff, but going after your former partner was unforgivable, the kind of thing you never come back from.

"Did you ever stop to think that maybe we were *quietly* working this case? And that now you've gone and let him know we're looking at him!"

Mal stared at Gloria, gutted, questioning every one of her assumptions. Was it possible that they were investigating the kidnapping properly all along? That she just threw a live grenade into the investigation?

She shook her head. "No. No, you were putting this on the father. You weren't looking at Ashley's killer at all. Don't turn this around on me."

"We were working every angle, Mal. Every single angle, and now you just let the killer know we're looking in his direction."

Mal couldn't believe Gloria's nerve. "This isn't about the case. This is about public perception. This is about the people, and maybe a commissioner or two, breathing down your neck, demanding answers. You're just pissed because I pointed out the obvious — that you're not doing your job.*"

Gloria looked as if Mal had smacked her. "How *dare* you. I've been working my ass off at this job. Doing everything in my power to find Jessi Price, *and* your daughter's killer, all while dealing with the political shit show I inherited, and fending off enemies at every step. Not all of us have the luxury of giving up."

"Giving up?" Mal wanted to pummel her. "You practically pushed me out!"

Gloria laughed. "Pushed you out? I fought to keep you! But you were a tornado, destroying everything in your path — your job, your relationships, and yourself. Look at you. A drunk. A drug addict. My God, is this how you honor your daughter?"

"Get out!" Mal pointed at the door, her finger shaking.

Gloria didn't budge.

Staring Mal down, she said, "Here's what's going to happen. I'm going to hold a press conference. I'm going to say that you are very much mistaken and that we're working several leads right now."

"Are you?"

"Never you mind what we're doing. You, my dear, are going to call your reporter friend and tell her that you're sorry — you were angry, drunk, or whatever the hell you wanna say. But you're going to take back every word, and insist that you have nothing but the utmost confidence in the department to do their job."

If Mal wasn't on the verge of tears, she might've laughed in Gloria's face. "Oh yeah? Why would I do that?"

"Because if you don't, I'll need a head to roll. Someone to take the blame. And Mike is lead on the case."

"You wouldn't."

Gloria shook her head. "If you believe that, then you haven't been paying attention."

"You have changed, haven't you?"

"I'm not the one who changed, Mal. I'm the same person I always was — a scrappy ass bitch who will do whatever it takes to help this community. You used to be like me. But now, hmm," she looked Mal up and down, then shook her head dismissively and marched out of the house.

Mal stared at the open front door, speechless.

Chapter 25 - Jasper Parish

JASPER WALKED BACK to his car.

Jordyn waited, legs sprawled on the hood, earplugs in and jamming to whatever was on her phone.

He held up the wallet, shaking it with a smile. "Got him!"

"What?" Jordyn smiled, showing the braces she so often tried to cover up. She jumped off the car and grabbed the wallet.

They climbed into the car, Jordyn going through the wallet's contents while Jasper started the engine.

"Where we going?" she asked.

"Going to his house. Gonna save Jessi Price."

"What then? If we let her go, we can't sit around and wait. The police will come looking for him."

"True, but we can't leave the girl locked up until this guy gets home. What if she needs medical attention?"

Jordyn nodded. "So, I guess we let him go. Let the cops get him?"

"I think that's our only move right now."

The house was ten miles away, in the unincorporated western-most edges of Creek county. Home to few, mostly farmers and poor folks who lived in double-wides on sprawling dirt and shrub patches of land. The kind of place without running water, lights, or any other city service. The kind of place you didn't want to break down in at night, lest you get hit by a truck or attacked by a bear or wild dog. The kind of place where you were as likely to be met with a smile as with the business end of a shotgun when you knocked on a door.

Jasper was definitely out of his comfort zone, turning off a paved road to barrel down a narrow stretch of dirt, trees crowding either side.

A red pickup was driving in the middle of the road ahead, straight at him.

Jasper pulled over enough to let the man pass.

He glared at Jasper from under the rim of his red Confederate flag cap. It might not have been a scowl, so much as the look you gave any stranger in these parts, but Jasper couldn't help but feel the weight of his gaze. There were rumors that some of the people out here belonged to the KKK, and they might not take kindly to a face like Jasper's snooping around.

Jasper glanced down at Jordyn's phone, with the GPS.

"I think it's down this street," she said, pointing right.

He turned off the main dirt road and onto a narrower one.

The street had one house, and it belonged to a killer.

Jasper passed the property, not wanting to pull up just in case there was someone else there, maybe a conspirator in the kidnapping. He parked at the end of the cul-de-sac, figuring nobody would spot the car unless they were looking for it.

They got out, went to the trunk, grabbed ski masks and

put them on. Jordyn also pulled her hoodie up over her head.

"You ready?" Jasper asked, patting to make sure his gun was holstered in his jacket.

Jordyn nodded.

He handed her the keys. "Shit goes South, you run back to the car and take proper measures. Understand?"

She nodded.

They moved past a large row of bushes and toward the house, ducking low as they approached.

The house was a small single-story home with a car port that looked like a holdover from the seventies. A vehicle sat in the carport under a cover. The front windows were open, a TV blaring sports talk.

Jordyn looked at her father, confused as they approached the front window on their knees. A curtain was blowing in the breeze of an oscillating fan, giving them intermittent glimpses of a television on the far wall, and the shadowy hints of a couch and lounger.

"Is someone in there?" Jordyn signed.

Jasper shrugged.

He moved away from the window and approached the front door, signaling for Jordyn to inch toward the street, out of sight so she could flee if shit hit the fan.

She shook her head.

But Jasper stared her down: *now was not the time to argue.*

Jordyn shrunk behind the large bush beside the killer's mailbox, and out of the way.

Jasper turned to the door, reached down with his gloved hand, and twisted the knob.

Locked.

He crouched low and headed around to the rear, hoping to find an unlocked door or a window to crawl through. But first he checked for any sign of a shed or other structure that could ruin a child.

The property was probably about an acre, but it had no other buildings so far as Jasper could see. It backed up to a forest, so there could be some makeshift dungeon farther back in the woods where the trees were thicker and the area darker.

The rear had two large windows on either side of two sliding glass doors. He crawled beneath the closest window and saw a thick brown curtain covering the sliding glass door. He checked the bottom of the track for a wooden bar, or anything which might prevent the door from opening.

Nothing.

He checked above for a lock or alarm contacts.

Still nothing, meaning he could probably lift the door off the track and slip inside, but that would make noise and should only serve as a last resort.

He placed his gloved hand flat on the glass and pressed, hoping to budge the door.

It did.

He smiled, sighed, and *very slowly* slid the door open.

The TV grew louder. He was reasonably certain that the TV was in the front and that he was about to invade the back — maybe a proper living room or bedroom. Either way, he hoped his luck would hold, and the room would be empty.

But it wasn't.

A heavyset blond in his late fifties, wearing a black tee and boxers, was holding a shotgun aimed square at Jasper's chest.

He fired.

Chapter 26 - Jasper Parish

JASPER JUMPED BACK as the shotgun exploded, falling back into the grass. Glass shattered above him.

He scrambled to his feet, raising his pistol in time to get a drop on the man charging through the open doorway.

"Put your gun down. I'm a cop!" Jasper yelled, trying to sound authoritative and defuse the situation.

"Bullshit," the man drawled, pushing his way through the brown curtain, agitated as it got in his way, shoving it aside with the barrel of his gun.

Once through the doorway, he took aim.

Jasper had nowhere to go.

Had no choice but to fire back.

He fired twice, one shot hit the man center mass, the other in his left shoulder.

He stumbled backward and fell through the broken window of the sliding glass door.

Jasper stared in disbelief at how quickly the situation had withered.

A dog barked. It wouldn't be long before someone called the sheriff's office.

He had to move, get the hell out of there.

He went inside, saw the man sprawled on the ground, eyes wide and terrified as blood pooled beneath him.

"Where is the girl?" Jasper asked, kicking the shotgun away.

The man struggled to respond, blood pouring from his mouth. "What girl?"

"Jessi Price. Where is she?"

The man looked confused.

Jasper mentioned the killer by name. "Don't play dumb. The girl you took with Richard Howell."

"I … *I'm* Rich Howell," the man said. "And I didn't t … t … take no girl."

The man's eyes went wide. Death claimed his body.

Jasper turned, examining the bedroom, seeing photos on the walls of the dead man and a woman Jasper presumed to be his wife. Then more photos of other adults, children, and what were probably grandchildren. A framed wedding portrait said "Richard and Susan Howell."

No.

Jasper raced from the room, searching the house for any sign of Jessi Price, or a dungeon. But all he found was a house belonging to an innocent man that he'd unintentionally murdered.

Maybe Richard is also the son's name. Maybe this is his father.

But of all the photos festooning nearly every inch of the house, none matched the man in the driver's license photo.

He was standing in the living room searching when the front door opened.

Susan was home.

The woman, a short, squat older woman with poofy blonde hair, looked at Jasper, stunned.

Then she screamed, and he ran.

JORDYN WAS SITTING inside the car, waiting.

"What happened?" she asked.

He couldn't talk.

He could only turn the ignition and get the car moving.

He raced down the street, passing Richard and Susan's house, not daring to look, afraid to see the woman he'd turned into a widow.

Rather than head back into town, he removed his mask and took the long way, heading farther west — less likely to pass sheriff's deputies approaching from the east.

After driving thirty minutes, and down several side streets, getting them good and lost, he pulled into a gas station, opened the door, staggered to the restroom on the side of the building, and vomited.

"What happened?" Jordyn asked, behind him, even though he never heard her coming. "Was Jessi there? Was she … dead?"

"No. I … I don't think it was his house."

"What?"

"And the man there. He had a gun. Shot at me. I had to … I had to—"

Jasper collapsed against the wall outside the bathroom, tears streaming down his face. His stomach churned, twisted as if someone had left a knife inside it.

His throat hurt, not just from throwing up, but from the scream he'd been holding inside.

"Oh my God, I killed an innocent man."

Chapter 27 - Mallory Black

MAL STARED at the television watching the empty lectern in front of the blue curtain with the logo for the Creek County Sheriff's Department emblazoned on it, wondering who would take the stage for the press conference. Would it be the Public Information Officer, Felicia Day, or would Gloria handle this hot mess herself?

Felicia, who was both younger and more eloquent than Gloria, handled most press conferences, sometimes bringing the sheriff up with her to be lauded for some major drug sting or other positive press. Felicia usually handled the negative stuff.

But Gloria was taking the stage this time. She must be *really* worried about her election odds.

Mal took a sip of her wine, sitting up and leaning forward on the couch, wondering what Gloria would say, and how Gloria would handle the questions about Mal's statements.

Her phone had been ringing off the hook since the story broke. Reporters from every paper and station wanted a quote. She'd ignored them all and finally had to silence her phone. She only allowed Mike's number through, but he wasn't calling.

So Mal sat alone, getting drunk, feeling like shit. What the hell had she'd been thinking? Gloria was right, talking to Presley was the wrong way to handle the situation. And it wasn't as if Gloria would be goaded into doing the right thing. Mal's drunken, drugged stunt merely alienated her from the entire department, Mike likely included.

Gloria updated the Jessi Price investigation, saying they were working on several leads but couldn't say more during an active investigation. Additionally, the department still considered Jessi's father, Luke Price, a person of interest.

After some more information, more or less a repeat of the known facts, including the girl and her father's description, photos of them, and the make, model, and plate number of his SUV, Gloria opened the conference to questions.

The first was from Presley Jennings, Channel 4. "Sheriff Bell, what do you have to say in response to former detective Mallory Black's statement that the department isn't doing everything possible to find Jessi Price? And that it's ignoring evidence that the Jessi Price case is tied to the Ashley Black murder?"

Gloria found a smile, but Mal saw through the facade, and right to the icy daggers she was shooting at Presley.

She braced the corners of the lectern and drew a deep breath. "Ms. Black has had a rough couple of years. I understand that she's upset and frustrated and that this case is bringing up a lot of feelings for her. She lost her daughter, and if I were in her shoes, I'd be devastated, too. Nothing can prepare you for the loss of a child, and I can't even begin to imagine the things going through her mind every day. But I would also remind you that Ms. Black is not part of this investigation, nor is she privy to details that we've not made public."

"Bullshit," Mal yelled at the TV. "You've got nothing, and you're not even trying to get anything!"

Several reporters tried to get a word in, but Presley beat them with a follow-up. "So, are you saying that the Jessi Price case is *not* linked to the Ashley Black case?"

Good question! Box her in. Make her give a concrete answer.

Gloria's smile widened, but Mal could see that she wanted to scream.

"As I said, this is an active investigation, and there are things we cannot go into without jeopardizing our efforts."

Mal shook her head, took another drink, and yelled at the TV. "Liar!"

Another reporter, a man off-camera, asked, "Any new developments on the Ashley Black case?"

Mal waited for more bullshit to spew from Gloria's mouth.

Gloria shook her head. "We're not here to talk about the Ashley Black case. If anyone has any other questions about the Jessi Price case, I will answer those to the best of my ability, but I won't be discussing any other cases today."

Another reporter asked, "Is Luke Price a suspect in his daughter's disappearance?"

"He is a person of interest," Gloria said before fielding a few softballs from reporters who were friendlier to the administration. After those questions, Gloria thanked everyone for coming, then left.

Mal stared at the screen dumbstruck.

That's it? Nobody else is going to press her?

What the hell?

Mal grabbed her phone from the couch and dialed.

"Presley," the reporter said. Mal could hear a lot of

background noise. She was probably still in the department's press room, surrounded by people.

"Hey, Pres. I just saw the conference."

"Hold on a second, let me go somewhere quieter," Presley said, as she navigated her way out of the noisy room and through a few doors. "Okay, I'm outside."

"What the hell?" Mal snapped. "I put my ass on the line by giving you enough to hold Gloria's feet to the fire, and that's the best you've got?"

"I asked her. She said it's an active investigation."

"You could've hit her with other questions."

"She wasn't coming back to me."

"Like that's ever stopped you. Come on."

Mal was quiet. Saying "come on" to someone then closing your mouth often got them to spill whatever they were holding back. It surprised Mal how often it worked, with both criminals and the general public.

Presley lowered her voice, "I got a directive from the top not to go too far down this road."

"Why the hell not?"

"Because if we're wrong on this, and it turns out the dad *does* have Jessi, then we look like we're interfering with a child abduction case."

Mal wondered if that was the truth or the cover story. She wondered if Gloria didn't reach out to someone more powerful and push Channel 4's news director in a different direction.

Channel 4's station was in Jacksonville, just north of Creek County, but that didn't mean the Creek County Sheriff couldn't wield some influence with the right people.

"So, fuck the truth then, eh?"

"I'm sorry. If you want to tell your side, I'm sure I could get you a spot."

"Yeah, so then it's about me, eh? The crazy, distraught

mother who is upset about her daughter's unsolved murder. I can see the narrative that Gloria's spinning and I refuse to play into it."

Mal hung up before Presley could say another word.

She threw the phone to the other end of the couch, then glared at the television, wishing like hell she was still a cop. Then she could be chasing the leads they were too lazy or scared to pursue.

Mal grabbed her remote and flipped through the channels until she found something to steer her mind away from the bullshit parade.

She stumbled across an episode of *Curious George* on PBS and remembered watching the show with Ashley when she was a toddler. Mal recorded the shows during the day then used them to help Ashley fall back asleep when she woke up in the middle of the night.

They'd lie on the couch side-by-side as the cartoon monkey calmed Ashley down. Mal didn't know if it was the colorful animation, the soft music, or the humor, but something about the show not only soothed Ashley but also relaxed Mal, making it seem like everything might be okay.

She remembered Ashley drifting off, occasionally giggling at something George had done, or watching her daughter's eyes as they got sleepy.

At the time, she'd been eager for Ashley to fall asleep, but now Mal would give anything to snuggle with her daughter in front of the TV, listen to her raspy little giggle, let her slowly drift off while holding Pinky Bear, or watching George chase the world's problems away.

Mal grabbed her pills from the coffee table, took two, and washed them down with the last of her wine.

Then she grabbed a blanket, pillow, and Pinky Bear from Ashley's room, brought them downstairs, and laid on the couch, drifting off to *Curious George*.

Chapter 28 - Jasper Parish

JASPER SAT ALONE in his living room, swaddled by darkness, his crime's weight like an anchor, weighing him down and piercing his soul.

His head was pounding. The sky was different. Blacker somehow. Same for the air. They both felt … wrong. He was dizzy, unsure whether it was from lack of sleep, or whether he was coming down with something. Either way, hell had descended.

After narrowly escaping the house without being caught by police, he'd come home, showered, and collapsed into bed. Jordyn tried talking to him, but he'd told her to leave him alone.

Now he wasn't sure where she was. The living room was dark, but it was still only mid-afternoon.

After sitting in the dark for over an hour, Jasper went to the fridge for a bottle of water then turned the TV to see if Richard Heller had made the news yet. The incident had, but the news had yet to release the man's name or any details beyond "the sheriff's department is investigating a suspected home invasion gone wrong."

He watched a recap of the sheriff's press conference where she more or less ignored Black's accusations that the department wasn't properly investigating the Jessi Price case. She looked, to Jasper, like every other politician on TV, spinning to keep the truth from dinging her popularity.

He turned the TV off, disgusted.

Jasper needed time to think, to decompress after what had happened. And he didn't want any more distraction from his thoughts. He kept seeing the innocent dead man sprawled on the ground, kept hearing the man's wife scream as he fled like a murderer.

How the hell did I become like the very men I kill?

He'd been a normal man once upon a time.

He'd been a cop who once protected life without needing to take it. He'd fired his service revolver only a handful of times in his dozen years on the force. He'd shot three people as a cop, all good shootings, never taking a life.

What happened to me? How did I get here?

"Dad?" Jordyn said from behind, surprising him.

Jasper turned to see her standing behind the couch holding a Diet Coke, wearing her coziest sweats and most threadbare sweatshirt.

"When did you get home?"

"A while ago. I was reading in my room, then came out for a drink and saw you sitting here in the dark like a weirdo."

She was smiling, hoping he'd laugh.

But Jasper was every kind of empty.

"What's wrong?" She plopped beside him on the couch and popped the tab on her soda.

"I killed an innocent man."

"It was an accident. You can't tear yourself up for it."

He looked at her, confused. "Aren't you the least bit upset?"

She took a drink of her soda, then nodded. "Of course I am, but what good does it do that man? He's dead. We can't bring him back. Besides, he shot at you first. If you didn't kill him, then *you* would be dead. And sorry if this sounds crass, but I'll kill ten innocent men to keep my daddy alive."

She smiled again.

"It's not funny."

"I'm just trying to make you feel better."

"I don't deserve it. I screwed up. I should never have brought you into this."

"What?"

"It's not right. Killing these people. And the worst part is, I knew something like this would happen. Or worse."

"What do you mean?"

"You shouldn't be doing this with me. It's wrong. You're going to get caught or hurt, and I don't know what I'd do if something happened to you."

"Nothing's going to happen."

"Something already *did* happen, Jordyn. An innocent man is dead."

She said nothing.

After a long moment of consideration, he said, "We can't do this anymore."

"Can't do what?"

"This. Going around and killing bad guys. No more."

"We made one mistake!"

"It's a person's life! He didn't deserve to die. His wife and family didn't deserve to lose him." Jasper met her gaze. Had he corrupted her so much that she didn't see the value in taking an innocent life?

"He was going to kill you. You didn't have a choice."

"We shouldn't have even been there! He's only dead because I broke into the wrong man's house. How could this have happened?"

"Fake ID?"

"Well, yeah. I looked at the other stuff in his wallet. A few dollars. A few freebie discount cards to make you think there were credit cards in there. Obviously a decoy. We should've considered that possibility before going in guns blazing. I screwed up, and there's no way to take it back."

She looked down, either avoiding his gaze or trying to think of some response.

Then she looked back up. "Do we let Jessi Price die? Because if we sit back, that's exactly what will happen."

He shook his head. It was practically buzzing. Between his headache and the vertigo, he could barely think straight, much less endure this conversation. "I can't do this anymore."

"We are *this close*. We know where he works. We can find him, get his real name and address."

"How will we do that? Keep riding the bus until we can follow him home? Don't you think maybe he'll notice his wallet missing and put two and two together, thinking someone's on to him? Maybe he'll even turn on the news and see that Richard Howell is dead, and realize it just might have something to do with the man who stole his wallet."

"All the more reason to act now. If he thinks that someone is on to him, what's his next step?"

"To get rid of the girl."

"Exactly."

"So, we need to act now. If we don't, that man's death was in vain."

Jasper looked at his daughter. Her eyes were wide, smile broad, and energy almost manic.

"Doesn't it bother you what I did? I mean, you don't seem the least bit shaken. This isn't right. The Jordyn I raised would be upset, would be crying with me. But you're practically giddy over the possibility of catching this guy."

She hugged him. "Do you want me to wallow with you? Is that what you want? For me to cry for a stranger, a man who pulled a gun on you? A man who would've killed you if you didn't kill him? Sorry. I can't do that. Yes, he might've been a great guy. And he might have been *innocent*, at least of anything having to do with Jessi Price. But he's dead, and we can't change that. All the tears in the world won't bring him back. Neither will taking the time to mourn a stranger, or sitting here in the dark. But it *will* kill Jessi Price. You tell me, what's more important? Feeling sorry for ourselves or saving this girl?"

Jasper sighed, long and deep. "You're right."

"I know I am. I'm always right."

She smiled playfully, still trying to get him to join her.

But Jasper knew he was years away from a smile.

"What do we do? It's not like we've got a lot of time if he's freaking out and trying to clean his mess. We can't wait at the bus stop all day tomorrow hoping that we'll find him catching the bus home, especially if he made me as the man who stole his wallet."

Jordyn eyed the laptop sitting on the coffee table in front of the couch.

"Check the school's website. See if they have pictures of the staff."

Jasper finally smiled. "Why the hell didn't I think of that?"

"Because I've got the beauty and the brains in this family."

He grabbed the laptop, searched for the school's

website, then clicked through staff pages at different grade levels until he finally found the man's photo.

"A kindergarten teacher," he said with a shiver, imagining how many of his students he was likely fantasizing about abducting. Hell, maybe he was even living out his fantasies through kids like Jessi Price.

Jordyn leaned in to get a better look at the man's face.

"*Now* we've got you, Paul Dodd."

Chapter 29 - Paul Dodd

PAUL WAS in a decent mood when he got home, despite his awful morning, and a call from Manny at the shop who said his car wouldn't be ready for a few more days because they needed a part that wasn't readily available. He'd have to catch a cab or take the bus tomorrow.

As he got out ingredients and prepared to make dinner — boneless, skinless chicken breast, Basmati rice, naan bread, Madras curry, and the assorted spices required for the dish — and tried not to think too much about Jessi stabbing him. After all, they had a special night coming up in three days, and he didn't want to tarnish the little time they had left together.

He always enjoyed the moments before the consummation best. It reminded him of being a kid, before his life went to hell, of the days leading to Christmas. There was excitement in the air, an electricity that made everything a bit more ... *real*. It made the rest of Paul's life, the long months he spent alone before he found another suitable companion, feel like a pale imitation. Like a life devoid of sensation, of waiting to happen. A life on hold.

But the weeks with his children were filled with special moments, ones he wanted to savor like a prime cut of filet or a bottle of Jordan Cabernet. He had this perfect little treasure waiting for him to explore, to touch, to taste. And it was only a matter of days.

Paul's only regret was that she wasn't enjoying her stay more. It was always better when the kids weren't scared. When they were under the illusion that this was part of some game, and that they'd be reunited with their family once it was over. Yes, it was a lie, and yes, he felt bad for not telling them the truth, but at the same time, it was a small mercy. Why make their last days on earth scary? Why let them know they were going to die? That served no one.

Long before he ever took his first kid, Paul had read accounts of serial killers who kidnapped children. Some had done some despicable things, treating them like animals, torturing them, and forcing them to endure horrifying final days, or sometimes weeks and years. Some kept them in cages. Others had brutalized the children ways before they died.

Paul could never do those things.

He wasn't a monster.

He loved children.

He loved their innocence. He loved their sense of wonder. He loved teaching them in school. He was the only person in their lives who cared about them. He saw so many parents come through his doors that didn't *deserve* to be parents. So many didn't even seem to give a damn about their kids. Many were neglectful. The worst were downright abusive and reminded Paul of his drunken mother.

Many parents didn't realize how lucky they were to have children in their lives. Many parents would slowly crush what made these children special, pulverizing their spirits until they were miserable little clones of themselves. Like that bitch, Mallory Black. She and her ex-husband were turning their daughter into a troll and didn't even see it. Mallory's self-righteousness after Ashley's death had pissed him off something fierce.

She acted like *she* was the victim. Like *her* life that had been destroyed.

She didn't own up to her actions that caused it.

That was why he found it so much fun to toy with her on her daughter's birthday. To remind her of how she failed as a parent and human.

Paul smiled, wondering how she reacted to finding the video he left for her. He wondered if she'd seen the surveillance footage of him standing over her, with her life in his hands.

A part of him wanted to shoot her. Destroy the bitch right there. But that would have been short-sighted. That would've ended her misery. And he wasn't ready to release her just yet.

He thought about his ex-wife, another bitch, and wished he could find a way to make her pay for stealing his daughter.

Tears welled in his eyes as he thought of Lily and wondered if his daughter remembered him. She'd been six when his wife left three years ago and took his daughter.

Lily was at that special age — right before things went bad, and it hurt him not to enjoy her now.

Thinking about his ex-wife soured Paul's mood. He was holding the blade to chop onions with a white-knuckle grip.

He looked down at his hand, feeling outside of his body.

He breathed in and out, smiled, relaxed his grip.

He turned on the small kitchen TV, wanting to check

in with the latest reports on Jessi Price or her stupid parents.

He loved watching the anchors, field reporters, cops, and so-called experts try and figure out what the hell was going on, what sort of "monster" could do this, and whether they'd ever find Jessi.

He loved being the only one who knew the answers while others stumbled in the dark, tripping over their stupidity.

The anchors were talking about some break-in which led to a murder that happened out west in the boondocks while Paul reduced the heat to let the chicken simmer and popped his naan in the oven.

He cleaned the cooking area, his eyes on the screen.

The reporter at the crime scene said a name which knocked him back.

Paul looked up at the screen to see a photo of Richard Howell of Cardinal Road dead, a victim of what authorities believed to be a home invasion gone wrong.

He stared in disbelief, wondering how a man sharing the same name and address as one of his aliases wound up the victim of a home invasion.

What were the odds?

He reached into his back pocket, where he kept his decoy wallet, to double check and see if it was the same name and address.

But the decoy wasn't in his pants. He checked his jacket pocket, where he kept his real wallet, just to see if he hadn't mixed them up or put them both there. But no, it held only his real one.

What the hell?

Paul went to his bedroom to check the top of his dresser where he always kept his wallet and keys — maybe he'd left it behind in his morning rush. He'd been plenty distracted. But no, it wasn't there, either.

Then, a flash.

The black man who bumped into him that morning.

Paul didn't get a good look at the man; he'd come out of nowhere, jogging or whatever the hell he was doing, and had bumped into him rather rudely.

But he hadn't just bumped into him, had he?

He picked my pocket.

Paul stared at the TV, but he wasn't hearing or seeing whatever it was showing. He was lost in thought, wondering if there was any connection between the man bumping into him and a dead Richard Howell.

It was too bizarre to be a coincidence. And in Paul's experience, nothing was ever just chance. Everything was connected to something. You just had to be smart enough to link the dots, and track things back to their origin.

He sat at his kitchen table trying to suss things out. The reporter said that Howell's wife, Susan, reported a black man with a ski mask standing in her living room when she came home. She couldn't make out his face, and he was wearing gloves, but she saw his neck and skin through the eye holes. She didn't have much of a description, but he was African American, and wearing a black hoodie — same as Paul's pickpocket.

There weren't a ton of black men in Pine Harbour, but he imagined it wouldn't be uncommon for those residents to have a black hoodie. Hell, Paul owned one himself. But the odds of a black man in a black hoodie picking his wallet on the same day that a black man in a hoodie broke into a home with the name and address of Paul's alias, were *astronomically* improbable.

It meant one of two things: either the man was a thief who was looking for someone who worked at the school and therefore wouldn't be home all day so he could go back in and break into his house at a leisurely pace, or he'd targeted Paul because he knew what Paul was.

Paul's heart pounded.

His face felt flush.

He ran his fingers through his hair, anxiety tightening his chest.

How does this guy know about me?

What trail did I leave, and who else might be on it?

And if he knows who I am and what I do, why not tell the police?

Is this guy fucking with me?

It seemed impossible.

Paul was incredibly careful when selecting his victims. He *never* picked kids from his school. And he never drove his own vehicle; he picked them up in a cop car he bought at auction, which he kept in a garage, rented under a different assumed name.

He stared at the photo of this other Richard Howell, and a tightness gripped his chest. This was too close to home for coincidence.

He thought of the black man. He hadn't noticed it at the time, but now, as he played the scene back in his head, he was certain that the man's eyes had met his, locking on for longer than necessary.

The man was on to him, toying with him, coming for him.

Or maybe he'd be sending the sheriff's department.

Either way, Paul was living on borrowed time.

And now he had to move everything up.

Chapter 30 - Mallory Black

MAL WOKE TO A RINGING PHONE.

She reached out blindly, feeling along the couch, searching until she found it. She opened her still tired eyes and saw a number she'd not expected to see — her ex-husband, Ray.

She answered, trying not to sound like she'd been sleeping in the middle of the day.

"Hey."

"How's it going?"

"Okay," she said, not sure what words might push them past the awkwardness. Their divorce had been relatively free of acrimony, but they'd barely spoken after Ashley's death. It was too hard for them both.

Ray had somehow moved on, found a new girlfriend, Julie. He'd probably marry her, have another kid, and pretend like the life he once shared with Mal and Ashley had never existed.

"I saw the story," he said. "Are you okay?"

"Yeah, I'm fine."

He was quiet for a moment. "You don't sound fine."

"What are you asking, Ray?"

"I'm just calling to see if you're okay."

"I'm fine."

"I'm in the neighborhood. Mind if I stop by?"

Mal sat up. "Why?"

"I just wanted to talk. Can I come over?"

"Yeah." She regretted it before she even said it, and wondered why the hell she agreed. "Um, when?"

"Fifteen minutes?"

"Okay."

After hanging up, Mal quickly cleared the living room of alcohol, pills, and the several reminders of Ashley.

She looked at herself in the bathroom mirror. Her eyes had dark circles, and her hair was a frizzy mess. She pulled it back into a tight ponytail then changed into jeans and a tee that disguised her hibernation through half the day.

She headed back downstairs, cleaning up a bit, all the while wondering why Ray was coming over. Was he worried about her after the news story, or was there something else? Had he broken up with Julie? Or maybe he lost his job. Ray was a photographer at the Creek County Chronicle, and the newsroom had gone through several rounds of cuts which he'd somehow managed to survive. Maybe the paper finally decided they didn't need photographers. Just put an iPhone into every stringer and reporter's hands, right? Always about the bottom line, to hell with quality.

She went outside, approached the unmarked car, saw it was Wilson and Reyes, and told them that Ray was visiting, so try not to shoot him when he showed up.

She went back inside and anxiously waited, still wondering why Ray was coming over.

Five long minutes later, the doorbell rang.

Mal answered, realizing that this was maybe the first time Ray had been home since after the funeral.

He stood on her doorstep, his blue eyes piercing as ever, and smile every bit as charming. Even after all they'd been through, all the time between them, a part of her wanted to hold him, longed to feel his mouth back on hers.

"Hey," she said, hoping her thoughts weren't too obvious.

"Hey," he said, hugging her.

She inhaled his scent. While it was slightly different now that he lived in a new house with another woman, there was still that bit of him that she'd always loved and still remembered.

They held their embrace for longer than either of them likely expected. Mal wondered if she'd been right in her guess that he split with Julie. If so, had he come over for a roll in the hay? And if so, was she willing? Mal hated to admit it, but her body longed for his touch, even if her brain recognized it for the awful idea it was.

She pulled away and met his eyes. He quickly averted his gaze as if she were seeing through him to the part he was trying to hide.

She closed the door behind him. "What's up?"

"Just wanted to see how you're doing."

Mal led him to the kitchen, where she'd already set out a pitcher of water and two glasses on the granite counter island. "Water? Something else?"

"Water's fine."

Clearly, he wasn't there for sex.

She poured two glasses of water, and took a drink, waiting for him to spill whatever was on his mind.

"So," he said after taking a sip, "what happened between you and Gloria?"

Mal wasn't sure what she should tell him, and certainly

didn't want him to worry about her. But it all started falling out of her mouth before she could help it.

"Jesus, why didn't you tell me about the first time the killer left something?"

"You would have just worried, and there wasn't anything you could do. Plus, you were living your new life. I didn't want to interfere."

She wasn't trying to sound like a martyr, but a part of Mal did want something from him, even if she couldn't quite figure out what.

"What now?" he asked. "Why are you even here?"

"I've got a protection detail. Surprised they didn't stop and frisk you."

He smiled, but his eyes were worried. "How long are they there for?"

"I dunno. I'm not worried. Let that fucker come back. I'll blow his ass away."

"Yeah, if you're not sleeping."

She hadn't told him the worst of it, how he stood over her putting the gun to her head. He would've freaked out. Ray was still a boy scout, wanting to protect her.

"I'm more worried about that little girl, Jessi Price. Gloria's not doing shit to find this bastard, and time is running out."

"Is that why you talked to the reporter, trying to light a fire under her ass?"

"Yeah, for all the good it did. She just does a press conference and buys herself more time to do nothing."

Whatever with the water. Mal went to the fridge for a beer. "Want one?"

"No thanks." Ray eyed her with his usual worry, treating her like a kid who didn't know any better. She already had a daddy, and Ray's overbearing behavior reminded her of one of the reasons their marriage fell apart. Now she felt stupid for wanting to sleep with him.

She flicked the cap off the beer, took a deep swig, and studied Ray's discomfort with a bit of nihilistic glee.

He took another drink of his water. "When's the last time you went to a meeting?"

She sipped her beer and smiled.

"You gave up?"

"Sorry, I know the 12-steppers help you, but if I wanted to be around a bunch of dysfunctional miserable fucks, I'd go back to work."

He looked exasperated. "I'm just saying, if you wanted to go back, I could go with you."

"Thanks, but no." She laughed. "I'm doing just fine without having sanctimonious people using me to feel better about themselves."

"I think you're missing—"

"I said no," she snapped, colder than intended.

Ray was quiet for a long moment, as if trying to work up the nerve to say something else. She hoped he wasn't going to harp on the benefits of 12-step meetings because damn, she was tired of that particular song.

"Have you considered maybe selling the house?"

She set her beer on the island. "I told you, I'm *not* selling the house."

"It isn't safe here."

"So, what you think if I move this creep won't follow me? He's a stalker, rapist, and murderer. I doubt he gives up easily."

"Can't you go into some protection plan or something?"

She laughed. "That's not quite how things work."

"I'm sure there's *something* you can do."

"Yeah, there is. I can stay right here and not fucking

run." She took another swig. "I'm not about to let some asshole kiddy rapist chase me out of my home. This is where we raised our family. This house has a history. And maybe that doesn't matter to you, but it sure as hell matters to me."

Suddenly, her eyes were welling with tears.

Oh, no. Fuck this.

She turned away, not wanting Ray to see her crying. Not wanting him to see how much it bothered her that he'd somehow moved on as if his previous life wasn't real, or didn't matter.

She heard him step up behind her.

She didn't turn.

He put his hands on her shoulders. "Is that what you think? That this house, that what we had doesn't matter to me?"

Mal bit her bottom lip. If she spoke, she'd never stop crying, and that was something she couldn't afford to do.

Mal had cried in front of Ray exactly twice in their marriage, and neither time had been from a moment of weakness. She hated this side of her and wished she could leave the room without it looking like she was being dramatic or fishing for pity.

"It's because I care that I think you should move. Not just because you might be in danger here, but because I think you'll never move on until you can get out of … out of *this place.*"

Ray sounded frustrated as if *this place* was a prison that trapped him in a past he couldn't wait to forget. But to Mal, it was a reminder of better days; a sanctuary of sorts. Clearly Ray didn't understand, because he was trying to start his life over.

But Mal didn't want a new life. She wanted her old one.

"I'm not selling the house." Mal knew how to get Ray out of her house. It was a bit cruel, but she knew it would work.

"You need money, Ray? Is that why you want me to sell? I mean, I know the value's gone up a lot, and hell, you could use the cash, right?"

"That's not it," he said, his voice terse.

"If you need money, just ask," she said, taking a drink.

He met her eyes, his flashing with anger or hurt. "You know what, never mind. Sorry I came."

Ray turned and headed toward the living room, then he walked out the door and closed it behind him without another word.

Mal smiled, even though she felt like a monster.

Chapter 31 - Jasper Parish

JASPER AND JORDYN sat outside the two-story home with the white picket fence in Bay Hill, a gated community in the northernmost part of Creek County. The house belonged to Rachel Dodd, Paul's ex-wife.

"Nice place," Jordyn said. "She must have a good job. Sure as hell ain't getting this on alimony from a teacher's salary."

Jasper hadn't looked up Rachel's job but agreed with Jordyn's assessment.

"So, what's the play?" she asked. "Why aren't we calling the cops on this asshole now that we have his address?"

"Because we don't know if he's keeping Jessi in his house, right? You said you weren't sure. If we call the cops and tip him off before knowing for certain, we might never find her. So, we talk to the wife, see what she knows, and maybe it helps us."

"I still don't understand why we need to talk to her. We know he's guilty if we find the girl in his house. Is that what you're worried about, proving his guilt? What if she's still close to him? What if she calls him the second we leave and tells the asshole that some big black dude, maybe the same black dude that stole his wallet, was over asking questions about him? What then?"

"First off, I doubt they're close. Call it a hunch. And second of all, just let me do things my way, okay?"

Jordyn smiled. "As long as you're not looking for a reason to wuss out."

"You sit in the car. I'll be back."

She sighed, threw her feet on the dashboard, and picked up her tablet. "Fine, I'll be here reading. Try not to shoot anyone."

He glared at her.

"Too soon?" Jordyn smiled, thinking she was cuter than she was.

"Did anyone ever tell you that you were nicer as a kid?"

Jasper closed the door and headed up the driveway, not waiting for his daughter's smartass response.

It was six o'clock, and there were no cars in the driveway. Hoping that Rachel wasn't at work, Jasper rang her doorbell and waited.

Shortly after he rang, a curtain beside the door parted and a brunette woman in her early forties peered outside.

"Yes?"

"Hi ma'am," Jasper said, opening his wallet and showing the PI badge he carried as one of his many aliases. "My name is Cole Houser, and I'm a private detective working a missing child case. I was hoping you could help me?"

He waited through her pause, hoping he wouldn't need to mention that this involved her ex-husband. That might scare her off. He figured the missing child case was enough to grease the cooperative wheels. Most people wanted to assist in a missing child case. Most people, however, didn't want to discuss their ex. Probably doubly so if he was a pedophile child rapist/killer.

She opened the door.

"Sorry to disturb you," Jasper said with a serious smile. "But I'm working on the Jessi Price case. Have you heard of it?"

Jessi Price was one county and an hour away, but it wasn't as if there were so many missing children cases that they didn't stick it out when they occurred anywhere within a few hours.

"Of course. How can *I* help?"

Jasper held up a picture of Jessi that he'd printed from a website, figuring it made his queries look all the more official, and maybe tug at Rachel's heartstrings. He wanted to take the conversation inside but first had to earn her trust.

"Well, Ms. Dodd, it's about your ex-husband, Paul."

The look on her face perceptibly shifted. It was a coin toss whether she'd slam the door in his face or break down right there.

"I think you can help me find Jessi." And there it was, that look of knowledge in her eyes. Yes, she knew what her ex-husband was. "May I come in to talk with you?"

"Um," she looked behind her as if trying to determine how safe it was to trust this stranger at her door. "Can I see your badge again?"

He handed her the wallet with his badge and fake ID. She gave it a cursory glance, as most people did, then opened the door wider to let him in.

Her house was as nice inside as it was outside, with a minimalist design that Jasper could very much appreciate. He spied a piano in the far corner of the living room, a few photos of a dark-haired girl that looked around nine or ten in her most recent pictures — clearly her daughter. Jasper wondered if she was home.

She led him to a large dining room table, pulled out a chair for him at the end, then sat to his right.

"What does Paul have to do with the girl?" She kept her voice low, lending to Jasper's theory that the daughter was home.

"I have reason to believe he could be connected to the disappearance, but I wanted to reach out to people he knew first. I don't want to throw Paul into the public spotlight if he's innocent. That can ruin a teacher's career, you know?"

"Why do you think he's connected?"

"I can't talk too much about the details, given that it's an active investigation," Jasper said, hoping she wouldn't press further. Saying something like that would usually rebuff people's questions. "But I was hoping you could help me, just to make sure we're not heading down the wrong path."

She nodded, then looked up and past him.

He turned to see the girl from the photos descending the stairs, still in her school uniform — beige pants and a white polo with a school's name and crest stitched in blue just above her heart.

"Hi, Lily," Rachel said, "Mommy's just talking to Mr. Houser. I'll call you when I'm ready to make dinner."

The girl looked at Jasper curiously, like she wanted to ask who he was but was either too shy or polite to do so. "Okay. Can I watch TV in your room?"

"Yes," Rachel said, clearly working not to sound impatient.

Lily bounded up the stairs.

Jasper waited until he heard a closing door, then

continued. "Can you tell me a bit about your ex-husband? Do you think he'd have any reason to take a child?"

Her eyes were starting to water. "I don't know. I would hope not."

"But you're not certain?"

"No."

"Why not?"

"I don't know if I should say anything."

Jasper considered pulling the photo of Jessi Price from his jacket pocket, but he didn't need to.

"I left Paul because I was afraid he might hurt our daughter."

"Why did you think that?"

"Stuff I found on his computer."

"What kind of stuff?"

"Naked photos and videos of our daughter in the tub, sleeping. They weren't sexual. And if there were like one or two, I might've chalked it up to a photo any parent might take. But there were *soooo* many. And then there was the stuff with other girls. And these weren't even close to innocent."

"Sexual?"

"Yes."

Jasper swallowed. No matter how many times he'd encountered stuff like this, it was never easy to hear, and always sickened him.

"What happened? Did you confront your husband?"

"If by *confront* you mean freaked the hell out, then yes, I confronted him. I asked him why the hell he had photos of our daughter like this. And I asked him who the other girls were."

"What did he say?"

"He said the other girls were from the internet, and

that he'd never touch a child. Weird as it might sound, I believed him."

"Why?"

"Because of what happened to Paul when he was a kid."

"What?"

Rachel took a drink of water, then wiped at her eyes. "Does it really matter?"

"Anything that might help us understand where his head is at can be helpful to ending this thing peacefully, and finding Jessi Price alive."

She swallowed hard then began the story.

"It all started when Paul was eleven. His father disappeared. Nobody knows where he went, but Paul figured he'd probably had enough of his mother's crap. His mother, Jean, was bipolar. Depending on the day, either overly nice or downright sadistic. Add to that a horrible lisp and kids calling him 'Odd Dodd' and you can imagine how hellish his life was. Paul had adored his father and felt rejected that his old man abandoned him and his sister. He hated that he'd basically been left to raise his three-year-old sister, Katie.

"Anyway, Jean was a waitress at some dive bar, made just enough to keep them in their house, with the little that was left going to drink and drugs. She was barely there for the kids. Worked at night and slept through the day. Paul wound up doing a lot of side jobs for the neighbors to keep food on the table for him and his sister."

Another swallow, another sip of water.

"When Paul was twelve, a new neighbor moved into the nice house at the end of the street. His name was Wes Richardson, and he was a single, rather wealthy realtor. Paul saw his car, a beautiful brand new Corvette, a car you'd obviously want to take good care of, and figured that he'd found himself the perfect client.

"Soon, Paul was washing the guy's car and cutting his lawn. In no time, he was walking the man's Husky. One night, during one of Jean's bad spells, she hurt Paul something fierce. Left bruises all over his face then told him to get the hell out of her house. It was raining, and Paul, not knowing where else to go, wound up standing on Wes's porch to escape the rain. Wes came home and asked him what happened. Paul broke down and told his new friend everything."

Jasper could see *exactly* where this was going.

"Wes invited him in then comforted Paul with pizza and cold Cokes. He convinced him to go home and work things out with his mom. Paul did, but he was also going over to Wes's place more and more. He even gave Paul a key and told him that he could crash there whenever he needed to. So, one week Wes had to go to some realtor conference in Salt Lake or something, and Paul had total access to the house while watching the dog. That was when Paul saw his first pornographic magazine, in a nightstand filled with a bunch them. This was his first exposure to a naked girl outside of his little sister. He was aroused but too young to know what that meant, or what to do with those feelings. He said he felt an immense amount of shame, yet he couldn't stop returning to Wes's stash, or looking for more. And then, in a box buried in the back of Wes's closet, Paul found a box of video tapes with names like *Missy's Spanking, Teaching Tina,* and other salacious titles that only fueled his curiosity. He debated for three days whether to pop one into the VCR. Finally, curiosity got the better of him. But this wasn't regular porn. There were children, in addition to adults."

Jasper sighed.

"Paul wasn't mature enough to know this was not normal. He doesn't think twice that Wes is anything but your everyday single guy. So, he never said anything to anyone because that would mean admitting to his snooping. Not only would he get in trouble, and a beating from his mom, but Wes would probably stop paying him for odd jobs, and would certainly never let him come over again.

"After a while, he practically lived with Wes. He'd watch cable, which he didn't have. He'd play video games, which he didn't have. And he'd eat and drink whatever he wanted, which he wasn't allowed to do at home. One weekend after Jean had an especially terrible episode, Paul went over to Wes's. That's when everything changed. He wasn't alone. Wes had a girl over, a pretty blonde in a bikini. Paul figured she was in college, but she could've been a teenager. Anyway, Wes and the girl, Julie, were drinking and smoking pot.

"Paul had seen his mother do both, as well as her friends, but had never tried either himself. Julie teased Paul, trying to get him to try a little. How could he say no to this girl with breasts falling out of a bikini top? He wanted her, and Wes, to think he was cool. That he wasn't just some stupid whiny kid from down the street. So, he had his first taste of beer and weed. One thing led to another, and soon Julie was letting Paul touch her. He was too messed up, and too excited to see how incredibly wrong this was or to find it creepy that Wes encouraged them both while he watched. Julie went down on Paul. He said he came immediately. But then he ran into the bathroom, embarrassed and scared."

Jasper sighed, wishing that someone had been around to stop Wes from turning Paul into a monster.

"Wes and Julie both talked Paul down, told him that what happened was completely okay, and even a normal part of growing up. Paul went home, again saying nothing and clinging to his secret shame. He avoided Wes for a month or so. But then one night he found himself back at his house. Julie was there. And it wasn't long until they were all at it again. This went on every weekend for a few months, Wes encouraging Paul to 'be a man' and have sex with Julie. Paul eventually did. On the couch. And as he did, Paul looked over and saw Wes masturbating. And rather than being disturbed or weirded out, Paul was happy that he pleased this man who had become like a second father.

"In the months that followed, Paul thought more and more about Wes, and even began to think of it as he masturbated in his bedroom late at night. He wondered if maybe he was gay. He felt such a mix of shame and lust, it was doing a number on his head.

"One weekend Paul went over eager to see Julie again. But she wasn't there. Paul was disappointed, but also excited. Wes told him that they didn't need Julie. They could do these things with each other. And that's how it all started."

"Jesus," Jasper said.

"Things went on for a while like this. Sometimes with Julie, and other times with only them. A few times with other girls or women. Paul said it was a confusing time, but also a lot of fun. Then he turned ten and everything stopped. Suddenly, Wes was too busy. He had some other younger boy doing his odd jobs. Paul was shut out and didn't understand why. He was devastated, started sneaking his mother's booze, weed, and pills. He was spiraling out of control, but Jean was too out of it to notice. Paul said that much of this time went by in a haze.

"By the time he was fourteen Paul was hanging out with other loser kids, drinking, doing drugs, and getting into tons of trouble. His mom had lost her job and was on welfare. She was always home, but never *really* there. One day, Paul and Katie, who was nine at the time, came home from school and their mother wasn't home, which wasn't anything new as she was always taking off for a day or two with whatever guy floated in and out of her life. But this time Paul had lost his key, so they were stuck outside. Then who comes along but Wes Richardson, asking if they'd like to have dinner.

"Soon Paul was back in Wes's good graces, doing odd jobs, watching his dog, back to making money. Things were good again. Paul thought perhaps he'd misjudged Wes's coldness, and that maybe it had been his fault. But—"

"Wes was targeting Katie?"

"Yes. And at first, Paul resisted, never leaving Wes alone with his sister or allowing her to drink or do drugs. But one weekend, Paul slept in. He woke up to nobody home then went over to Wes's and found Katie in his jacuzzi with another teenage girl. She wasn't even wasted or drunk, but she enjoyed the affection. Paul was pissed but didn't want to rock the boat. He figured if Katie wanted to let Paul and the other girl do stuff to her, who was he to stop them?"

"I don't know, only her *brother?*" Jasper said, disgusted.

"Yes," Rachel agreed. "But the way Paul explained it, Katie had always been flirtatious with boys and men, always craving attention. He often called her a slut, so I guess that was his way of justifying allowing this all to happen. Wes was also now paying Paul and Katie what was a ridiculous amount of money for them, each week. Money that put food on the table, and helped them feel secure. Anyway, this next part Paul confessed through tears. A few months into this rekindled relationship, Wes had one of his girls over. Lots of drugs and booze. One thing led to another and … Paul wound up having sex with his sister."

"Oh, God, no."

"And Wes recorded it."

Jasper closed his eyes, shaking his head. He wasn't sure where the story was going, but he needed to hear the rest if only it gave him leverage with Paul if he had to negotiate for Jessi's freedom rather than kill for it.

A part of Jasper felt terrible for the young Paul Dodd, an innocent kid who never had a chance at being normal. A kid who was screwed over by a father who left, a crazy drug-addict mother, and by a pure demon — the rotten recipe to fashion the man who would go on to kill Ashley Black and kidnap Jessi Price.

But Paul was no longer an innocent. Now he was the monster, and someone had to stop him.

Rachel continued. "Eventually, Wes began having sex with Katie while Paul watched, joined in, or screwed whatever other girl Wes had roped into his sick little parties. This all continued for a bit until Katie turned ten, which was incidentally the time she started getting breasts."

"And then he kicked them to the curb?"

"Yep."

"But Katie didn't take it well."

"What happened?"

"She told her mother that Wes was raping them both. She didn't mention that Paul had sex with her or that Wes had filmed it, but the minute the shit hit the fan, Paul was terrified that the cops would find out and that he'd be arrested too."

"Did they find out?"

"No. They never did. Paul doesn't know what happened to the video Wes recorded, but no cop ever asked about it. And it never came up in trial. It was as if it never happened. Their mother died shortly after the trial. Paul and Katie were both sent into foster care. Paul was adopted by a good foster family. They were supportive and made sure that he did well in school. He quit hanging out with drug addicts and started making something of himself. He enlisted in the Army after graduation. Was in Special Ops or something; he doesn't like to talk about that time. But he got a full scholarship from the Army, then came home, went to school, and got a teaching gig. He was living a normal life. Somehow, he managed to escape his abuse relatively untarnished. Katie wasn't so lucky."

"What happened to her?"

"She had the opposite experience, bounced around from home to home, never got along with other kids. She was sexually abused and eventually ran away. Paul didn't hear from her for a long time. She reached out a few years ago. She was living in Portland and got herself into some trouble. Heroin, I think. She asked Paul for money. He said he couldn't help her unless she went into a treatment facility. That was the last time they ever spoke."

Rachel took another drink of her water, then stared at Jasper. Finally, she said, "Paul isn't a bad guy. Yes, he has this other side, a deep, brooding side that he'd go into every so often. I figured it was from his abuse, or maybe things he saw in the Army. That stuff messes with everyone, right? But I didn't think he was *bad*. At least not enough to ever hurt his own child."

It looked like she believed it. "Then why the divorce?"

She blinked back tears. "I guess because I couldn't be certain. And if anything ever *did* happen to Lily, I'd never forgive myself. The way he explained it was that he didn't *exclusively* like kids. He said he loved me more than I could know, and I think that he meant it. Paul wasn't one of these pervert child molesters. He *hated* that he was attracted to children, that he was so twisted at an early age. How do you come back from that? How do you cure that? He loves kids, in the platonic sense of the word, and teaching. Can you imagine if he went to a shrink and told them what he was feeling? How quickly he'd be ostracized and out of a job?"

Jasper hated how she was defending her ex-husband, but also knew it must've been hard for her to reconcile the man she loved versus the things he hid, and now the fact that he might have kidnapped a child. She was clinging to illusion even as truth's light eroded the facade.

"He said he'd never hurt Lily or any kid. Said that he knew all too well how it felt to be a victim and would never put that on anyone. I believed him. That's why I didn't report Paul to the police. I just wanted him out of our life. I demanded full custody, and he said he wouldn't fight it. I thought this would be easier, on all of us. Just make him go away. I never thought he'd touch a child. I … I should've said something."

Rachel was starting to crack, realizing that her inaction might cost another little girl her life. She looked at Jasper, face in anguish, desperate for absolution.

But he wasn't the one to forgive. And there could be no solace, at least not until Jessi Price was alive and home with her parents.

"Do you know where he is now?" Jasper already had an address for Paul, but given that the man had used a decoy, his public info could also be false.

"Yeah, now and then I get mail and send it to him."

"May I have his address?"

Rachel stood, went into the study, then returned a few moments later with a piece of paper. She handed it to Jasper.

He looked down at the address. It was the same one he

already had. "Does he have any other places that you know about? Places he might hide a child?"

"No, not that I know of."

Jasper stood, thanked Rachel for her time, and was about to head toward the door when he stopped and turned. "Did you happen to keep any copies of the things you saw on his computer?"

Rachel's eyes moved ever so slightly, giving her away even if she attempted denial. But she didn't. "Yes, I did."

"Could you make me a copy?"

"Um … I … I dunno."

Jasper could understand her reservations on a few levels. One, she'd be handing over photos of her daughter to a stranger. Two, she probably wondered if her having these things would make her liable either criminally or for withholding evidence.

"Okay, you don't need to give me a copy. But I suggest that you put one in a safe deposit account and inform your lawyer that if anything happens to you, that copy goes straight to the police."

Rachel crossed her arms over her chest, eyebrows furrowed. "You don't think he'd come after Lily or me, do you?"

"I don't know. But we ought to take care of this, just to be on the safe side."

"Do you think I should call the police and give them the evidence?"

Jasper didn't want that. At least not yet. He needed a chance to move in on Paul before the sheriff's department. He was the only one who could guarantee Jessi's safety and ensure that Paul was taken care of once and for all before the monster could hurt anyone else.

"No need to thrust yourself into the headlines just yet. That wouldn't be good for you, your daughter, or Jessi

Price. Just make a copy, and I'll be in touch soon. I'm working with a few deputies make sure this is done as quickly and as quietly as possible."

Rachel looked ever so slightly relaxed. "Thank you, Mister?"

"Houser. Cole Houser. And thank you, ma'am."

Jasper left.

It was time to end Paul Dodd and save Jessi Price.

Chapter 32 - Mallory Black

MAL LINED UP HER SHOT, aimed down the sight, and fired at the target, a gray paper silhouette on a cardboard backing showing vitals in dark circles for the head and heart.

She emptied her Glock 22, half heart-shots, and half head. None missed.

So many times, she'd pictured her daughter's killer on the receiving end of her gun. She had no idea what he looked like, and that made it harder to imagine, and therefore prepare, for his death; but she could at least be certain that with practice she wouldn't flinch once eye-to-eye with the opportunity.

She'd always been a great shot, one of the top in her graduating class at the academy. Since leaving the force, Mal had hit the range at least three times a week, and she'd only improved.

Mal smiled and hit the button to bring the target closer, examining her results with no small amount of pride. She replaced the target, then sent it back to ready her next shot.

She thought back about Ray coming to her house, saying that she ought to be attending meetings. Mal could admit to having a small problem, but it wasn't like she was off the rails like after Ashley's death.

She was managing fine.

What did Ray know? He was living his new life with Julie. He wasn't there with her and didn't see how well she got along most days.

Could an addict make such precise shots?

She lined up her shot and aimed again.

The first one missed, and so did the second.

But the third found its home, as did every one after.

She scowled for allowing thoughts of Ray to ruin her game.

She recalled her target, tore off the sheet, and was about to line up a new one when her phone buzzed in her back pocket.

She pulled it out and saw a text from Mike: *Got something to show you.*

She gathered her stuff, left the range, removed her headphones, and went to the car.

Inside, she turned the engine to get the air going and dialed Mike.

"Hey, Mike. What have you got for me?"

"We ran the names of people at the coffee shop, cross referenced them with times, and I've pulled a few photos for you to look at. Where you at?"

"Westside Shooting Range."

"Hang tight; I'm about five minutes out."

FIVE MINUTES LATER, to the tee, Mike pulled up alone in his unmarked car.

"Where's your partner?" Mal asked when he got out of his car.

"Back at the precinct running down leads."

Mike opened a manila folder and spread its contents on top of her trunk. "I pulled driver's license photos from the DMV. Any of these men look familiar?"

Mal had no idea what her daughter's killer looked like, nor did they ever land any credible suspects. But it was possible that these photos could trigger a memory of someone she'd never considered — maybe a guy she locked up years ago, or someone on the periphery that she'd never viewed as a suspect. Sometimes missing data, like who was in the coffee shop spying on her, was the missing link that allowed a person to finish the puzzle.

"These are all the guys at the coffee shop at the time of the login to my cameras?"

"All that we've not already ruled out."

There were eleven photos with names and DMV info attached. She picked up the closest one and examined it, waiting for some recognition.

Nothing.

She moved to the next, then the third.

Something clicked on the fifth.

Mal stared at the photo of the handsome man with the brown curly hair and the piercing blue eyes.

He looked so familiar, yet she couldn't remember any context.

She looked at the name. Paul Dodd of Cantille Street.

But there were no ringing bells.

She wondered if he was one of her drunken one-night stands. He was prettier than her usual type, but a hookup was possible. Mal hated that her life was so out of control that she couldn't remember if she'd slept with a man.

Before Ray, there had only been one other man. Since Ray, she'd lost count.

She stared at the photo trying to shake something loose.

Then it hit her.

The toy store.

The morning Ashley vanished.

She'd been looking for that Kewl Chic doll and had run into this man in the toy aisle.

He'd made small talk. She thought maybe he was even flirting. Then she was interrupted by a call from work; the burglary turned double homicide.

She hadn't thought much of him at the time, or since — until now. Even in the days after Ashley went missing, and anyone she'd ever met was practically a suspect, she'd never thought of the man in the toy store. She'd always seen that as a random encounter.

But now she knew better.

Paul Dodd had been stalking her even then.

Plotting, planning, and brazen enough to bump into her the day he planned to take Ashley. She stared at the photo and finally had a face to go with two years of rage, pain, and hate.

"Him," she said, handing the paper to Mike. "It's him."

Chapter 33 - Jasper Parish

JASPER'S HEART raced as he stepped out from the dark woods, hopped the fence, and landed in Paul Dodd's back yard — practically pitch black beneath the new moon.

There were lights on in the windows along the back of his home, but the blinds were all drawn so that Jasper couldn't see inside.

He adjusted his ski mask, tightened his gloves, then reached back and pulled his backpack around to his front, unzipped it, and withdrew the pistol. He'd already done a Google Maps search to see photos of Paul's home and yard. It was the only house on this side of the street with a fully fenced-in back. He double checked to make sure there were fences on either side.

Jasper patted his front pocket to make sure his cell hadn't fallen out. He'd need to call Jordyn — parked at a nearby gas station — once he was done killing Paul and saving Jessi.

Paul's house didn't have any doors along the rear, meaning he'd either need to climb in through a window or circle around the front and hope nobody spotted him picking the lock.

He crept up to the closest window along the back and pressed his gloves against it, trying to slide the window open.

But it wouldn't budge.

He tried the other windows: same results.

Why can't things ever be easy?

He crept toward the side of the house, hearing the muffled sounds of classical music from the other side of the walls. He wondered if that was where Paul was keeping the girl.

He continued along the side of the house, reached the tall privacy fence's gate, slowly unlatched it, and peered into the front yard.

Jasper froze when he saw movement on the sidewalk.

He watched shadows form the shape of a rotund man walking a Chihuahua.

The dog sniffed the ground, taking forever, looking for a place to do its business.

Come on.

Being so close to his kill, and yet unable to reach him, was a torment to Jasper. He wanted to get inside and get this over with. He didn't even intend to take his time with Dodd as he had the others. No ritual of knocking him out and then waiting for him to wake for a speech about why he deserved to die. No drawn-out process to make Paul regret his sins.

This would be quick and efficient, so he could ensure that Jessi was alive and well. Then he would call the cops so they could come and get the girl after he was long gone.

This one wasn't about a kill.

This was about saving a life.

And though he hated Paul Dodd for the hell he'd put

Mallory through — a hell that Jasper had followed on television in the weeks and months that followed Ashley's disappearance — this wasn't even about revenge for the Black family.

This was about Jessi Price.

Oh, yeah, if this isn't about the kill then why the hell didn't you just call the police in the first place? Let them know where to find the girl?

Because I can't trust the police not to screw this up. Especially after that press conference where they threw Mallory under the bus.

The man and the tiny dog finally moved on.

Jasper opened the fence and made his way into the front yard.

He spied a few other people out for late night walks along the cul-de-sac, but fortunately for Jasper, Paul's front yard had plenty of trees and shrubs, making it easy to stay out of sight as he made his way to the front door.

The porch was dark, comforting Jasper as he retrieved his lock picking set and worked the door.

He had it unlocked in less than a minute.

Hopefully, he wouldn't trigger an alarm.

Jasper swallowed hard, gripped his gun, and crossed the threshold into the killer's home.

Chapter 34 - Mallory Black

GLORIA'S OFFICE was the last place in the world Mal would've expected herself to be this morning. But there she stood opposite her old boss, waiting for the woman to deliberate on what she and Mike had just told her.

Gloria looked up over her glasses. "And you think he has Jessi Price?"

"Yes."

"But we have no evidence?"

"Other than my hunch, no."

Mike took the ball. "But we've got this guy on possible burglary, logging into Mallory's account, stalking, if not outright being Ashley's murderer. So, is it a reach that this Dodd also has Price? Maybe. But not by much."

"I'll never get Judge Cansell to green light a search warrant tying this to Jessi Price."

"We don't need it for Jessi. We go after him for breaking into my house. We just need to get in the door. We find evidence of Jessi being there, then we call the judge and update our warrant. Or, we can use exigent circumstances."

Gloria looked back at the packet on Dodd. Former military, honorable discharge, a teacher, divorced due to irreconcilable differences. His wife had sole custody of their nine-year-old daughter. He had no record — unfortunate for them as that might have helped make their case. Maybe some B&E, stalking, or indecent exposure — *anything* to nudge Gloria's eventual *yes*.

She met Mal's eyes. "And you said this guy came up to you the day Ashley vanished? You're *certain* it's him? I mean, how do you remember something like that, a random guy in a store, especially given everything else that happened that day?"

"I'm one hundred percent sure it's him. You forget my stellar memory?"

Gloria looked again at the papers, then back at Mal. "Okay. I'll call Cansell. We'll get eyes on Dodd's house and inlets into his neighborhood. Then we get SWAT to stage at Riverview Elementary. I want a clean operation. No more shit shows this week. Understand?"

Mike nodded.

Gloria looked at Mal. "And you?"

"Can I ride with Mike?"

"Yes, but you're on as a consultant only. And I don't want you anywhere near the crime scene. Got it?"

Tears stung the corners of her eyes. "Yes, ma'am. Thank you."

Chapter 35 - Jasper Parish

JASPER SLIPPED through the monster's living room undetected, moving toward the left side of the house where the loud classical music was still playing.

He'd already given a cursory glance into the kitchen and living room to the right, finding no sign of Dodd or the girl. The only rooms left unexplored were behind the four doors to the left, all of them closed.

Probably three bedrooms and a bathroom. Maybe one of the rooms had been converted to a child's prison.

He entered the hallway, gripping the gun, prepared not just to shoot, but to deflect an attack if Paul was waiting behind a door.

His heart raced as he neared the doors. Music was louder, disorienting Jasper as he approached the first one.

He couldn't help but feel like he was about to enter a trap.

He slowly twisted the knob, then turned.

The door opened into a dark bedroom. He let it swing all the way open to ensure that Paul wasn't hiding behind it.

The room was empty except for a few boxes at the far end.

Time for the next door.

He approached with the same caution, reached the door, twisted the knob, then let it swing open as he took a step back, ready for whatever might be waiting.

A bathroom — a clear glass shower stall with nowhere for Paul to hide.

Jasper approached the third room, where the music was coming from, carefully gripping the pistol as he reached out for the knob.

His fingers closed around it.

He was about to twist the knob when his phone buzzed.

Only Jordyn had the number.

Something must be wrong.

He fished the phone from his pocket and peered at the screen:

COPS COMING. GET OUT!!!

Chapter 36 - Mallory Black

IT ALMOST FELT like old times for Mal.

Except that Mike's new partner, Skippy, was riding shotgun, and Mal was in the back seat of the squad car. But everything else was the same — the adrenaline rush, the suspense of not knowing what was next that heightened her senses, and a creeping unease in the back of her mind, a dread that could only be defeated by moving forward and eliminating the threat. Everything blended to create a feeling that you got used to as a deputy, a feeling she was surprised to find herself deeply missing.

She'd longed for the old camaraderie. Not only did you share a history with your brothers and sisters in blue, but after a while, those were often the only people you could *truly* relate to. They were the ones who understood the dark sense of humor and ability to disconnect one needed to get through the job's worst parts. They didn't look at you like a monster when you shifted from talking about recovering a body from a lake to the latest sports results with no transition.

They were the ones that had your back, maybe even

saved your ass a time or two. They were sometimes more like family than your actual blood, especially since you spent more of your waking days by their side.

Had things gone differently following Ashley's death, they'd still be Mal's family.

"Here we go," Mike said from the front seat. They rolled up on Dodd's home, a one story house at the end of a cul-de-sac.

The SWAT team pulled up in their unmarked SRT van.

Mike and Skippy got out of the cruiser. Mike opened Mal's door and they watched as the six SWAT deputies hopped out of their van and headed to the front door with the battering ram. Two of the deputies peeled off of the six, heading to the rear, in case Paul tried to make a back-door escape.

There were also deputies positioned at the end of the block at the neighborhood's only two exits, just in case Paul somehow got by them.

Her heart raced, watching the SWAT team breach the front door and pour into the house.

All was quiet as they waited for any word — by radio or in-person, as deputies emerged with a suspect and, with any luck, Jessi Price alive and breathing.

Waiting was always the hardest part. While homicide detectives on TV spent their careers busting down doors, that wasn't quite how it worked in real life, unless it was a situation where the SWAT team could never arrive in time. Detectives usually had to stand back and wait, missing all of the action inside.

And that was always a trial for Mal.

She had to do something to exert her rush of fear and adrenaline. Take down the bad guy, rescue the victim, anything other than waiting.

No one spoke as they waited, as if a whisper might jinx them, as if a single syllable could be the difference between finding Jessi Price alive or dead.

Mal stared at the open front door wishing she could go inside, hating the waiting. She needed to know — did they get Paul? Is Jessi alive?

She kept staring, waiting for something, anything.

But she never expected the explosion.

Chapter 37 - Jasper Parish

JASPER RACED through the woods trying to get as far from Dodd's neighborhood as possible when a deafening explosion rented the air around him.

What the hell?

He flashed back on the sensation that had attacked him just before Jordyn's call, that he was walking into a trap. Loud music blaring from the room, the doorknob he was just about to turn.

Had Paul Dodd improvised an explosive device?

Jasper remembered Rachel saying that she thought he was in Special Ops. Jasper hadn't given it much thought at the time, particularly in light of the other revelations. He was an idiot for not at least considering the possibility that the man would have laid a trap.

Jasper wondered if the explosion had killed any of the deputies. A deep chill — *he* could've opened the door if Jordyn hadn't called.

Did she have one of her visions, or was this pure chance?

Jasper could no longer discount things such as fate or a hidden, controlling hand pulling humanity's strings.

Nearby, sirens wailed.

Roads would soon be crawling with emergency work-ers, sheriff's deputies, and probably federal agents. He had to reach Jordyn before roadblocks were raised.

Jasper's breath was ragged as he reached the edge of the woods, tore off his ski mask and gloves, then stuffed them into his backpack.

He could see the lights of the small shopping plaza through the tree line ahead — the Gas 'N Go where Jordyn was parked. He was about to walk out toward the street when sirens and flashing lights rounded the corner.

He stepped back into the trees, holding his breath, praying the lights hadn't revealed him.

Four cars zipped by, one after the other.

And then they were gone.

Jasper took in a deep breath then headed across the street.

He found Jordyn sitting in the passenger seat, staring at him anxiously.

He entered the driver's side, threw his bag in the back, and fastened his seatbelt.

Her eyes were wide with worry. "What the hell happened?"

"I think Dodd rigged an explosive."

"Was he in the house?"

"I don't know. I don't think so. I think he's onto us."

Jasper started the car and pulled out of the station, heading down the road, eager to flee the neighborhood.

Several ambulances and fire trucks whizzed by as Jasper gathered speed.

Jordyn swallowed. "Was Jessi in there?"

Jasper shook his head. "Not if Fate has any heart at all."

Chapter 38 - Mallory Black

THE LEFT HALF of their suspect's house exploded, and Mike, Mal, and Skippy ran inside as fire engulfed the still-standing half, searching for any survivors.

Mike was first through the door, yelling for his comrades.

They heard a scream from the rear where Sgt. Doug Carter lay on the ground, covered in blood, staring down at a large metal pipe or maybe the leg of a chair that had pierced his gut and sent him to the ground, bleeding out.

Mike and Skippy tended to Doug.

Mal fell to her knees, covering her nose and mouth with her shirt pulled up over the bottom half of her face. She yelled for the deputies she couldn't see, then called out to Jessi.

No response.

There might be survivors. Deputies could be lying somewhere deafened by the blast, unable to hear her.

She crawled to the room where the explosion occurred, but couldn't see anything through the flames and smoke, save for the burned husk of an officer lying face down on the floor. She reached down to pull him out. She might not be able to save him, but she could at least drag his body out.

But he was burning hot, and Mal had to drop him.

As Mike and Skippy lifted Doug, Mal spun toward the kitchen, searching for anyone that might have been thrown across the living room.

She saw nobody. Just a door at the end of a hall, with a padlock outside.

She crawled toward it, screaming, "Jessi!"

Flames licked the walls behind her. Soon the hallway would be swallowed by flames, along with the rest of the house.

If Jessi was in this room, Mal had to save her.

She stood, banged on the piping hot door, and screamed, "Jessi!"

No answer.

She was soaked with sweat, her breath short. The house was about to be ashes, and Jessi Price might still be locked inside a spare room turned dungeon.

She grabbed her gun and yelled, "Get down on the ground, Jessi. I need to shoot at the door."

Mal coughed, gagging on smoke, her lungs on fire as she waited an excruciatingly long moment to give the girl time to get out of the way.

She raised the Glock and fired.

The first shot ricocheted somewhere, but the second split the lock wide open.

She returned the gun to her holster and wrenched the lock open, hoping there wasn't another nasty surprise behind Door Number Death.

It was dark, but Mal could see that it was a little girl's bedroom.

"Jessi?" she called out, running inside.

Nothing

She bent to look under the bed but saw only darkness.

"Jessi!" she coughed, feeling faint, dizzy, hot enough to die.

She saw the closed door, maybe a bathroom.

Maybe Jessi was inside.

She went to the door, tried the knob, and opened it to more nothing.

Shit!

She turned to leave, but couldn't see beyond the wall of flames and smoke.

She tried to draw a deep breath of air, something to hold as she raced back to safety.

Instead, Mal collapsed to the ground.

Chapter 39 - Paul Dodd

PAUL LISTENED to the radio report on the explosion.

Soon his name and photo would be on every TV station, every news site on the web, all over Facebook, and his secret was out.

Paul Dodd, teacher and monstrous pedophile, serial rapist and killer, is wanted in connection with the disappearance of Jessi Price and the death of however many cops died in the explosion.

Life as he knew it was over.

There was no return from this.

The cops would be talking to everyone he worked with, to his bitch ex-wife. Probably to Lily.

Do you know where your daddy is hiding?

It wasn't enough that Rachel had poisoned his daughter against him, now the media would follow. Kids would mock Lily at school, teasing her for being the daughter of the kiddy rapist/murderer.

Her life was ruined, too.

And for that, he felt the most remorse.

For that, Paul wanted to crawl up into a ball and cry.

But there wasn't time to cry.

There was only time to run.

Fortunately for Paul, he'd been arranging for this day like a doomsday prepper would get ready for the apocalypse.

And not unlike the preppers, Paul had a secret bunker in the woods an hour northwest of his home, on a large piece of land that Wes had gifted to him. A place that nobody, outside of Wes, could tie him to. A place where no one would ever find him. Or her.

A place with enough provisions to keep him alive for at least three years. A place where he could lay low until he was presumed dead, or change his appearance enough that he could maybe start over.

But that was a long time away.

And he had to reach his bunker first.

He glanced back to make sure Jessi was still asleep in the back of his car.

She was.

Perhaps worst of all, Paul's plans for her birthday celebration were now a tangled mess.

He couldn't kill her now.

The bunker would be lonely. It would be a long time before Paul could find another girl.

Jessi would have to live a bit longer. The downside was that she didn't want to be there. After that incident with the knife, there was no going back to the farce that she wasn't a prisoner.

The silver lining: he could enjoy her longer. Eventually, she'd bend to his will. Because out in the middle of nowhere, buried in an underground bunker, nobody would ever hear her scream.

Chapter 40 - Mallory Black

MAL WOKE WITH A GASP.

Mike was kneeling over her body, eyes wide, relief washing his face. "Oh my God, I thought we lost you."

She struggled to sit. Bursts of light pierced her vision.

She looked back and saw the burning house, fire-fighters streaming in, others attacking it with a hose.

She remembered passing out in the house. "Did you—"

"Save your ass and give you mouth to mouth? Yes," Mike said. "Why the hell did you stay in there?"

"I was looking for Jessi."

Mal finally managed to sit up and looked around, searching for any sign of the girl, either with one of the EMTs or among the dead pulled from the fire. "Is she?"

"No sign of her yet," Mike said, then he called over to one of the paramedics asking them to take a look at Mal, get her some air, and whatever else she might need.

A young, short Latina woman responded, asking Mal a series of questions, checking vitals before leading her to an ambulance where she checked Mal's oxygen level and blood pressure before strapping an oxygen mask onto her face.

Mal sat in the back of the ambulance staring at the chaos of the burning house, the firefighters trying to extinguish the blaze, the dead officers, and the two other injured survivors. Sheriff's deputy vehicles pulled up as additional units arrived on the scene. Early responding reporters and news vans lined the perimeter, eager for the scoop.

All because of a monster named Paul Dodd. The same man who murdered Mal's daughter, destroyed her life, and was now about to annihilate another family's.

Mal thought she knew hate before, particularly in the months following Ashley's death: an endless void that consumed her every waking hour.

But that was nothing compared to the hate she felt now.

Now that she had a name to put to the monster.

Now that he'd struck at her other family.

He had to be caught.

He had to be stopped.

He had to pay for his crimes.

He has to die.

After the paramedic removed Mal's mask, she found Mike in front of Gloria's car, talking to her alone, likely filling her in on everything that had happened.

Mal approached.

Gloria turned to her. "You okay?"

Mal nodded. "Yeah, just a little smoke."

She wasn't sure if Mike told Gloria that Mal would've been dead if not for him, but she wasn't about to throw him under the bus over a few missing details. After all, Mal wasn't supposed to have gone inside. Best to say nothing, in case Mike was covering for her.

Gloria met Mal's eyes. "So, I guess you were right on

this guy. The firefighters managed to stop the fire before it ruined his secret dungeon, and damn it if that isn't the same room as in the video of Ashley."

"Do we know if he has Jessi?"

"We won't know for certain until forensics can get in there. But as of right now, Paul Dodd is a suspect."

"I want to help catch this bastard."

"You almost died in there," Gloria said, her eyes narrowed. "You need to go home and relax. We've got this."

"I want to help."

"You no longer work for the department, remember? And I'm sure I don't need to tell you that it's a big conflict of interest to have you working the case, especially now that we know this is the man who probably killed your daughter. It's already going to be a media cluster fuck. We need to do this as clean as possible, Mal. I'm sorry."

"Bring me on as a consultant. *Something.*"

"We'll call you if we can think of a way you can help. Meanwhile, I want you home and relaxing."

Mal was about to protest. Gloria cut her off with the last thing Mal expected, a hug.

It had been forever since they'd been good enough friends for a genuine embrace. Forever since Mal had felt anything other than anger at her former boss.

This was disarming, short-circuiting her protest.

Mal wondered if the hug was heartfelt, or merely a tactic to calm her, especially in front of the cameras.

Gloria held her tight, then softly said, "I'm glad we didn't lose you tonight."

Tears wanted to fall, but Mal refused to let them.

Gloria pulled away and met Mal's eyes again. Hers were wet as well.

"I want to catch this fucker as badly as you do. But we

need to do it right. There will be no shortage of high-priced lawyers wanting to take this case, land themselves some celebrity, get the book deals and all that bullshit. We can't give them any ammunition to weaken the case. You got me?"

Mal hated how right she was, but facts were facts, and this case just went from local news to national tabloid. Spotlights on the department would be supernova-bright. Even the best departments couldn't stand up to that sort of scrutiny, that second-guessing and armchair coaching. Things were about to get chaotic. The FBI would surely be more involved. And as much as Mal hated the bench, she had no choice but to warm it.

Mal nodded. "I've got you."

Gloria turned to Mike. "Why don't you take her home."

THE FIRST HALF of the drive was Mike talking about the SWAT members that died, and how he'd just been to a picnic with one of them, Lars, last weekend. The guy was about to have his first kid, and now he was dead.

Mal said, "God I hope we catch this fucker. *And* I hope he resists. Please, Jesus, let him resist!"

Mike laughed.

Mike had never been one for excessive force. He was very by-the-books, enough to be an occasional pain in the ass to work with. To see him practically looking forward to physically punishing Dodd saddened Mal. Paul had made one of the nicest guys on the force want to hurt someone. Mal wondered if Mike wanted to go as far as she did, and put a bullet in the fucker's head.

She didn't want to ask, nor offer up her bloodlust.

These were the sorts of conversations that could come back in a courtroom to haunt them, cost them their careers, even land them behind bars if circumstances were just so.

Best to say nothing.

Laugh it off and let him vent.

They drove in silence until Mike finally said, "So, what was it like?"

"What was what like?"

"Dying? And coming back? You see lights or anything?"

"I don't remember anything."

"Really? You didn't see anything?"

"Just darkness. One minute I was in that room, and the next I was looking up at your big ugly mug."

"Damn, girl. I guess you *are* going to Hell. Good thing I saved you. Still time to repent. You can come with us to church on Sunday."

Mal laughed. Mike was a devout Catholic, and they'd had numerous conversations about faith over the years. He always teased her about being an atheist, though she was less an atheist than an agnostic, and always enjoyed the banter.

Mal smiled. "Thanks again for the rescue, though I'm not letting you save me from Hell. I'm looking forward to it. Gonna go down there and kick Satan's ass."

"I bet you will. Shit, probably take over the place."

"Damn straight. And I'll take all the Paul Dodds and make sure they're in a special room where they can *really* get what they deserve."

"I like that." Mike laughed. "You'd be an excellent devil."

A sly grin. "Enough to make you change teams?"

"Don't get carried away."

They drove in silence for a while longer, punctuated only by a few somber radio transmissions.

As they pulled up to Mal's, she said, "Thanks again."

She reached over and hugged him, squeezing him hard, then let go.

His eyes were watering. "It was good having you back by my side. I've missed it."

"Me too," she said, climbing out of the car.

"You really should come back."

Mal smiled, then turned and headed toward her house.

Halfway to her front door, she glanced across the street to see her assigned deputies sitting in their car. For the first time, she wasn't annoyed by their presence. She waved at them, then at Mike as he pulled away.

Finally, Mal unlocked the door and entered her empty house alone.

Chapter 41 - Jasper Price

JASPER LAY on the couch in his apartment's darkened living room, bathed in the blues and whites of the television news, numb as he stared at defeat.

Paul Dodd had escaped.

His trap had killed three sheriff's deputies and seriously injured two others.

As far as anyone knew, he was on the run with Jessi Price.

The girl's final hours were ticking down. She was only alive so long as Paul needed her, so long as she wasn't a burden.

There was no way he could flee the country with her as his captive. No way he could legally cross the border into Canada or Mexico. His only option was to hole up somewhere.

"You think he has a place already picked out?"

Jordyn was sitting beside him on the couch, staring at the TV. "What?"

"Sorry," Jasper said, standing. He went to her bedroom

225

and grabbed the blanket from her bed. By the time he returned to the couch, she was zonked out again.

He covered her with the blanket, then leaned down and kissed her on the forehead.

He was glad she'd stayed behind. Had she come inside, it might be her in a body bag on the news. Maybe both of them. This disaster only confirmed Jasper's decision to cut her out of the vigilante business — at least the up close and personal stuff. He'd still use her visions, so long as he decided to continue, but even that felt tenuous.

He could have easily died and left Jordyn an orphan. Yes, she was technically an adult, but she wasn't ready to be on her own. Not to mention the hell of burying her father only a couple of years after her mother — that was more than any child should endure, and might just break her.

He needed to free himself from this.

But he couldn't yet.

Jasper stared at the Missing Child photo of Jessi Price flashing on-screen, remembering how helpless he felt when trying to warn Mallory Black that her child was in danger.

He'd been afraid to go directly to her, scared to intervene. Either one would've put him in the crosshairs. The police would've wanted to know *how* he knew that Ashley Black was in danger. They would've assumed he was working with the kidnapper. What was his alternative? To tell them that his daughter was psychic?

Even if he managed to convince them that it was true, the trouble wouldn't have gone away. Shadowy men in dark suits would appear wanting to run tests on Jordyn.

Soon, they'd both end up in some CIA black site, forced to help them find bad guys, eliminate threats, or whatever secret psychic warfare the government was up to. Jasper would've once thought that those secret projects were the stuff of conspiracy theorists, but now he knew that at least one person was truly psychic and had to consider that there were others as well.

Whether they were somehow gifted, or chosen by Fate, as Jasper believed, the result was the same — people in positions of authority would use them to maintain their power.

Jasper would rather rot in prison than see that happen to Jordyn. He'd confess to any number of crimes if it meant keeping her gift a secret.

He stared at the photo of Jessi Price, wishing he could go back in time two years. He could have stopped Dodd before the man made his move. He could have trailed Ashley and waited for Paul to come get her.

Sometimes life was less about what you did than what you didn't.

Had he stopped Paul then, so many lives would be different now.

Ashley would still be alive.

Mallory's life wouldn't have fallen apart.

Jessi Price would be safe with her family.

And three cops would be going home to their families tonight.

If only he'd stopped the monster.

He sat next to Jordyn, watching the news and hoping that somehow Paul was caught and Jessi saved.

He got up, went to his bedroom, picked up one of the burners, and dialed a number that he promised himself he'd never dial again.

Chapter 42 - Mallory Black

MAL LAY in Ashley's old bed, drifting off to the siren song of her opiates when her cell phone started to scream.

She looked at the caller ID. The number was blocked.

Her heart raced.

What if it's Dodd?

"Hello?"

And then a voice spoke, one she hadn't heard in two years, yet hadn't forgotten — the man who left the voice-mail warning her of Ashley's kidnapping.

"Hello, Mallory."

"Paul?"

"No. I'm not the man you're looking for."

"Then who are you?"

"Someone who's sick of seeing bad people do awful things to good people."

He sounded tired, or maybe drunk.

If he wasn't Paul, he had to be connected somehow.

She had to get him talking.

"People like Paul Dodd?"

Another laugh. "People like Paul Dodd."

"How do you know him?"

"I know lots of people. It's my job."

"How did you know my daughter was going to be taken?"

"That's also part of my job."

"Then why didn't you tell me more, give me a name? Something I could've done to save her?" Mal tried to bar the anger from her voice.

"I didn't know his name then. I do now."

"What else do you know?"

"Not enough. I'm still looking."

"Who are you?"

"A friend."

"Friends tell each other their names."

"You'd be surprised the secrets friends keep from one another," he said with a slight chuckle. "Tell me, Mallory, do you think it's ever okay to kill a bad guy?"

"What are you asking?"

"If you could go back in time and kill Paul Dodd before he killed your daughter, would you?"

Mal wondered if this man was recording her. She wasn't sure why he would be. It wasn't as if he could use a recording against her. In Florida, you had to get permission before capturing someone's audio communications.

"Well? Would you do it?"

"Yes. I'd do anything to get Ashley back."

"What about now?" he asked. "If he turned himself into you right this second, would you kill him?"

"No, I'd arrest him."

"But you just said you'd kill him to save your daughter."

"I was assuming you meant that I'd somehow found where he was holding her. Then yes, I'd shoot him to save her. But if you're asking if I could kill him right now, in cold blood, if he turned himself in? Then no."

"Even after all that he did to *your daughter*, and is now probably doing to Jessi Price, you *still* wouldn't kill him? I'd think you'd want justice."

"It's not my place to decide if he lives or dies. That's up to a jury. Murdering him now, that wouldn't be justice. And it wouldn't bring my daughter back. It would make me no better than him."

"I think you're lying, Mallory. Either to me or yourself. I think if you saw him right now, you could kill him quite easily. And you'd probably *enjoy* it."

And then he hung up.

Thursday Oct. 19

Chapter 43 - Jasper Parish

"Hey, wake up, old man. We've got work to do."

Jordyn gently shook him.

Jasper opened his eyes, noticed the bright light spilling through the half-opened blinds.

"What time is it?" He squinted, trying to make out the time on the cable box.

"Nine. Rise and shine."

Jordyn was showered and dressed, seemingly ready to head out.

"What work are you talking about?"

"I had a thought."

Jasper sat up. He badly needed to piss, but that could wait. "Okay, I'm all ears."

"If Wes made Paul into the monster he is, what are the odds that they're still in touch?"

"Wes went to jail."

"Yeah, but that was what, twenty years ago, maybe more? How much you wanna bet that he's out? And if so, what if Paul got in touch?"

"Why would he do that?"

"He was trying to please the man, practically pimped his own sister out to the guy. He was pissed at Katie for ratting on them. I'm thinking that Paul probably had to testify with her and that he's felt like shit about it ever since."

"So, what? You think he reached out to apologize?"

She smiled. "That's *exactly* what I think."

Jasper stood, told Jordyn to hold on, then went to the bathroom.

He stood there pissing, careful not to get any on the seat or floor.

The more he thought about Jordyn's hypothesis, the more it made sense.

He came out of the bathroom smiling. "Okay, let's see if we can find this guy."

Less than fifteen minutes later they knew that Wes Richardson got a fifteen-year sentence, out in nine for good behavior. He was retired, living an hour north, fat off of real estate holdings that had gone into a blind trust during his lockup.

Jordyn laughed. "Man, there are people doing weed with more time behind bars than this rapist."

Jasper shook his head.

Jordyn stopped chewing on the end of her pen. "Okay, so we have a name and address. Do you think Paul went to his old mentor's place?"

"I doubt it. If Rachel told us about Wes, she probably told the detectives. Paul has to know that'd be a bad idea. But that doesn't mean they haven't talked before now."

"You think Wes knows where Paul Dodd is?"

"Only one way to find out. You ready for a drive?"

"Want me to be the getaway car?"

"No, I might need your gifts on this one. If Wes refuses to talk. Maybe you'll pick up on something."

"I knew you couldn't do it without me." Jordyn smiled and hit Jasper with her blanket.

He smiled back, but their play was bittersweet. Jasper hoped he wasn't putting Jordyn into danger — especially after trying to get her out of the vigilante business.

"We're done with this," he said. "Soon as Jessi is safe."

Jordyn's smile disappeared. She simply nodded.

Chapter 44 - Mallory Black

AGAIN MALLORY WOKE to a raging headache and her ringing phone.

She rolled over in Ashley's bed and grabbed her cell from the nightstand, part of her hoping it was her mystery man calling to finish last night's cryptic conversation.

But it was Mike.

"Yeah?" she answered.

"How would you feel about coming with me to an interview?"

"Where's Skippy?"

"He woke up puking his guts out."

"He a drunk like me?"

"Nah, probably too much Paco's Tacos last night."

"So, who are we interviewing?"

"Rachel Dodd. Ex-wife. Lives up in Bay Hill."

"You didn't interview her last night?"

"We brought her to the station while the victim's advocate kept her daughter company, but I didn't get much from her. She did confirm finding some stuff on his computer a few years ago and was worried that we were going to arrest her for not coming forward. Said she didn't know if the stuff was illegal or fell into the whole "nudity as art" thing. Plus, she was scared of her husband. She demanded a divorce and got sole custody, and then he was out of the picture. She said she doesn't know anything about him now. She consented to a search, but I don't think we got anything worthwhile."

"Why do you want me to talk to her? You think she knows where Paul is?"

"I don't know. I mean she was upset, so maybe it's that, but I felt like she was holding something back."

"Like what?"

"I don't know. Just something."

"What makes you think I'll get it out of her?"

"Because you were always better at this than me."

"About time I got some recognition for my stellar people skills," she joked. "So, Gloria's okay with me interviewing her?"

"I didn't exactly tell her."

"Oh, shit. The Boy Scout is leaving the campground and his pack?"

"It's an informal interview. We don't need to bring her in, we just sit down and talk at her house. She was skittish last night, especially given how her ex is all over TV. Plus, being at the station probably didn't do much to relax her. Maybe we'll have better luck in a calmer place, with you taking lead."

"Okay. Gimme twenty minutes."

"Thank you."

She hung up, then looked at the nightstand and the bottle of pills she'd managed to avoid opening all night. A minor but important victory, proving she *could* sleep without the pills.

Now she was paying the price with a raging headache,

and couldn't imagine effectively interviewing someone in such a condition.

Mal opened the bottle, palmed a single pill, then washed it down with some water.

She put the bottle back in the nightstand, then went into the bathroom and showered.

THEY ARRIVED JUST BEFORE 10:15 in the morning, but they weren't the first. That honor belonged to the media vultures, staking claim to positions with Rachel Dodd's home in the background while updating the masses that they would be "live from the suspected killer's home."

Forget that Paul Dodd no longer lived there.

Forget that his wife wanted nothing to do with him.

Forget that these people were harassing a woman and her innocent child.

Only ratings mattered. If the public demanded you stand in front of a house and put on a sideshow, you fucking stood in front of a house and put on a sideshow, no matter whose life you might ruin.

They parked in the driveway behind a blue SUV, and a patrol car with a deputy keeping watch over Paul's wife and daughter.

Mike and Mal approached Deputy Childress, a barrel-chested former boxer turned deputy in his fifties. He had a tight afro and big, thick black-framed glasses. Deputies called him Smiles because it had been years since one had found his face.

"Hey, Sam," Mike said. "Just wanted to follow up on last night's interview with the wife."

"Sure thing. Hey, Mal. You back on the force?"

NOLON KING & DAVID WRIGHT

She smiled. "Not officially yet. But this one's doing everything he can to get me back, though."

"Hasn't been the same without you," Sam said, almost smiling.

"So, how's it going here? Media staying away?"

"They try, but she doesn't want to talk."

"How is she?" Mal asked. "And her daughter?"

"Shaken. And pissed that our guys left a mess for her to clean."

Mal followed Mike to the front door, standing behind him as he rang the bell.

After a moment, a woman peered through the curtains in the window next to the front door.

Mike flashed his badge, even though they'd spoken last night. "I just have a few follow-up questions, Ms. Dodd. Won't be but a minute."

Mal heard Rachel unlocking the door, two locks and a security chain.

The door opened a bit, revealing a nervous-looking brunette, eying Mike and then Mal. "Come in," she said, her voice raspy and eyes red.

"Thank you for your time, Ms. Dodd. My partner's sick today, so I brought my former partner, Mallory."

Mal noticed that Mike was careful not to misrepresent her as a detective. Nor did he offer her full name — a good decision as it was only a matter of time before the media picked up that Paul Dodd wasn't *just* a suspect in the disappearance of Jessi Price.

Rachel led them through her living room, where her media center drawers were pulled out and laying on the floor. Games, tech, and cables were scattered everywhere, remnants of last night's search. She took them past the kitchen, where drawers had also been pulled out, many still littering the floor, then sat at the dining room table.

"I'm sorry about the mess. Would you like some help putting everything back in place?"

Rachel complained rather than answering Mal. "They took my computer. They took all of our family videos. They took my daughter's Nintendo! Did they *really* need to take her Nintendo?"

It wasn't as if the detectives stormed in and took her stuff by force. They'd asked for permission, and she had consented. But Mal wasn't about to argue. Rachel likely felt helpless, overwhelmed, as though swept in a tide being carried to sea. It was more important to listen, let her feel understood.

Mal said, "We'll get the Nintendo back to you as soon as possible, Ms. Dodd. The same with your other stuff. Did the deputies explain why they needed these things?"

"I ... don't remember. The past twelve hours are all tornado and fog."

"We want to check under every stone, to see if there's anything that might tell us where Paul took Jessi Price."

"He definitely has her?"

"Yes, forensics came back this morning with a positive match on hairs found at the scene. We've got an APB for him and his vehicle. Amber alerts, too. But we don't have a clue as to where he went."

"Oh God," she said, head crumbling into her hands, crying.

Mal looked up and saw Rachel's daughter, Lily, standing at the foot of the stairs, wrapped in a blanket.

Rachel turned to her. "Are you done napping, Lily Bear?"

"Yes," she said, coming toward them.

Mal watched the girl approach, holding her blanket tightly around her. She thought of how Ashley used to carry a security blanket when she was a bit younger than Lily. Her "wubbie."

"Hi," Mal said as the girl stood beside Rachel, hugging her.

"Hi," she said, her voice soft. The girl's eyes were red, just like her mom's. Mal wondered how much she knew about why the sheriff's department was looking for her father. Did she know what he did? Or was her mom keeping her in the dark as a gentle mercy?

"These officers are here to ask a few questions. But they'll be leaving soon, and then we can make lunch."

Lily looked at Mike, then at Mal. "Why do you want to know so much about my Dad?"

Mal blinked. She looked at Mike, then back at Rachel. She wasn't about to tell the girl anything that Lily's mother didn't want her to know.

Mike said, "We're just trying to find him so we can ask him some questions."

"What kind of questions?"

"We think he might know where a little girl is. A little girl about your age who went missing, and whose family wants her back."

"Is she one of his students?"

"I'll tell you later, sweetie," Rachel said. "But for right now, can you help me out and start putting the stuff away in my bedroom?"

"Okay." Lily sighed, clearly not wanting to leave the dining room or the discussion.

"Thank you," Rachel said.

"Bye!" Mal waved.

The girl waved back then headed slowly up the stairs.

After she was gone, Mal leaned close to Rachel and said, "He has the girl. The only question is how long until he kills her."

Rachel's eyes went wide. "*Kill?* He could never kill a child."

Mal wanted to disabuse the woman of this lie. Wanted to tell her that not only had he killed her daughter, but he'd also been sending gifts and stalking her ever since.

But telling her that much could screw up the interview. So she told her just enough. "We have reason to believe that he's already killed."

"What? No. Who?"

"We can't go into that as it's an active investigation. Let me just say that we have credible evidence that he's done this before, and that he's about to do it again if we can't find him. Do you have *any* idea where he might have gone?"

"What? You think he called me? I haven't spoken to him in more than a year. He hates me."

"All the more reason to help us find him."

"What do you mean?"

"We have a deputy posted outside your house in case he comes back, but we can't keep him there forever. The sooner we find your ex-husband, the sooner you and Lily will be safe. The sooner we can return Jessi Price to her family. Does he have any summer homes or friends with houses he might be staying at?"

Rachel shook her head. "No, not that I know of."

"How about family? We've got …" Mal fished the notebook from her jacket and glanced at it. "He has a sister, right? In Portland? Any other relatives?"

"No, she's all he had. And he hasn't spoken to her in forever."

Mal picked up on something in Rachel's voice, in her eyes. Maybe the same something that Mike had sensed last night, but couldn't extract.

"*Why* hasn't he spoken to her?"

Rachel looked at Mike, then Mal. "Do I need to go through this again? I already told the private detective. Don't you all share info?"

Mike leaned forward. "What private detective?"

"Um, his name was Cole Houser. He was working on behalf of Jessi Price's family."

Mal looked at Mike. He gave a subtle shake of his head to indicate that he'd never heard of any Cole Houser.

"When did you talk to him?"

"Yesterday."

The day Paul's house blew up. A coincidence? Mal didn't think so.

"What did he look like?"

"Um. A black man, late thirties, *maybe* early forties. Very short hair. Good looking. Broad shoulders and arms. He had that look that some male cops and military have."

"What look is that?" Mal asked.

"I dunno, stoic?"

"I'm not sure we've met him yet," Mal said. "Everything is so hectic right now. I don't want to be a pain, but could you please tell us what you told him?"

Rachel got up, grabbed a Diet Coke from the fridge, and offered one to both Mike and Mal. They declined. She sat back down, took a drink, then told a story about Paul Dodd being abused as a kid by a neighbor named Wes Richards. The man had molested both Paul and his younger sister, Katie, then Katie told her mother and wound up sending Wes to prison.

Judging from Mike's expression, and the way he was sitting forward on the edge of his seat, scribbling into his notebook, he hadn't heard any of this last night.

After Rachel finished her tale, Mal asked, "Do they still speak?"

"I don't think so. Two and a half years ago was the first

I ever heard of the man. For all I know, Paul could've made him up to get me feeling sorry for him. He didn't want me turning him into the cops."

Mike asked, "Do you think he was lying?"

Rachel shrugged, defeated. It looked like she was trying not to cry. "Well, apparently I don't know Paul all that well if what you say is true, about him taking Jessi Price and maybe being a murderer."

Mal tried fishing for more information, but Rachel was exhausted and seemed to be empty.

"Thank you for your help," Mal said, standing. "Because of you, we might be able to save Jessi Price."

Rachel reached out and hugged her. Mal was startled but managed not to show it. She hugged the woman back, awkwardly embracing the wife of the man who had murdered her daughter. The woman might have stopped all of this before Paul ever touched Ashley if only she'd had the courage to turn him in.

Mal couldn't understand why Rachel hadn't said something sooner. Had she been worried that turning Paul in would have ruined his life, or perhaps her and her daughter's life? Was she afraid that people would whisper as they passed.

Oh, there goes the pedophile's wife. How could she not have known? I wonder if he touched their daughter.

Rachel's fear, or weakness, allowed Paul to become the monster who killed Mal's daughter, and had now taken another girl. Everything would be different now had she acted then.

But she hadn't.

And as much as Mal sympathized with the woman, she could not erase the residue of anger she still felt for her.

Rachel pulled away and said, "Good luck finding Jessi."

Mal followed Mike out of the house and to their car. He was on the phone, likely with Gloria judging from his tone.

She got in the car and waited. He stood outside, still talking. Something big must be happening, judging from the way Mike was getting increasingly animated, waving his hands and talking louder.

A few minutes later he got in and keyed the ignition. "They found Paul's Infiniti."

"What? Where?"

"At the shop. Went in yesterday morning. Mechanic said he saw Paul on the news, with the APB, and figured we ought to know he's not driving his car."

Mike pulled away from Rachel's house.

"Shit," Mal said. So now what? He obviously couldn't ask a neighbor to take him and his victim somewhere, right? Does he have another vehicle? Remember, he picked up Ashley and Rebecca in what they thought was an unmarked cop car. He could've bought one at auction."

"Not that we know of. Gloria's checking with the local cab companies and ride sharing services to see if he's called."

"And you don't have anything from his cell, right?" Mal assumed that they didn't; otherwise, they'd be triangulating his position and closing in, rather than asking Paul's ex-wife where he might be.

"No, he hasn't used his cell since yesterday. Likely ditched the SIM card. Probably using a burner."

"So, what now?" Mal asked.

"What do you think of this Wes guy?"

"He's worth looking into. Maybe if we can get *his* cell records, we can find out if Paul is calling him from another number. We get the number to his burner then triangulate to find him."

"You're assuming he's calling him and not texting with some anonymous service."

"True. But it's still worth a shot. I mean, he's not careless, but he's also not a cutting-edge hacker. He used a coffee shop to break into my security site, leading us to him in the first place. I'm thinking he's only moderately tech proficient, and maybe dumb enough to use a phone to contact Wes."

"Let's hope. So, you think we ought to head up there?"

"Oh, you want *me* to go with you?"

"Well, look how much you got out of Rachel."

"True. I am good." Mal smiled. "You sure you don't want to check with the boss?"

"She already said yes."

"Really?"

"I guess we must be desperate," Mike joked.

Mal punched him hard in the arm. "Just drive."

Chapter 45 - Jasper Parish

FOR A MAN who went to jail for raping children, Wes Richardson had done embarrassingly well for himself. His waterfront home was in The Oasis, gated on one side with sand on the other, an hour south of Creek County.

Getting in was simple enough, using the dial pad at the unmanned gate to punch in the emergency code shared by most gated communities.

From there, Jasper drove to the man's house, parked in front, and pulled out a bouquet of flowers. Then he rang the doorbell and waited.

Wes peered out what looked like a living room window, saw Jasper's flowers and delivery cap, then moments later opened the door.

Jasper dropped the flowers and tazed Wes.

He rattled on the ground as Jasper kicked the door shut, flipped him over, and cuffed the fucker's hands behind his back.

Jordyn waited outside. Jasper would make sure the house was clear before bringing her in.

"You don't have to kill me," Wes cried out. "If you

want money, let me get to the safe. I'll give you everything I've got."

"Well, that sure is kind of you, sir. But I'm not here for your money."

Wes kicked out at Jasper.

But Jasper cocked him across the back of his head with the taser, then pulled out his gun and aimed it at Wes. "Who else is in the house?"

Wes took a moment to answer. "No … nobody. It's just me."

Jasper wasn't sure if he was stalling, trying to determine what answer was most likely to keep him alive, or covering for someone else.

"I'm gonna ask you one more time. If you're lying, I will kill everyone in here. Who else is in the house? I don't care if it's a guinea pig or a person. I want names."

Wes nodded, "It's j-j-just me."

"Okay, let's take a walk." Jasper pulled the man to his feet. "Where's your kitchen?"

"Why?"

Jasper hit Wes in the head again. "Don't ask. *Do.* Now take me to your kitchen. It's fine if you wobble."

Wes followed the order, leading Jasper through the immaculate house. The place was a museum, or at the very least a photo shoot. The ceilings were high, the walls were textured, and if the floor wasn't marble, it was a decent approximation. The gourmet kitchen wasn't just spacious; it seemed to have two of everything: two refrigerators and freezers, two islands, and two gorgeous cobalt blue Viking ranges. On the far side of the kitchen was a long glass table surrounded by eight black metal chairs. Everything was immaculate.

"Have a seat, Wes," Jasper said, pointing to one of the chairs. "We're gonna have a little talk. Answer my questions, and you get to live. If not, I'm afraid we're going to get your nice, clean house very, very messy."

Wes was cuffed and tied to the chair, naked from the waist down, sobbing, as Jasper made a show of going through his kitchen drawers and pulling out one knife at a time, searching for the perfect one.

"Ah," he said, pulling out an eight-inch Hanzo knife, "this one looks just right."

"What do you want from me?"

"I already told you. I'm going to ask you some questions. And I need answers. Are you ready to answer me?"

He nodded, barely breathing a *Yes*.

"Hold on one second." Jasper set the blade on the counter, then went back to the living room and opened the door for Jordyn.

"Where is he?"

"In the kitchen. Just hang back in here and listen. Let me know if you get any vibes."

"Why can't I go in?"

"He's not exactly decent."

"What are you *doing?*"

Jasper smiled. "Having some fun."

Jordyn rolled her eyes. "Whatever you say."

She sat on the couch and crossed her arms.

"Remember, don't take off your hoodie or get hairs anywhere."

"Yeah, yeah." Jordyn was already annoyed that she couldn't use her phone at the crime scene, and had to remove her SIM card to ensure they didn't pop up on any cell tower tracking.

Jasper returned to the kitchen. Wes's chair was about six inches closer to the counter.

Jasper looked at him and smiled. "Tsk, tsk, Mr. Richards. I can't leave you alone for a second now, can I?"

Wes's eyes widened as Jasper grabbed the blade and sliced him across the chest.

The wound wasn't deep, just something to prove he meant business.

Wes screamed.

Jasper raised his fingers to his lips and told him to hush, or else.

Wes did as instructed, wincing.

"So, where did you get this knife?" Jasper asked, balancing it in his hand. "The weight is really well distributed. I like it. It's hard to find a reliable blade. Where did you buy it?"

"I don't know. It was a gift from a friend."

"Well, you can tell your friend that he or she has exquisite taste in knives. Is he or she a chef?"

Wes looked annoyed, confused by Jasper's line of questioning. He shrugged. "He's an amateur chef, yes."

"Ah, I figured as much. Either a chef or a murderer. The right tool for the right job, am I right, Wesley?"

Wes nodded, looking down at the blood trickling from his cut.

"Don't worry; it's only a flesh wound. You ever see that Monty Python bit? Man, they don't make comedy like that anymore, eh?"

Wes stared up at Jasper, angry and confused.

Just where Jasper wanted him.

"Okay, okay, I get it. Enough chitter chatter. You want to get down to business. Let's do it. I'm here about an old friend of yours. Might you guess who I'm inquiring about?"

"I haven't a clue."

Jasper made a buzzing sound. "Wrong answer, Wesley."

He swung the knife swiftly just under the last cut, giving it a twin.

"Fuck!" Wes cried, glaring at Jasper. "Just tell me what you want!"

Jasper stood in front of the man, just far enough that he couldn't reach if he tried to kick him. "I want an answer. Where is Paul Dodd?"

Jasper watched the man's face and saw that glimmer of recognition mixed with a bit of *oh shit, that's why you're here* in his eyes.

Jasper moved to Wes's side, holding the blade near his chest. "You're not going to insult my intelligence and pretend that you don't know who Paul Dodd is, are you?"

Wes shook his head.

"Good. Now tell me where he is."

"I don't know."

Jasper closed his eyes and sighed. "Really? You're going to make me cut you again?"

"I swear, I don't—"

Jasper sliced him on his left leg. Not too bad, but certainly painful.

Wes screamed.

Jasper wasn't too worried about noise. The home was large and on nearly an acre. Plus, there were landscapers at work on two of the three closest houses, so plenty of machines to drown them out.

Jasper looked down at the injury and the blood spilling all over Wes's once-gleaming kitchen floor.

"Man, you are making such a mess."

"I said I don't know where Paul is. We haven't spoken in years."

Jasper shook his head. "Forgive me if I don't believe you."

"I swear."

Jasper held up his finger. "Don't go anywhere."

This time he took the knife with him, heading upstairs to search Wes's home office. Sitting on his desk, Jasper spotted a laptop, open to email.

He grabbed the laptop, carried it downstairs, still open, and set it on the kitchen island with the knife beside it. Then he searched Wes's email, right there in front of him.

"What are you doing?"

"Just checking to see if you have anything from Paul."

"I already told you I haven't talked to him in years. Why are you even looking for him?"

"Oh, you haven't heard? He kidnapped a little girl."

"What?" Wes said, eyes wide.

Jasper wasn't sure if the man was feigning shock or not.

"I swear, I don't know anything about him taking a girl."

Jasper smiled. "I'd like to believe you, but it's hard to trust a pedophile."

"I'm not a pedophile."

Jasper picked up the knife, "Do we need to play this game again?"

Wes flinched. "I'm not a pedophile *anymore*. I go to therapy."

Jasper slowly lowered the blade. "So, you're saying I won't find any child pornography on your laptop?"

"Heavens no!" Wes said, as if deeply offended.

Jasper laughed. "Are you *sure?*"

"Absolutely," Wes said, glaring at Jasper, practically challenging him.

Jasper pulled a flash drive from his pocket and plugged it into the USB port on the computer's side.

"What are you doing?" Wes asked.

"I find it hard to believe that a pedo can change his spots. Yeah, you might lay low for a while. Maybe you don't rape a kid for a few months. Maybe even a few years. And bravo, society thanks you, sir. But surely you still *look*, even if you can't touch, right?"

"I told you I'm in therapy. I have a girlfriend."

"That's nice. Is she in high school?"

"No. She's a woman. We're getting married. I've changed."

"Here's the thing about that," Jasper said, still holding his smile, "pedophiles aren't exactly known for changing. I get it. You can't help liking what you like. But … I'm thinking that most people *won't* understand when they see the sorts of things you've been looking at online."

"I told you, I'm not looking at shit!"

"You sure about that?" Jasper turned the laptop so that Wes could see the horrifying images and videos that Jasper was loading from his flash drive onto the computer.

Wes's eyes looked ready to roll from their sockets.

"No! I didn't download that shit. *You're* putting it on my computer!"

"Yeah, I don't think the police will believe you. How about your girlfriend? What do you think *she's* going to think?"

"Fuck you."

"Wrong answer," Jasper said with another buzzing. He grabbed the blade, walked back over to Wes, and sliced him across his right bicep.

Wes screamed.

"Don't be such a baby. These are all minor wounds. You like minors, right?"

Wes glared at him, gritting his teeth, holding back on whatever he wanted to spit.

Jasper closed the laptop and removed his thumb drive.

"Okay, Wesley, are you familiar with ransomware?"

Wes shook his head.

"Well, the short of it is, your computer is now infected with a virus that has locked all your data. You can't unlock or wipe it. You can't do *anything* until I give you the key. I took the liberty of loading some of this stuff to the cloud, too, just in case you think getting rid of your computer will save you. In short, I own you."

"Please," Wes begged, tears spilling from his eyes, "I told you, I'm a changed man."

"Well, now's your chance to prove it. Help me find your old buddy, Paul. What better way to show the world you've changed than by being a hero? Helping to get a little girl back to her family? Nobody has to know I'm also blackmailing you to do the right thing. That'll be our little secret."

Wes stared at the ground, mulling the offer.

"Or you can be a good friend and go to jail for a long time. Your call, Wesley."

Wes was bawling. "Let me call him. I'll convince him to turn himself in and let the girl go."

Jasper shook his head. "No. We're past that point. He also killed three cops. There's no way he's going down without a fight. Hell, if he's cornered, he'll probably kill the girl before killing himself. I'm not willing to risk that."

Wes kept his eyes on the ground.

Jasper put the blade on the counter, then came over to Wes. In his most soothing voice, just inches away he said, "Listen, man. I know you're changing. Despite what I said, I *do* think people can change. Even pedophiles like you. I think you feel bad for what you did to Paul and his sister a long time ago. Probably like you owe him. Is that right?"

Wes nodded, not meeting Jasper's eyes.

"Yeah, I thought so. So now you feel almost guilty for turning him in. But that's the best possible outcome. You obviously cared for him, right?"

"I loved him like a son."

Jasper didn't bother asking Wes if he considered fucking someone the same as loving them. It was time to play good — *sympathetic* — cop.

"Right. I get it. And you don't want to see him dead, do you? Because that's what will happen if you don't tell me where he is. The cops *will* kill him. This is the only way he gets out alive. The only way that girl ever sees her family again. Come on, Wes, do the right thing."

He looked up when Jasper called him Wes instead of the mocking Wesley. Then he nodded. "Okay. But if I help, I don't want my name in the paper. I don't want him to know it was me who gave him up."

"That's fine. We can do that."

"And I want that shit off my computer."

"Consider it done."

"Okay, I own a piece of land in Hendricks, about an hour northwest of here. I bought it for Paul, as a gift to make up for what I did to him and his family."

"What's on this land? A house?"

"No, an underground bunker. It's not too deep, but it is hard to find."

"So how do I find it?"

"There's a hidden folder on my computer. It has everything you need."

Jasper opened the laptop, unencrypted the ransomware lock, and found the folder. He scanned the documents to make sure they were legit, dragged them to another flash drive, then scribbled the address in his notebook.

Jasper closed the laptop and returned to his spot in front of Wes. "Thank you, for doing the right thing."

Wes nodded. "Can you let me go now? Please."

Jasper turned and grabbed the Hanzo.

"You see, Wes, I'd love to believe that you've changed. I

mean you came a long way today, and for that, I give you credit. But then I think about this," he said waving his hands around, "how you're up in this nice place after ruining so many lives. And that just doesn't sit right with me."

"I did my time," Wes said, indignantly.

"Let's talk about that, Wesley, shall we? How long a sentence did you get? Fifteen years, out in nine for good behavior? Now let's look at the sentence your victims are still serving. Paul's life is ruined. He killed at least one girl, which in turn destroyed her family. Now he's about to murder another. And then there's Katie, strung out on drugs, ruining her life. They, and countless others, are still serving for *your* crimes, while you're living it here in your fancy gated community, with your girlfriend, acting like a changed man. But the way I see it, you're still a pile of shit."

Jasper glared at Wes.

He was breathing through his nostrils, his face red. Surely he wanted to explode, but didn't dare upset the man holding a blade so close to his skin.

Jasper looked down at Wes's shriveled manhood and shook his head. "Cock or balls, Wes — which is responsible for your sins?"

"What?"

"I asked which is responsible for your sins? I mean, you had to know in that thick skull of yours that it was wrong to be raping kids, right?"

Wes nodded.

"So, I'm thinking either your balls or your cock are to blame. And that's the only way we're gonna get any real change. Which is it?"

Wes shook his head. "No. You don't have to. I swear I'll never—"

Jasper yelled, "Pick one or I'm picking both, just to be on the safe side."

"No, please—"

"Your choice," Jasper said, then plunged the blade, taking both.

Chapter 46 - Mallory Black

MIKE AND MAL arrived at Wes Richards' house at 12:40 PM, meeting with a St. John's County Sheriff deputy, Calvin Hodges — more leverage to question Wes if he didn't want to play ball.

Hodges was a big black dude with a shiny dome and giant arms. He'd barely said a word, let alone smiled, since their arrival at the house. Clearly, he wasn't happy to be out here.

Hodges knocked as Mal tried to look through the open window beside the front door into the house.

No answer.

Hodges knocked again.

Still nothing.

"I'll head 'round back," Hodges said, "see if anyone's home."

Mike and Mal nodded, staying put at the front door.

"So," Mal said, trying not to laugh, "you gonna be the good cop or bad?"

"Let Hodges be the good cop," he joked.

Mal laughed. "Seriously, what's his problem? You piss on his Corn Flakes this morning?"

"Not that I know of. Never even met the dude before today."

"Well, he doesn't like you," Mal teased.

"Me? Maybe it's you he doesn't like, Mad Dog. Maybe he heard about your drunken brawls."

Hodges appeared before she could make her smart-ass response, his eyes even more serious than before.

"You all need to check this out."

They circled the side of the house while Hodges called in a signal seven to dispatch.

HODGES WENT INSIDE to secure the scene. Since no one could search the house until the violent crimes unit could get a search warrant, Mike and Mal were shit out of luck.

Mike told Hodges to give him a call if he needed anything — he had to get back to the station. Hodges didn't seem keen on having Mike and Mal bail after dropping a homicide in his lap, but he didn't press the matter or make them stay.

Mike's phone rang on their way to the cruiser.

Mal got into the car, waiting while he talked to someone at the precinct.

Mal looked at her phone and saw a voicemail from Ray. It was from last night, but the hectic morning kept it from notice.

She pressed play then listened to her ex.

"Hey, Mal. Just wanted to say I'm sorry how things went down. I didn't mean to pressure you to sell the house. I want whatever's best for you, and … well, even though we're not together that doesn't mean I stopped caring about you or stopped wanting the best for you. I'll leave you alone. But if you need anything, anything at all, just reach out. I'm here for you."

There was a long pause as if Ray wasn't sure how to close the message. He was with someone else now, so he wasn't about to say that he loved her or anything like that.

After a long moment, he awkwardly closed with, "Okay … bye."

She smiled. He was still so clumsy, just like in high school.

She was the cool, artsy drama girl. He was the nerd into *Dungeons & Dragons*. On paper, they never should've worked. He certainly wasn't the type of guy she'd been interested in before. She'd been into pretty boys with questionable sexuality and even more questionable fashion. Boys who were into the same music as her and seemed cool and mysterious.

Guys like Ray were dorks. Not enigmatic.

But they wound up sitting next to one another in art class. They didn't talk much for the first few months. Why, she wasn't sure. Maybe because Ray was so awkward, and she was lost in her own world, passing notes between classes, reading them, and doing all the other stupid things she did as a teenager.

On her fifteenth birthday, Ray handed her a charcoal sketch.

It was amazing.

And the first time anyone had ever drawn her. His attention to detail, not to mention the embarrassment on his face when she hugged him, was crushing.

They became friends.

It was nothing more than that for a long time, but they had a surprising amount in common. Far more than she ever would've thought before talking to him. They liked the same books and TV shows. They were both into art. He wasn't into drama, but still, they had plenty of other things to talk about.

He was a closet Cure fan, and wanted to start a cover band, but didn't have any other friends into that style of music.

The more Mal learned about Ray the more she liked him. But everything changed when she dated Vic Russo, the school quarterback. She wasn't sure why, given her former infatuation with effeminate boys, she was dating a jock who treated her like shit.

Vic was insanely jealous of Ray.

One day, Vic and his boys saw her and Ray sitting together at lunch. He lost his shit because they "seemed a bit too close."

With the wisdom of age, Mal knew that despite his machismo, Vic was secretly insecure. The type of boy who shrinks into an abusive man. But at the time she didn't get it, thought maybe *she'd* done something wrong. So when Vic told her to choose between Ray or him, she had to let Ray go.

She didn't do it overtly. She took the chickenshit way, avoiding him and withdrawing. It was easy to do in school since they only had art together. But it was harder on evenings and weekends, times they used to talk on the phone for hours or hang out at the park. Ray lived right around the block.

One weekend, Ray managed to catch her walking home from the store and offered her a ride in his new car.

One of Vic's boys saw it.

That Monday in school, Vic and his boys beat him bloody.

Mal was hanging with her friend, Becki before school,

when a sudden buzz circled the commons area and whispered turned into a roar — a fight outside!

They ran out and saw Vic and his boys pounding on Ray.

He never stood a chance.

For the first time, Mal saw how cruel Vic and his stupid jock friends were. She broke up with him on the spot and apologized to Ray for not being a better friend.

He confessed that he liked her. And though she'd never considered him boyfriend material before, something clicked. Maybe maturity. Maybe seeing him in a different light. Either way, they'd been in love since.

Madly.

More in love than she ever thought possible.

Years passed, and they each became absorbed in their jobs. They'd changed, even if neither wanted to admit just how much.

But it was too late to break up. They loved their daughter and had to find a way to make their family work.

Until they couldn't.

Mike opened the car door, dragging Mal away from Memory Lane.

"We got something."

"What?"

"You know the ride sharing service, Pik-Up?"

"Yeah."

"Well, they had a driver pick up Paul Dodd last night."

"I thought he ditched his phone."

"I'm assuming he did as well, but he needed a valid Pik-Up account to get a ride, so he needed his phone one last time to leave town."

"Where did they take him?"

"That's the thing. They brought him out West and dropped him off at Holy Trinity Church."

"A church?"

"That's where they dropped him off, but that's not where he went."

"What do you mean?"

"Well, fortunately for us, a lot of these ride sharing services don't just track your pick up or drop off, they also want to know where you go from there. They say it's to determine safe drop-off points and to improve their core services, but I think they're tracking so they can serve local ads to people on their phone. A huge business in local advertising."

"So where did he go?"

"A warehouse."

"Let's go!" Mal said.

"Henry and Simmons are already there, waiting for us."

Mike started the car and smiled at Mal.

"What?" she asked.

"The look on your face. You can pretend all you want, but you miss this job something fierce."

"Just drive, Mike."

"Okay ... *partner*."

Chapter 47 - Jessi Price

JESSI WOKE up woozy from Officer Bob's medicine.

She wished he'd never made her drink it.

Jessi knew he probably wasn't a cop, but she still thought of him as Officer Bob. She supposed he *could* be an actual officer. She also supposed that bad guys could be cops. What better way to hide from the good cops than right under their noses?

Her right hand was cuffed to the metal bars on the headboard. Part of her wanted to pull against the cuff, cry out, and scream. But then Bob would make her take more medicine, or maybe hit her.

So Jessi pretended that she was still sleeping, peeking through barely opened eyes, trying to see where Bob had brought her last night while she was out.

A small room with two beds, a couch, a TV, a bookshelf, and stacks of food and water all along the walls. There was something weird about the place, but she couldn't figure out what it was at first. Then she realized that there weren't any windows.

There weren't any in her room at the other house,

either. But the rest of that house had windows. Jessi saw them when she first got there, when she still believed she was waiting for her father.

This place felt different.

Like it wasn't really a house.

But she did see a ladder leading up into a hole in the high ceiling along a far wall.

A ladder!

A way to escape!

But first she'd have to get the cuffs off, and Jessi doubted he would ever leave her alone or un-cuffed. He'd never trust her after she tried to stab him.

Bob was sitting on the couch, his back to her, watching TV.

Suddenly, she heard her name.

Her ears perked up. It was hard not to sit up and open her eyes to see the screen. But if Bob knew she was awake, he'd probably turn off the TV. Then she wouldn't hear what the people were saying about her.

"The Sheriff's department is asking anyone with information about Paul Dodd or Jessi Price to contact 1-800—"

His name wasn't Bob. It was Paul Dodd.

I knew it.

I knew he was a bad man.

She kept her eyes closed.

She heard a familiar voice, her mother. "Please, mister. Bring my child home."

"Mommy?" Jessi said, no longer able to pretend she was sleeping.

Paul turned the TV off and spun around to look at her.

"Turn it back on!" Jessi screamed.

"No."

He turned his back on Jessi, ignoring her.

"I knew it! You're not taking me to see my dad! You stole me!"

Paul said nothing.

Jessi screamed as loud as she could. "Help! Help!"

He laughed. "Scream as loud as you want. Nobody's gonna hear you."

"Where are we?"

"Neverland."

Paul clicked the TV back on, but quickly turned the channel, finding some old sitcom that Jessi's parents used to watch. She wasn't sure of its name.

"I want to go home."

"Too bad."

"I thought you were going to take me to see my Daddy."

"Oh, you'll see him soon enough."

"I want to see him now!" Jessi screamed.

She didn't care if she made him mad any more.

After the stabbing, Jessi had to apologize a lot. Had to tell him that she was sorry and that she was just scared. Had to lie to him to keep him from being so mad.

And it had worked.

But Jessi wasn't going to fake it any longer. Paul was a bad man, and she couldn't pretend he wasn't.

"I want you to bring me to my Daddy now."

"Be careful what you ask for."

"What do you mean?"

He jumped off the couch, ran over to her, then dropped to his knees beside the bed and looked Jessi in the eyes. "You want to be with your Daddy again, do you?"

"Yes."

"Right now?" His smile was weird, his eyes wild like her cat when he rolled in catnip. And it wasn't just his wild eyes. Paul's entire face had changed, like he was no longer pretending to be nice.

Or no longer hiding what he really was.

"Yes, I want you to take me to my Dad. Now."

He reached into his back pocket, pulled out his phone, and swiped at the screen.

And for the first time, Jessi wondered if maybe she'd been wrong. Maybe he *was* going to call her father, and reunite them.

She leaned forward trying to see the screen, anxious. Her heart was pounding, happy butterflies fluttering in her stomach.

Would her complaining finally get him to bring her home? Jessi didn't care if he brought her to Mom or Dad, as long as she was away from *him*.

He found whatever he was looking, then turned the screen so Jessi could see.

"What is this?" she asked, looking at a photo of her father sitting in a corner of a dark room she didn't recognize.

Paul pressed the picture. Jessi realized it wasn't a photo, but rather a video. The person shooting the video — probably Paul — moved closer.

Her father was tied with rope. "What did you to do to my daddy?"

She heard her father's voice begging, "Please. Don't."

Then Paul's ugly laughter.

"Please, I have a family."

"*Had* a family," said Paul's voice. "Don't worry, though, I'm taking care of them next."

Her father screamed bad words at the man.

Then the phone was set down.

Jessi could see only the bottom half of her father, on his knees.

She saw Paul's feet walk out of the shot.

Then a loud sound in the background — a familiar sound that she couldn't quite place. Then, as Paul walked back into the frame, she saw the source — a chainsaw.

Her father screamed.

And then there was blood.

So much blood.

Jessi screamed as she watched her world ripped apart by the bad man.

"You killed him!"

Paul returned the phone to his pocket, then got up close in Jessi's face, smiling. "Yeah, I killed him. And if you don't stop being a little bitch, you're going to join him. Do you understand me?"

She didn't answer.

She *couldn't* answer.

Jessi finally lost it.

She threw herself at him, as much as she could while cuffed to the rail.

Her mouth closed around his ear.

She bit.

Hard.

Paul screamed.

Blood flooded her mouth, tasting like hot metal.

She wanted to bite his ear straight off.

She twisted, biting harder.

Then she felt the blow to the back of her head, and she let go, falling backward into the bed.

"Ah, you are a spirited one!" Paul laughed even as blood gushed from his left ear.

"I hate you! I'm gonna kill you!"

Paul laughed harder.

"You have that backward. I'm going to kill *you*. But not before I fuck you so hard that you'll beg me to kill you."

He grabbed Jessi by the back of her hair. The metal cuff bit into her wrist hard as he yanked her up.

He pulled her face to his, then licked at her mouth, trying to stick his tongue past her lips.

She screamed, squirming, kicking at him.

Paul grabbed her by the neck, hard, slammed her against the headboard, and squeezed so tight that she thought he might break her head right off.

She stopped kicking.

Stopped screaming.

All she could do was stare into his evil eyes.

And wet herself.

"Now that I have your attention," he said as he slipped his hand across her chest. "It's about time we make a woman out of you."

He reached down.

And Jessi screamed.

Chapter 48 - Jasper Parish

Jordyn rode shotgun in silence.

"What?" Jasper asked.

"I don't get it."

"Get what?"

"Why you did *that* to him."

Jasper wasn't sure if she'd seen the lengths to which he'd hurt the man before finally ending his misery.

"He was a rapist. He deserved to die."

"Even though he did his time? Even though he'd changed? You saw his computer. He didn't have any illegal stuff on it. Did he?"

"Maybe he had it somewhere else. Maybe he doesn't have any kiddy porn at all. I don't know. But he's still a monster. He ruined people's lives. He made Paul. If not for him, Paul wouldn't have killed Ashley. Or kidnapped Jessi Price. You get that, don't you? Plus, gave Paul a place to hide, and continue hurting Jessi."

Jordyn said nothing. Just stared out the passenger window.

"Okay. I get that he deserved punishment. Maybe even deserved to die. But *that?* What you did to him?"

"What?"

"You tortured him. Even though he helped by giving you Paul's location. You cut off his … stuff … and shoved it in his mouth. Why?"

Jasper shook his head. "I don't expect you to understand."

"You're right. I don't understand. This seems to be more about you than him. Like you *enjoy* killing. You *enjoy* the torture."

"Wait a second. How is this different from me setting that Jeff guy on fire after wrapping him in his snuff film tape?"

"He was a bad guy *still* doing bad things. You were dispensing appropriate justice. I didn't think that was for you as much as this was. Don't get me wrong, Dad. I *do* enjoy stopping these monsters. Keeping them from hurting more people. But this is something different. What you did to him is like the kinds of things we try to stop monsters from doing."

Jasper turned to her, stunned. "Are you saying that I'm like them?"

"I didn't say that."

"But you're thinking it."

Jordyn kept staring out the window.

Jasper focused on the road but felt like his daughter had stabbed him in the gut with her accusations. How could she say he was becoming like the people he hunted? Did she not see the distinction between his brand of justice and the evil fueling the *real* bad guys?

He wanted to lash out, blast her for acting entitled, but he couldn't yell at Jordyn. Because deep down, he saw the truth in her words.

He *did* enjoy torturing Wes Richards.

Enjoyed the man's screams as Jasper removed his manhood.

Enjoyed the power of holding the man's life in his hands, giving him just a bit of hope that he might get through this, then snuffing it out.

Does that make me a monster?

Jasper had never truly considered the question. He didn't think he was a monster, but he also knew that none of the monsters he'd put down ever saw themselves that way. They always had reasons that drove them. An internal logic, no matter how twisted. They weren't mustache-twirling bad guys doing evil stuff for shits and grins. They were broken, often too much to see what they were.

He glanced again at Jordyn.

Is that what she thinks of me? That I'm just like them?

And at that moment, he hated himself enough for the both of them.

"You're right," he said softly. "I don't know what came over me, but you're right. I went too far."

Jordyn stayed silent.

"I thought we were doing good, but maybe you can't do this sort of thing without it changing you. Without it turning you into the monsters you're hunting."

"You're not a monster," Jordyn finally said, still staring out the window.

Yeah, if that's so, why can't you look at me?

Jasper pulled up to their apartment building and killed the engine. "Yeah, but I'm also not proud of what I did. If I can't look you in the eye and respect my actions, then I'm not worthy of being your father."

Now she looked at him. Her eyes were welling up.

"I suggest we abort the mission."

"What? What about Paul and Jessi?"

"The cops can handle it."

"What about stopping the other bad guys?"

"I don't know. We'll figure something out. Or maybe we ignore them. Why ruin our lives with an endless battle? I spent most of my life fighting for other people while ignoring you and your mom."

"But you were helping people."

"Yeah, for all the good that did. Bad people still do terrible shit. And how did Fate reward me for doing good? By giving your mother cancer. I never got to spend the time with her that she deserved. I don't want to lose you, too. Maybe my purpose has been wrong all along."

He put his hand around hers, braiding their fingers their.

For a moment she seemed so tiny, like the little girl she once was, rather than the young woman she was becoming.

"I love you, Dad." She unstrapped her seatbelt, leaned across the console, and rested her head on his shoulder.

"I love you, too, Jordyn."

Chapter 49 - Mallory Black

PAUL DODD's warehouse unit was crawling with deputies and FBI agents, now working with the sheriff's department on the case.

Gloria introduced them to Special Agent in Charge Terry McDaniels, a white-haired man in his early fifties wearing a gray suit and blue tie that matched his eyes. Mal had met the man two years ago when he came in to help with Ashley's case. He wasn't like the FBI agents you saw on TV who came in and pushed around the local cops. He was always supportive and seemed to have a decent head on his shoulders. He also seemed to take it hard when they came up blank on Ashley's killer.

McDaniels informed them that this was a priority case with every available resource assigned.

Mike updated McDaniels and Gloria on the Wes Richardson situation.

McDaniels asked, "Do you think Paul Dodd killed him?"

Mike answered, "Makes sense. If Wes knew where he

273

was, Paul wanted to tie up loose ends, make sure nothing is leading us to him."

McDaniels put a finger to his lip, then looked at Mal. "What do you think?"

"I'm just a consultant," she said, holding up her open palms.

"Yeah, but I can tell by your expression that you have reservations."

She glanced at Mike, not wanting to mess with his investigation. He gave her a look: *Go ahead.*

"Well, this crime's level of violence seems odd to me. I mean he severed the man's penis and balls then shoved the penis in his mouth. From what we know of Dodd, he practically worshiped Wes. Even though the man raped Paul and his sister, Paul still talked to him. Hell, he was mad at his sister when she got Wes put in jail."

"Do we like the sister for this?"

Mike said, "As far as we know, she hasn't talked to Paul in years. Last his ex-wife heard, the sister was in Portland."

"We have people looking into her," Gloria said.

McDaniels asked, "Do we know how often Paul and Wes talked?"

"We pulled Paul's cell phone records and found that he called Wes at least once a week, talking for at least a half hour at a time. Going back about three years."

"If not Paul," McDaniels said, "who else might have done this?"

"I still like Paul for this," Mike answered. "I can't imagine who else it might be. Another victim, maybe? Or Paul could have staged the scene to throw us off, figuring we wouldn't expect that level of violence from him."

"The timing is too suspicious to be someone else," Gloria said. "I think we have to operate on the theory that

Paul did it, likely to cover up whatever Wes knew about his plans."

"Did we get anything from the house that can help us find him?" McDaniels asked.

"Forensics is still there. We couldn't find a computer in the house, though we did find a modem and a box indicating that he had at least one laptop. I'm thinking our suspect took it with him."

"What about you all? Get anything here?" Mal asked.

Gloria said, "A couple of prints, but nothing else. The warehouse manager said that Paul, who went by the name Richard Howell, had a car. One of those old patrol cruisers sold at auction, painted black, with a dome light and everything."

Mal said, "That's the car that picked up Ashley and her friend, Rebecca."

"What name did you say?" Mike asked.

"Richard Howell. Same name as that murder vic from the other day."

"Well, *that's* weird," Mike said. "Any connection?"

"I've got Cooper and Billings looking into it."

Mal said, "If they're not connected, there sure are a lot of weird coincidences around this case."

McDaniels nodded. "We've got a BOLO on the car. Nobody's reported anything yet, though."

"So, where do we go from here?" Mike asked.

Mal's phone buzzed in her pocket. She pulled it out and saw *PRIVATE* on the screen. "Will you excuse me?"

"Yeah," McDaniels said.

She walked away from the trio, and out of the warehouse, beyond the yellow tape, then answered. "Yes?"

"Hello, Mallory."

It was him.

The man who had warned her about Ashley.

The man who had called her after the news segment, sounding drunk, asking if she thought it was ever okay to kill, wondering if she would kill her daughter's murderer if given a chance?

Mystery Man.

"Hi," she said, wondering why he was calling, now of all times. Did he know something about this case? She couldn't help but think that he did. "What have you got for me?"

"Got?" he asked, surprised.

"You know stuff I don't. I have no idea how, and right now I don't even care. Right now, I just want to know where Jessi Price is. Can you help me?"

"I can," he said.

Chapter 50 - Paul Dodd

PAUL HATED THIS PART, when fantasy crashed hard into the reality of what he'd done.

Jessi was curled up in the bed, covered in her blanket, crying.

Paul was sitting in the far corner of the bunker, disgusted with himself and his appetites.

Somehow, with each of the six girls he'd taken, it was always the same. Months of anticipation, months of fantasy, months of dreaming of that first moment when he'd finally touch their bare skin. When he'd finally be able to ravish their bodies.

And in his fantasies, they always welcomed his touch as he'd welcomed Wes's. As his sister had welcomed Wes. As his sister had welcomed *him*.

But the girls he took were different.

They always resisted at first, because they didn't know better. They didn't know how good he'd make them feel. They didn't understand yet.

But he'd teach them.

But not once did they ever appreciate the moment for what it was.

Never did they come to welcome his touch.

Never did they come to love him as he'd loved Wes, or his sister.

And that broke his heart.

It made Paul feel even more like a monster than he already did.

Now he felt like a broken pervert who defiled a child. Who, in a moment of anger and sick lust, had ruined her.

He stared at the blanket and the crying shape beneath it.

Her cries cut into his soul.

Just twenty minutes ago, he hated her. He hated her smart mouth. He hated the burden of having to hide her, the burden of having to bury his love for children. And in the act of violating her, he only wanted to hurt her, and empty the evil seed inside him.

At that moment, he'd been so alive.

But now he was practically dead.

Her whimpers under the blanket only reminded Paul that he was a monster. He hated thinking of himself that way, as someone capable of hurting a child.

And that's what he saw her as now: *a child*.

Not an object of his sexual desires, but a broken child, crying for her mommy.

He hated himself.

He hated his sickness.

A part of him wanted to put her out of her misery to put him out of his.

But another part wasn't ready to let her go. Because it knew that guilt was temporary. Desire would return, and he'd need Jessi as an outlet. It would feel as earth shatteringly good as it had the first time.

Followed by more self-loathing.

The cycle usually ended just after the girl's tenth birthday.

It was Paul's ritual. His way of exorcising yesterday's demon. Of punishing the girl that would become a woman who would become a bitch.

But now that the sheriff's department was onto him, now that he could no longer exist undercover in the real world, that limited his ability to find new girls.

So, this one would have to last a while longer.

He hoped that she'd become bitchier after her tenth birthday. If he could hate her as he had come to hate Katie, it would be easier to keep doing this to her. Maybe, eventually, he wouldn't feel remorse.

Maybe she'd even come to like it.

Come to love him.

Though Paul wasn't sure that he wanted her love. Not if she was already this ungrateful and bitchy. Maybe this would all be more fun if he could continue to hate her.

He could probably keep her for at least a year, but Paul wasn't sure how long he could manage after that.

Little girls had a shelf-life, after all.

Wes had his reasons for losing interest in kids at around ten, a reason he never explained to Paul, a reason Paul never had the courage to ask. He assumed that nine and under were Wes's preferred ages. Same for Paul. He'd tried to examine it over the years and had never really figured out the why. Was a part of him trying to relive his incestuous relationship with his sister? Or his relationship with Wes? Would he have been like this had Wes never come along, or would he have been attracted to women his own age?

And if that were the case, would the desire to kill still be there?

He didn't think the desire to kill came from Wes. Wes hadn't ever killed anyone as far as Paul knew. Maybe he wouldn't have gone to prison if he had.

No, those particular seeds must have come from his mother. But Paul didn't want to think about her now, or he might lose it and kill Jessi.

If Wes hadn't made Paul a pedophile — assuming he was responsible —would he still need to kill?

Would he be murdering women after he slept with them?

It seemed unlikely.

He hadn't planned his first kill.

Her name was Marissa Rodriquez, a foster child who always hung out at the park he went to on the weekends with his daughter. He'd used Lily to get close to the girl, groomed her for a while before finally convincing her to get into his car. She actually liked him, thought he was funny.

He hadn't come up with his birthday ritual and hadn't planned to kill her.

He simply wanted her. He brought Marissa to the bunker, drugged her, then made love to her.

Afterward, the realization hit him like a sledgehammer: *what do I do now?* If he let her go, she would go to the police just like his sister.

His life would be over.

He'd go to prison.

He'd probably be subjected to rape on a daily basis.

He knew he had to kill her.

And he hated it.

Because of all the girls he took, she was the one who seemed least repulsed by him. She liked him, until the moment he took her virginity.

After that, she was scared of him just like all the others.

Paul hated that he had to kill her.

He wasn't even sure how to go about doing it, so he wound up making her drink a concoction of Kool-aid laced with sleeping pills.

He thought he was being gentle, doing her a mercy.

But watching her asphyxiate in her sleep, choking to death, hardly seemed merciful.

It terrified him.

There was even a moment where he thought about trying to save her. But his nature's better devils warned against it.

Paul never saw himself as a murderer. But then, suddenly, he was. He needed the birthday ritual. It helped to remove himself from his actions and see what he was doing as a gift.

He was celebrating their innocence.

Preserving them as perfect little children.

They'd never grow up to disappoint their parents or become vacuous self-obsessed bitches. They'd never grow up to raise children they didn't even care about.

They were going out on top, and he was helping them.

But as Paul sat there alone in the aftermath of reality, listening to Jessi's hitching cries, he found it hard to justify what he was doing as kindness.

The birthday ritual was a lie he told himself so that he could continue to do what he needed to do. It was self-preservation, and to pretend otherwise was ignoring reality.

It was funny how he saw things with perfect clarity in moments like this, saw himself as he truly was.

Paul wished he could carry this self-awareness through his normal life. Maybe he wouldn't be a slave to his desires or stuck where he was now, running from the law, life as he knew it over.

Paul wanted to cry.

But a beeping alerted him to a threat outside.

He stood, went to the four security monitors on the wall, and saw a stream of cars and vans on the dirt road leading to his bunker.

They'd found him.

Paul screamed.

Chapter 51 - Mallory Black

THE BUNKER WAS RIGHT where Mal's mystery caller promised, in Timucua County, a plot of undisturbed woodlands abutting the Timucua National Forest, a place that people often went to disappear, or make sure that bodies did. A place trekked by hunters, tree huggers, and few others.

The Timucua Sheriff's Department chopper found Paul's car dumped in the woods about a half mile from the bunker, which increased the likelihood that he and Jessi were hidden underground as Mal's mystery man said that they would be.

Two perimeters surrounded the bunker by dinner time.

Mal and Mike stood outside the mobile command unit RV. The scene was a flurry. More than fifty people led by the FBI, including the Creek County Sheriff deputies and SWAT team, local officers from Timucua County, paramedics, and a host of others, all with two jobs: *save Jessi Price and apprehend Paul Dodd.*

They gave the bunker's barely visible square hatch a

wide berth of nearly fifty yards. You couldn't have officers tromping all over the grounds given that there could be booby traps hidden in the nearby woodlands.

Two members of the SWAT team trained in explosives ensured a clear path to the hatch where the FBI's crisis negotiator would soon attempt to make the first contact by way of a throw phone.

After that, the ball was in Dodd's court.

Being underground with only a single access point, and holding a child hostage, the FBI couldn't exactly lead a full-on assault to take him out.

This required a crisis negotiator's delicate touch. There were four on scene, two from the FBI and another two from Creek County Sheriff's Office. It paid to have as many negotiators as possible — you never knew who was most likely to reach the suspect. Someone like Paul would be far more likely to respond to a male negotiator than a female. But there was a female negotiator on hand, just in case their profile was wrong, and a woman's touch was needed.

Even with the right negotiator standoffs could drag on for days, during which time the number of people on-scene would multiply, swelling anxieties, along with the potential for negotiators and SWAT to start getting pissed at one another, with the SWAT team wanting to take the fucker out while the negotiators aimed for a peaceful resolution.

Meanwhile, the outer perimeter turned into a tent city of media outlets, all vying for the scoop.

And as the hours ticked, the pressure to do something increased until something *had* to give. All too often, these sorts of situations ended when the suspect realized he was fucked. That he was out of options, and may as well go out with a bang, make everyone remember his name — murder-suicide.

This was the worst possible outcome for the authorities, but probably the best and most-hoped for among the media vultures. If it bleeds, it leads. And if the victim is a child, the ratings go wild.

Mal wished she could pause time before they made the first contact with Paul Dodd and everything got out of hand.

She wanted a crack at convincing him to surrender.

Mal wasn't a crisis negotiator, though she'd had some training. The man was obsessed with her, going to the extreme of sending her "gifts" and breaking into her house to put a gun against her head as she slept. Mal sensed there was some connection to exploit.

She headed inside the mobile command unit, approached SAIC McDaniels, who was talking with Gloria and Robert Tellison, the FBI's first negotiator.

She looked at McDaniels. "I want to try talking to him."

Gloria looked like she was going to weigh in, but McDaniels beat her to it.

"With all due respect, Ms. Black, you're a civilian, and I don't think that's a good idea."

"The man is obsessed with me. He broke into my home and stood over me as I slept. He could've killed me, but didn't. I think I can reach him."

She had worked with Tellison once before. He was a six-foot-four thin, bespectacled black man who reminded Mal more of a university professor than law enforcement. He said, "I won't say no outright. Let's keep you as an option."

Classic negotiator response, avoid a hard no to pacify her, or at least avoid conflict.

McDaniels added, "I'd also suggest that Dodd isn't obsessed with you so much as he's using you to relive whatever he did to your daughter. You're not the object here — merely a vessel to achieve his needs. Your engagement could *increase* the odds of him killing Jessi Price."

Mal hadn't considered that. "Shit. Maybe you're right. I don't want to screw things up. But if you need me, for anything, I'll be here."

"Thank you," McDaniels said.

Mal met Gloria's eyes. She seemed relieved that Mal was backing down rather than escalating this into an argument.

Mal headed back outside the RV where Mike was pacing, a huge wad of gum forming a giant ball in his right cheek.

"Man, the department really ought to let you guys smoke again. You look like a fucking hamster."

"Whatever," Mike said. "So, what's the word inside?"

"Nothing. I was just availing my services, should they be needed."

"Yeah, they gonna try sarcasm as a negotiating technique?"

"Fuck you, hamster."

Mike laughed.

Mal joined his pacing, staring over at the bunker's hatch, barely visible through the surrounding brush. The bunker was something you'd never see unless you stumbled upon it by accident or knew exactly where to look.

"This fucker thought everything through," she said.

"I just hope they're both still down there. That we're not wasting all our resources and time while he's swapped cars and is crossing state lines."

"We'll know soon enough. I think Tellison's about to make contact."

"I wonder if he knows we're here," Mike said. "You

ever been in a bomb shelter? Not sure how deep it is, or if it's soundproof."

"I'd guess fifteen feet deep, maybe more, depending on the water table in these parts. I have a feeling he knows we're here, though. He probably has cameras in the trees."

Mike looked around, chewing on his wad of gum, and sighed.

Mal asked, "So, is this all over the media yet?"

"I haven't looked. But if not, I'm sure it will be soon."

Mal thought of Jessi's parents turning on the news, maybe seeing reporters in the woods outside the second perimeter, learning of the standoff, and the hell they must be going through.

Mike asked, "So when are you gonna tell me more about your tipster?"

"I told you I've got no idea who he is."

"He's gotta be connected to Paul somehow, don't you think? Or maybe Wes? Maybe a third member of their sick little tribe?"

"I considered that. But, I dunno. That doesn't feel right."

"How else could he have known that Ashley was in danger? Or where Paul took Jessi?"

"I dunno. But let's not look a gift horse in the mouth."

"And you tried getting him to come in?"

"He wasn't having any of that."

"Sounds fishy as hell," Mike spit out his gum, dug a fresh pack from his jacket, and shoved several new pieces into his mouth. "You think he's the guy that Paul's wife mentioned. The private investigator?"

"Definitely possible."

"We need to get with her again, maybe bring a sketch artist."

Mal nodded. "Maybe he really is a P.I.?"

"Working for the Price family?"

"Well, you'd have to ask them. I'm thinking maybe he works for someone else, though, and *that's* why he's keeping to the shadows. Maybe he works for Paul, or, more likely, Wes. Maybe he got a bit too close to what they were doing but didn't want to come forward publicly."

"Lawyers," Mike said with a resigned sigh, "gotta make everything complicated. What do you think he'd be doing for Wes?"

"I don't know. Could be real estate stuff. Maybe he accidentally discovered some shit he wasn't supposed to."

"And calling you is his way of reaching out without screwing up his reputation for discretion?"

"Maybe," she said.

"What if he's not a P.I.? What if he's an accomplice? Or maybe, like I said before, a pervert like Paul. Except maybe he's only into *watching* kiddy porn, not kidnapping or raping kids. Maybe he's a customer of Paul's?"

A flash of anger burned in Mal's gut at the thought. She imagined, not for the first time, Paul recording what he did to Ashley, then selling or sharing it with other pedophiles. Her daughter's innocence stolen on repeat, alive on the internet forever, swapped in videos via anonymous message boards and chat rooms. She had no reason to believe that he'd done that. Nobody from cyber crimes or the FBI had reported seeing photos or videos of Ashley during their daily treks on the dark web. Still, she couldn't help but imagine a bunch of sick fucks getting off on Paul violating her baby girl.

Mal wondered if any of them were aware who Ashley even was. If she was just another anonymous victim, or if they knew her identity. Maybe that was part of the appeal, getting off to a dead girl getting raped. Maybe he'd even recorded himself killing her, then shared, traded, or sold that.

She'd seen enough horrors in her time as a detective and was rarely shocked by the heinous shit that people did to one another. But this was the worst of the worst — exploiting a child for sexual gratification, then sharing that crime with the world.

If people *were* out there watching her daughter's final moments, Mal hoped they every one of them died horrible deaths.

"Thanks a lot," she said, punching Mike in the shoulder.

"What?"

"I hadn't thought of my mystery guy as an accomplice until now. There was a time after Ashley died when I assumed the killer was calling just to mock me. But recently, I started thinking that wasn't the case. That he might be a good guy."

"Frankly, I'm surprised that you thought *anyone* was good. I thought you were the pessimist between us."

"Oh, you didn't hear? I'm an optimist now."

"Yeah, right."

She stared as Gloria, McDaniels, and Tellison stepped out of the mobile command unit and started talking to some other deputies and FBI agents while preparing to make the first contact with Paul.

Mal turned to Mike. "You think he might be an accomplice?"

"Don't know. But I think we ought to try and find him."

"Agreed."

Mal watched as Tellison, with his bulletproof vest beneath his blue FBI jacket, approached the bunker's hatch holding a throw phone.

Before Tellison reached the hatch, a man's voice commanded, "Stop."

The voice was coming from a speaker system that wasn't just coming from the hatch's door, but from two or three points around them in the woods. Dodd had set up speakers around his bunker. Mal wondered how much he'd prepared for this day, and what other surprises he might have planted around them.

Bear traps? Mines? Bombs?

And again, surely there were cameras.

Paul was probably watching her now.

Tellison introduced himself, then told Paul that he wanted to leave the throw phone at the hatch so they could talk more directly.

But Paul said, "I don't want your phone."

"Shit," Mike whispered.

Throw phones weren't used just to speak with the hostage taker. They had miniature cameras that the FBI could use to get eyes inside the building, determine the layout, see whether it was rigged with traps, and, maybe most importantly, what condition the hostage was in. But they couldn't do their job if the hostage taker refused to take it.

Mal wondered if he knew the phone had a camera. It wasn't common knowledge, but it could've been something he used in the military. Or maybe he studied police technology and techniques like many serial killers did. There was at least one profile of the Unsub who killed Ashley that said he might be involved in law enforcement. That was close to ex-military

"I don't want to talk," Paul said. "And I don't have any demands. I just want you all to leave me alone."

"Give us Jessi, and we'll leave you be."

His voice ice cold: "Jessi isn't here."

Mal froze from the inside, hearing the murderer who killed her baby, broke into her home, and terrorized her.

He was so close, yet so far away.

She wanted to hurt him. Grab him by the throat and end his worthless life. She couldn't do that, nor would she risk her freedom to kill him.

But a girl could dream.

"We know she's in there," Tellison said. "We just want to bring her back to her parents."

"I said she's not in here! Now *please* get off of my property."

Tellison looked back at McDaniels, standing just outside the mobile command unit, then back down at the hatch.

"We can't leave here without Jessi. We know she's with you."

"Yeah? How do you know that?"

"We've got surveillance of you bringing her here," Tellison lied.

Mal couldn't believe he'd tell such a blatant lie. Of all the things he could've said, why choose something like that?

Paul's laugh crackled over the speakers. "Yeah, is that so? Then what's she wearing?"

"Okay, you got me," Tellison admitted. "I'm lying. Obviously, we didn't see anything. But we have credible intelligence that puts Jessi with you."

Mal wondered if Tellison's lie was just so he could get called on it, then "admit" the truth. Another tactic to forge a connection with Paul.

"She's not here."

"Well, we still need to check. If you'd just let us take a look inside, we can be on our way."

"Leave. Now."

Tellison wasn't budging. "Your ex-wife Rachel and your daughter Lily, they're worried about you, Paul."

Paul didn't respond.

"I'd like to tell them that you're okay. Why don't you open the hatch so we can talk?"

"How dare you use my daughter's name to try and get me to open my door to you? Leave! Now!"

Tellison was walking a fine line between engaging Paul and pissing him off. Mal hoped he wouldn't go too far and get Jessi killed.

"I'll talk to my boss, Paul. In the meantime, can we get you anything? Food? Water? Does Jessi need anything?"

Paul said nothing.

Tellison walked back to the mobile command unit, defeated, but with his head held high.

And now, the waiting.

Chapter 52 - Jasper Parish

THE HOSTAGE NEGOTIATION with Paul Dodd was all over the news by nightfall. Reporters were coming "live from the scene" standing in the woods, likely right outside the second perimeter, updating TV anchors with the scant information they had.

Everything was going through the FBI, who would neither confirm nor deny that Paul Dodd was the person they were attempting to negotiate with.

Jordyn sat on the couch beside Jasper, eating from a giant blue bowl of popcorn. He wanted to ask her if she found this entertaining, but knew she tended to eat when anxious. And they were both on edge, waiting to see how this would play out, and if Jasper had made the right decision in turning this over to the sheriff's department, and now the FBI, rather than tending to business himself.

"How long you think this'll go on?" Jordyn asked.

"Could be days."

"*Days*? Come on, people have to sleep."

"You can sleep if you want. I'll wake you if anything happens."

"I'm good," she said, despite her tired eyes.

He got up, went to the kitchen, and poured himself a glass of wine.

He went back to the couch, sat, and took a sip of his Pinot Grigio. It was crisp, and it made Jasper think of a porch swing on a hot day. Just one more way to give his brain an escape.

"Wine?" Jordyn asked, eyebrows arched.

"I need something to take the edge off. And *popcorn*," he said with an eye roll, "doesn't do the trick for me."

He smiled, then took another sip.

His cell phone rang.

Jasper looked at the screen and saw Lenny's number.

"Hey," Jasper said, getting up and answering the phone.

"So, this shit on TV. That's you?"

"Yep," Jasper said, walking into his bedroom and softly closed the door.

"And they said that the sheriff's department had received an anonymous tip. That you, Mr. Anonymous?"

Jasper laughed. "It wouldn't be anonymous if I told you."

"I thought *you* were going to take care of this." Lenny sounded almost disappointed.

"I thought you wanted me to give up this life."

"No, I wanted you to keep Jordyn out of it. Big difference."

"Well, now we're both out. You should be happy for me."

Lenny was quiet.

After a long moment, he said, "Of course I'm happy for you. You've done great, son. Now enjoy some much-needed time off."

Lenny hung up.

Jasper felt like he'd let the old man down.

He flashed back to the eighth grade, playing point guard for Lenny's summer basketball team, and the coach's one big rule: *never waste his time.*

You showed up to practice. You kept your nose clean. You did what you said that you'd do.

Practice was three times a week, on top of their two scheduled games. Five days of basketball, which was great when Jasper was younger and more into it. But as high school approached and Jasper began to notice girls, he grew more interested in his social life than sports.

He became specifically more interested in a girl named Staci who had started showing an interest in him. She was pretty, smart, and the first girl to give Jasper the time of day. One day she asked him to take the bus to the mall with her. This was the first time they'd be hanging out without her friends and seemed like the perfect opportunity to move their relationship along.

Jasper blew off practice that day.

Staci spent half their trip to the mall talking about some other boy she liked, Jasper's friend Jake. So not only did he ditch the game for nothing, he felt stupid and guilty.

He dreaded the next game, figuring that Lenny would lay into him in front of the entire team. Ask why he didn't show up, or call, just left his teammates high and dry?

The next game, on a Friday night, was supposed to be epic, against their biggest rival. Jasper's stomach churned like it was making ice cream. He entered the gym, hoping that a missed practice wouldn't affect his game and Lenny wouldn't yell at him in front of everyone, or make an example of him as he had other kids in the past.

But Lenny didn't say a word to Jasper.

He made the team do their drills just like usual.

Jasper wondered if Lenny had somehow missed his

absence. Had he overestimated his importance to the team? He was the starting point guard, but they had a second one who was decent enough. Maybe it didn't even matter if Jasper showed up for practice.

Jasper went through the drills, finding himself almost upset that Lenny hadn't pulled him aside to ask about his missed practice.

But Lenny said nothing.

Then the game started, and Jasper, for the first time in two years was sitting on the bench. And there he stayed for the entire game. Jasper was afraid to ask when he'd be going in. This was his punishment, and Lenny was making a point. Jasper asking why would be an insult to the coach and his team.

So, he sat there and watched.

Watched the backup point guards make ten turnovers.

Watched his team lose by fifteen points.

Watched his screw-up cost the team an important win against their biggest rival.

Watched his teammates avoid him as if he wasn't even there.

They didn't sit near him on the bench.

Didn't ask why he wasn't playing.

He was ostracized, no longer part of the team, but still forced to sit and watch, like a ghost unable to interact with his family.

Even worse, Jasper's mom usually got off work right before the fourth quarter. She was always there for the end of the game and to take him home.

But not that night.

After the game, Jasper couldn't make eye contact with Coach.

He headed to the locker room, fighting tears, desperate

to get his bag and go to the parking lot where his mom would be waiting.

But she didn't show up after the game, either.

Kids left with their parents and the parking lot steadily emptied. Jasper felt more alone than at any time since his father's passing.

He sat on the curb no longer able to keep his tears from coming.

The door opened behind him, and Jasper heard Coach's voice talking to one of the gym's employees.

He wiped the tears from his face, wishing he could disappear so Coach wouldn't see him.

But Jasper needn't have worried.

Coach and the other guy walked right by him, toward their cars, carrying on their conversation as if Jasper wasn't even there.

The men got in their cars and started to leave.

Jasper's heart was breaking, a million pieces everywhere.

Coach's car turned from the exit, heading back toward the gym instead.

The car's lights washed over Jasper, making him feel exposed and vulnerable.

Here it comes.

Coach pulled up, rolled down his passenger side window, and said, "Your momma's not coming."

"What?"

"I told her not to."

"Why?"

"Get in the car."

Jasper did, slowly, dreading what was to come.

They drove a few minutes before Coach finally spoke. "You know why I benched you tonight?"

"Yes, Coach."

"Tell me."

"Because I didn't show up to practice."

"Why else?"

"I dunno."

"Really?"

"Because I let the team down?"

"Now we're getting somewhere. But that's not all of it."

"What then?"

"What's my number one rule?"

"Don't waste your time?"

"And why is that?"

Jasper repeated something the coach had said to them many times when they weren't playing full-out at practice. "Because you don't have to be here. You've got a day job that's hard, and you could just as easily be sitting home watching TV."

Coach smiled. "That's part, but not all of it."

"What is the rest?"

"If I invest in you that means you'd better damn well be investing in yourself. It's one thing to waste my time, but to waste your own? That's the biggest sin."

Jasper wasn't supposed to say anything. Just sit there and let it sink in.

"We get one go 'round in this life, son. The things you spend your time on will define you. They'll shape the rest of your life. Now I'm not gonna ask why you missed practice. But I do have to know if it was worth more than being part of the team?"

"No, Coach."

"Because if you found something better, by all means, son, go do that thing. Life's too short to do stuff you ain't happy doing."

"I'm happy playing on the team, Coach."

Coach looked him up and down. "Good. I'm happy having you here."

And that was the last time Jasper ever missed practice or let down Coach.

Until now.

He returned to the living room to see Jordyn passed out on the couch. He pulled the blanket over her body, kissed his daughter on the forehead, then went to bed.

Chapter 53 - Mallory Black

It was just after midnight and Tellison's three attempts to make progress with Paul Dodd were all met with nothing.

Mal and Mike sat at a small table inside the mobile command unit with Gloria, Tellison, McDaniels, and Timucua County Sheriff Samuel Johnson, eating cold pizza, several hours old.

It was going to be a long night.

Possibly a long few days.

If the standoff went too long, Gloria would likely reach out to the local RV dealer to supply a few vehicles for key personnel to sleep between shifts.

Sitting in the center of the table, atop the pizza boxes, were tons of papers and reports from field agents who'd spent the entire day and evening interviewing pretty much everyone Paul had ever worked with, gone to school with, served in the Army with, or lived nearby. This was still early going, with plenty of interviews to conduct over the next few days, all in hopes of finding something that might give them an edge in ending this with Jessi returned to her parents. But so far, they'd found nothing to give Tellison an opening.

Every attempt to speak to Paul had been met with a command to leave.

Mal was claustrophobic thinking of Jessi down in that bunker with the same monster who'd stolen, raped, and murdered her daughter.

Mal imagined the little girl huddled in a corner, crying, terrified, with no idea what might happen next. Help was right above her. She could hear the voice of at least one FBI agent wanting to return Jessi to her parents, but this monster stood in his way.

How long until he killed the girl and then, as so many cowards did, turned the gun on himself?

Mal's heart felt almost bruised, knowing that Jessi's walls were closing in around her. She could feel the RV's walls collapsing, too.

She needed to get out of there.

"I need some fresh air." Mal grabbed her water bottle, stuffed it halfway into her front jacket pocket, and headed out the door.

She walked fast before Mike would inevitably follow, thinking she'd wanted to talk alone.

But she didn't want Mike around.

Mal needed solitude.

She walked away from the RV, away from the clusters of spotlights, deputies, and agents, venturing toward the dark woods, not even caring that they might be booby-trapped with God-only-knew-what.

She just needed to be out.

And once alone, standing in the darkness, inhaling the crisp, cold October night air, she tried to calm her rising anxieties by slowing her breath, closing her eyes, and focusing on the present.

She closed her eyes, tuning out the sounds of chatter, the hum of the generators and the RV, finding a relative quiet to settle.

But as she tried to calm herself, Mal kept picturing Jessi Price, some twenty feet below, trapped with the monster.

Then Jessi was replaced with Ashley.

Even though she knew that her daughter was dead and that she only imagined Ashley in danger, it still sent Mal into a blind panic, desperate to do *something*.

She reached deep into her coat pocket, found the pills she'd avoided all day, popped the cap, and shook a few into her palm.

A branch snapped behind her.

She turned to see Mike staring, first at her, then at her dropped bottle of pills. A white-hot heat rushed to her face as she fell to her knees and fished pills from the grass and dirt, quickly returning them to the bottle and hoping to avoid her old partner's scrutiny.

She returned the bottle to her pocket, without taking a pill, hoping Mike would say nothing.

"You okay?"

She swallowed and nodded. "Yeah, just need some fresh air."

He was quiet, maybe deliberating whether to ask about the pills.

He nodded instead. "Okay, well, if you need me I'll be in the MCC."

He walked away, branches breaking underfoot.

Mal's heart pounded. Her breath short. Shame burrowed in her gut.

But she didn't care about the shame as much as relieving her anxiety. Otherwise, it might spiral out of control and into a full-blown panic attack.

She grabbed the bottle again, shook two pills into her palm, popped them into her mouth, then washed them down with her water.

She closed her eyes, waiting for the familiar euphoria. Only these days it was more of a gentle calm, a return to normalcy only the pills could provide.

There was some euphoria, but it wasn't the same as it had been in the early days when the bliss had lasted so much longer.

Now it was a spike, enough to stave off the depression and anxiety she suffered through the day. It had gone from recreation to necessity.

Addiction, she heard Ray in the back of her mind. *You're an addict, Mal.*

She thought about him coming to her home, to *their* home, offering help. She'd been so bitchy, flat out rejected his offer then made him feel terrible on top of that.

There was a time she wouldn't have dreamed of hurting Ray. He was a genuinely nice guy and didn't deserve a shitty wife who was more concerned about her job than her home life.

Nor did Ashley deserve a mother who wasn't nearly as present as she should've been.

Mal had failed as a wife.

As a mother.

And as a deputy.

Now she was nothing more than an addict, forced to sit on the sidelines and watch while a bad man did terrible things to innocent children.

She was helpless.

And then in a moment of odd clarity, Mal realized she *wasn't* helpless.

She had one card left to play.

A way to redeem herself and to possibly spare Jessi.

Mal knew what she had to do.

Tears welled in the corners of her eyes. She hated that the pills made her so emotional, but that was often the only time she wasn't numb. In an odd way, Mal enjoyed feeling something, even if it was pain.

She reached into her inside pocket, fished out her cell phone — the new one, not the one that Paul may have compromised — and dialed Ray.

After a long moment, his tired voice answered, confused.

"Hello?"

"It's me."

"Mal? What number are you calling from?"

"It's a new phone."

"You okay?" he asked.

She could hear him getting up out of bed, probably so as not to disturb Julie. She wondered if his new lover was there, looking at him, perturbed at his ex-wife calling, interrupting their time together.

"I need to talk to you."

"Okay. What's wrong?"

"I'm sorry about what I said."

A pause. Then, "It's okay. I understand."

"I'm not sure you do."

"What do you mean?" he asked.

"I'm not even sure *I* understand."

"What is it, Mal?"

"I'm about to do something very stupid, Ray."

"What are you going to do?" Concern raised his pitch by several octaves. "Where are you?"

"I'm standing twenty feet above the man who murdered our daughter."

"What are you talking about?"

"Have you seen the news? Paul Dodd?"

"Yeah. Wait, is … is he the man that … killed Ashley?"

"Yes."

"And you're there with the Feds and the sheriff's office?"

"Yes."

"What are you going to do, Mal?"

She told him.

"No. You can't do that."

"Someone has to do something. He's going to kill her."

Ray was quiet until he finally said, "Mal, you know I love you, right?"

Silence.

"Please, Mal. You called because you're not sure this is a good idea. Right?"

"I called just in case I didn't make it out of this. I wanted you to know that I … I'm sorry. For everything."

She hung up and slipped the phone back into her pocket, ignoring the buzzing as Ray tried calling her back.

She reached into her other pocket, took out her pills, said "fuck it" and swallowed another two.

She turned around and looked at the hatch. It was thirty yards away, several lights all aimed at it, illuminating the immediate area like a football field. There was no way she'd make it all the way there without someone trying to stop her.

Still, she had to try.

Mal started toward the hatch, walking briskly, without looking at any of the other agents or deputies along the fringes.

Twenty yards away and still no one said a word.

Every instinct in her body told her to turn around, stop

before she got herself arrested, or worse, got Jessi Price killed.

But Mal couldn't stop.

If she could just talk to Paul Dodd, she could get him to trade Jessi for something he wanted more.

Chapter 54 - Jasper Parish

JORDYN'S SCREAM woke Jasper immediately.

He sat bolt upright in bed, adrenaline flooding his system.

He grabbed his gun from the nightstand, then ran into the living room, weapon aimed, sweeping the area, ready to kill whoever was dumb enough to break into his house.

But no one was there.

Only Jordyn, crying.

"What is it?"

"She's going to die."

"Who?"

"Mallory Black."

Chapter 55 - Mallory Black

SHE WAS ten yards from the hatch.

Mike called out, "What are you doing, Mal?"

"What needs to be done," she said without stopping or turning to see if he was alone or standing with others who might not be so polite while trying to stop her.

Gloria called out, "Stop, Mal!"

She reached the hatch, not daring to look back at her former colleagues.

She looked down at the hatch and called out, "Open up, Paul!"

It looked even more impenetrable up close. The hatch, raised about eight inches out of the ground, was a square gun-gray metal blast door with a screw-on steel cap covering a deadbolt lock and four portholes, one along each side, where a person could look outside before opening the door.

A speaker was built into the top.

It crackled to life.

"Well, well, well. Look who decided to pay me a visit."

"Let's talk, Paul."

"Okay, talk."

"No, I want to come inside."

"I don't think so."

"I have an offer for you."

"Oh? Go on."

"A trade. Me for Jessi Price."

"What are you doing, Mal?" Mike shouted from behind her.

Mal didn't answer, and couldn't look at Mike. She held her focus on the hatch, awaiting Paul's response. "Why would I give you the only leverage I have to get out of here?"

Confirmation. He admitted to having Jessi.

"Because you don't want Jessi. You want me."

Paul laughed. "Now why would I give up my pleasurable company for your disagreeable temperament? Plus, I'm sure you wouldn't come down here without trying something."

"No tricks. Paul. A straight trade. I think you want to talk to me. I think you *need* to talk to me. Let's face it; there's no way they're letting you leave here, especially if anything happens to that girl. You let me in, and we'll work something out. Just you and me."

Paul said nothing.

Mal hoped that she guessed correctly. That he did have some obsession with her, whether it was *her* or the connection to Ashley didn't matter in the end. As long as Mal could get down there and set Jessi free.

"How would this work? How do I know this isn't a trick?"

"Obviously, you have the upper hand. I won't do anything stupid that might jeopardize Jessi's life. You open the hatch. I come down. You make sure I'm unarmed or whatever you need to do, then send Jessi up the ladder."

"And then what?"

"That's up to you. But no tricks. I promise."

"Tell everyone that I want the area cleared, they all need to go up the service road. If I see a single cop, FBI agent, sniper, anyone, other than you, I kill the girl. Got that?"

"Got it."

Mal turned around and finally saw the disappointed faces of Mike, Gloria, Tellison, and McDaniels.

She approached them.

Tellison laid into her first. "What the hell are you doing?"

"I'm getting her out."

"We don't trade hostages!"

Mal glared at him. "Why not? I don't care what happens to me. I just want that girl safe and back with her parents. You can send the Army in after Jessi's free; I don't care."

"And what if he doesn't free either of you? Then we lose two to him."

"I won't let him hurt her," Mal vowed, meeting Gloria's eyes, then Mike's.

Uncharacteristically, neither said a word.

She wasn't sure if this was their way of supporting her, or if they simply saw no point in arguing after her deal with Dodd.

"Let her do it," Gloria said.

Tellison looked baffled. "What?"

McDaniels agreed. "Yeah, let her do it."

"And then what?" Tellison asked.

"I'll either figure something out," Mal said. "Or, I won't."

Chapter 56 - Mallory Black

MAL WAS ALL ALONE, just outside the swaths of light focused on the hatch.

Every deputy and agent had backed up, along with all emergency personnel, per Dodd's demand.

It was just her, the monster, and Jessi Price.

Paul's voice spoke over the intercoms. "Now remove your clothes."

"What?"

"Remove your jacket, your shirt, pants, and your shoes. Leave your weapon, your cell phone, and any other belongings on top of your clothes. You may keep your underwear on."

Mal didn't allow him to see her annoyance, assuming he was watching her via closed circuit cameras. She shook off her jacket, all too aware that she was leaving her gun and pills behind.

She took off her shirt, boots, and pants.

Mal set her gun and one of her two phones on the clothes, leaving them on the ground. Then she stood there, almost naked, the cold air pimpling her skin.

Mal wasn't sure if Paul wanted her to feel vulnerable as she entered his domain, or if he asked her to strip so he could see she wasn't packing a gun or anything else to try and apprehend her.

Either way, she wasn't about to let him get the upper hand. She didn't need her clothes or her gun for strength. Mal had all she needed to defeat him in her head.

She stepped toward the hatch and heard a metallic thud — the lock sliding open.

The door raised with a hydraulic hiss, probably opened from some remote control below. Paul was nowhere in sight.

She reached the opening and peered down into darkness.

She couldn't see anything except a dark, carpeted floor.

Paul called out, this time not on the intercoms, his voice a hollow echo, caroming off the walls.

"Step down then stay with your face to the ladder. Don't turn until you're instructed."

She climbed over the lip, carefully using her bare foot to find a rung.

She began her descent. The door slowly shut above her with a THUNK.

There was the sound of a lock sliding home.

Mal was trapped, but she kept going, bracing for a bullet to the back of her head.

Her feet hit the carpet.

She stopped.

A loud sound of metal exploded beside her.

She jumped — a pair of handcuffs thrown by Paul. "Put your hands behind your back and cuff yourself."

"Is this really nec—"

"Now!"

His rage was an echo that rattled her body.

She reached down, grabbed the cuffs, and followed his order.

"You may turn around now."

She slowly turned, finally coming face to face with Paul Dodd.

In some ways, it was like seeing a celebrity in person for the first time. She'd watched him on video, though she hadn't been able to see his face. When she did get a name, then access to his driver's license photo, social media, and all the other photos they managed to find, she was able to start putting a face to her daughter's killer. A face she imagined putting a bullet through. But seeing him up close, in person, was unsettling. He was scarier as a concept than as a man.

He was average build, slim, and didn't look crazy at all. He was, as she remembered thinking at the toy store when they first met, handsome.

It was hard to reconcile the monster in her mind with the man in the flesh.

She might have doubted he was the same man if not for his gun, and the sobbing girl on its end. His other hand was on her neck, his smile like a Cheshire's threat. "Welcome to my humble abode."

Jessi was no longer the cute, innocent, fun-loving kid in the school photo that served as her missing child pic, taken when she still knew what it meant to be a happy, normal little girl.

Everything was different now.

Her hair was a mess.

She was wearing a long pink tee, with seemingly nothing underneath.

Her eyes were haunted, ringed by circles of midnight.

She looked like a ghost of the child she was.

Mal's heart broke. She forced herself not to tremble. "Has he hurt you?"

Jessi nodded.

Mal wanted to kill the fucker four times.

If she wasn't cuffed, she might've tried to end him with her hands. A bullet was too fast for a fucker like that.

"You'll be okay," Mal said. "People are waiting to take you back to your parents."

"My daddy is dead."

Mal looked at Paul.

"Whoops," he said with a dismissive shrug and The Good Son's smile.

"Okay, you got me down here. Let Jessi go."

"And have your stormtroopers bust down my door? I don't think so."

"You said you'd let her go." Mal held her calm. She couldn't afford to lose the little control she had left.

"Have you learned nothing in all your years as a cop? Why let her go when I can have you both?"

"Because if you don't send her up, you're right, they'll be sending the stormtroopers down."

"I don't think so."

"I'm the only thing keeping you alive right now."

"And I'm the only thing keeping you *both* alive," Paul snarled. "Remember that. Now, why don't you take a seat over there on Jessi's bed?"

He nodded toward one of the two beds before moving the gun just enough to remind her that Jessi Price might not always have a head.

Mal walked over to the bed with its sheet half off the mattress, blanket balled atop the pillow. She tried not to think of the ways Paul may have already soiled Jessi on that bed.

She sat.

Paul told Jessi to join her.

Jessi walked over to the bed and sat beside Mal, close enough to hear her rapid breathing and see the pulse trying to escape her neck.

Paul looked at them both, a fat canary in his mouth. "Wow, so here you are, in the flesh! I must say you look much prettier when you're not passed out drunk."

Mal said nothing.

She stared at Paul, giving him nothing.

"Swooping in here like a mama bird to save the chick! That's really something; I'll give you that."

He stepped closer, his eyes on Jessi. "Say, Jessi, do you think this nice lady is a good mommy?"

She looked up at Mal, her eyes red, lip trembling. Then she looked back at Paul and nodded.

"What was that? I can't hear you."

"Yes, sir."

Paul smiled and shook his head. "I'm sorry. She was *not* a good mommy. If she were a good mommy, I never would've taken her little girl. Just like I never would've taken *you*, if *your* mommy had been good."

Jessi said nothing. Her arms were crossed, fingers tightly grasping them, as if flesh could protect her from the devil, rather than tempting him.

Mal wasn't sure where Paul was going, but she had to be careful. He had a gun, and she was cuffed. Her only chance was to play passive, then wait for him to slip. If she could lure him close enough to her, she could use her feet to knock him down, and maybe incapacitate him. Then Jessi could get the keys and free her.

Plans galloped through her mind. So many variables, and with each one she sought the best possible means to take Dodd down and rescue Jessi.

"Like your mommy, Jessi, Miss Mallory is no longer

with her husband. It's always a shame when parents can't find a way to stay together. The children always suffer. I would never disturb a happy home. I would never have picked you, Jessi, had your family been together. Nor would I have taken Ashley, or any of the others."

He smiled as he said *others*, taunting Mal with the knowledge that he alone had, knowledge that could help other parents of missing or murdered children.

Only the killer knew how many he killed.

Mal wondered if he bought into his bullshit about only picking kids from broken homes, or if these were the lies he told himself to justify his actions. Maybe he didn't buy a word of it and was only hoping to inflict pain, to put all of the responsibility for Ashley's death on Mal.

Either way, she wasn't about to give in.

"Tell me, Mal. Do you ever wonder what you could've done differently to save her?"

Mal said nothing.

She stared into his dark eyes, trying not to let her rage show through.

"I asked you a question, Mal. Please don't make me angry. I would hate it if you made me take it out on the child."

Jessi flinched, fingernails digging deeper into her arms.

"Of course I do."

"And how does it feel to lose your child like that?"

"Why don't you tell me how it feels to kill a child, to take a little girl from her mother?"

His smile faded. "The first time was rough. To be honest, I didn't want to do it. But I had to, or she'd tell. And I wasn't going to prison." He stared at the ground. Mal was surprised to hear the regret in his voice and see it in his pensive stare. "I liked her."

"What was her name?" Mal asked.

Paul looked up. He seemed ready to tell her, but then that smile returned.

"You're good, Mal. But I'm not playing."

The fact that he wasn't telling her the name made Mal hopeful. If he were planning to kill her, then he wouldn't care what he gave up. He would likely want to boast, knowing it would never leave these walls.

For the first time since slipping on the cuffs, a ray of hope pierced the gloom. "You said the first time was rough. Were the others easier?"

Paul stared at Mal as if trying to decide how to answer.

In Mal's experience, and in the things she'd learned while at the Academy, serial killers often liked to talk about themselves. They go through their lives with a pitch black secret they could never share. Once caught, they opened up. There is a freedom in no longer worrying about what's coming behind you.

But even if he fit the personality type, Mal wasn't sure if Paul was there yet. He might still have some illusions that he could figure his way out.

He finally answered. "Have you ever come upon a stray animal hit by a car? It's the saddest thing ever. Here you have this animal that was living a horrible life, unloved, hungry, struggling just to survive, and then BAM, it's hit by a car, a car that keeps moving as it lies dying on the road. It watches as other cars pass, scared and confused. Then you happen upon it. You look into its eyes and see its pain. You see its confusion. You also see that there's no hope for that poor animal, and the only thing you can do, the only *merciful* thing you can do, is put it out of its misery."

"So, that's what you're doing? Putting these kids out of their misery?"

"Yes."

"You don't see the hypocrisy? It's *you* who are hurting

317

them in the first place. If you didn't steal them from their families, they wouldn't need your … *mercy*."

"They were hurt long before I came along. Their lives were on a downward trajectory."

"Bullshit," Mal snapped.

Paul glared at her. "Do you know that your daughter cried herself to sleep almost every night in the weeks before I picked her up?"

"What are you talking about?"

"I watched you and Ashley for months before making my move. Used your in-home security cameras. I couldn't believe how much you ignored your child's pain. She wished for you and Ray to get back together, but you were too damned selfish to see."

The world was yanked from beneath her.

The thought of this monster watching her family for months before taking her daughter was a sledgehammer to her psyche.

"All that time you spent wondering what you could have done differently to save your little girl, the answer was simple: *pay attention to your daughter*. I never would've come into your lives if you had. I would have found someone else. There's no shortage of shitty parents ruining their children's lives."

Tears stung her eyes.

"*You* did this to her, just like Jessi's mommy. You are the architects of your pain, *not me*. I am providing a mercy."

Jessi buried her face in her palms, sobbing.

Mal saw a surprising glimpse of pain in Paul's expression. It showed an empathy that many killers lacked, that many killers *couldn't* feel.

It might be the leverage she needed. "Is this what you call mercy? Is Jessi's life somehow better because of what you've done?"

"I'm going to release Jessi from her pain."

"You still don't get it, do you?"

"What?"

"We can recover from our pain. We can still lead normal, happy lives, no matter what life does to us. You're not giving these kids a chance to save themselves."

"Yeah, I've seen what happens to these kids when they grow up. They become twisted, terrible people. *Mean.* Innocent girls turn into monstrous bitches who can't help but inflict their pain upon others."

Mal laughed. "Wow, pot meet kettle."

"I am not like that."

"No? You're not acting out your childhood pain upon others? You're not taking out what Wes did to you and your sister upon the world?"

"I don't expect you to understand."

"Oh, I understand completely. As unique as you think you are, you're not, Paul. Thousands of kids are abused every year by people like Wes, and many kids turn into abusers, just like you."

"I am not an abuser."

"Keep telling yourself that."

"I never touched my daughter."

"I bet you wanted to, though," Mal said with a smile.

Paul pointed the gun at her forehead. "Watch your mouth."

"And what then, after you raped her? Would you have to kill her, too? As a *mercy?* Face it, Paul, you sit here talking about how *other* people are to blame, how parents ruin their kids, don't love them enough, whatever. But that makes *you* even worse. Because you know the attention and love a child needs, and you find these supposed lost children in need of love, and what do you give them? Nothing. You *take!* You steal their innocence to fulfill your sick perversions. And then when you can't look at yourself in the mirror anymore, you kill them so they don't remind you of what you are: a lying hypocritical monster who wouldn't know the first thing about real love."

Paul stared at her.

He looked close to exploding.

She needed to give him another kick, something to shove him over the edge.

"You're pathetic. You're not even a man. The best thing your wife ever did was to divorce you before you could ruin Lily. But hey, there's still time. Maybe she can find a real man to raise your daughter. A man who—"

Paul jumped from his seat, gun falling to the ground as he rushed her, hands raised to choke the life from her throat.

Perfect!

Mal raised her feet and kicked Paul square in the jaw.

He fell back screaming

She leaped from the bed as Jessi scurried to a corner of the room.

Mal raced towards Paul, hands still bound behind her. She had to incapacitate Paul, quickly, before he managed to stand or get the gun.

He started to sit up.

Mal's only shot was to kick him in the kneecap.

She raced toward him, then slid, bringing her left foot straight at his knee.

He rolled out of the way, surprisingly fast, then sprang to his feet.

Mal was on the ground, struggling to stand, hands pinned beneath her, pain splintering her right shoulder and both wrists.

Blood streamed from Paul's broken nose as he glared at

Mal, eyes full of hate, rage, and a darkness she'd never seen so close and personal.

Paul screamed as he charged her.

She tried to roll out of the way but was too late.

His hand seized the back of her hair, grabbed it tightly, and yanked Mal to her feet.

Paul pushed her fast toward the closest wall.

She managed to use her left heel to kick down hard on the top of his right foot.

He screamed in surprise but didn't let go of her hair, their momentum rushing them toward the wall.

She turned her head to the side just before it would've smashed her face.

The pain was like lightning striking her skull.

She felt dizzy, sick to her stomach.

She fell to her knees.

Suddenly, a scream.

"Stop it!"

Mal looked up to see Jessi holding Paul's gun.

She was aiming at him with shaking hands. "Let us go!"

Paul raised his hands. "Woah, woah, woah. You know how to use that thing? Miss that shot and you could bring this whole thing down on us."

"He's lying!" Mal shouted. "Shoot him!"

Jessi fired.

Paul fell to the ground screaming.

Eyes wide, Jessi dropped the gun and ran toward Mal.

"Get the gun!" Mal yelled.

The girl turned around, too late.

Paul was already standing. If he'd been shot, Mal couldn't see any blood. More likely Jessi missed, even at that close range, and he faked being shot.

He grabbed the gun, turned it on Jessi, then cocked his arm back and walloped her across the head.

She dropped like a sack to the ground.

Eyes closed.

Not moving.

Mal screamed.

Paul grabbed Mal by the back of the hair again and shoved the gun against her temple. "You fucking cunt! Look what you made me do. I wasn't even going to kill her. I was going to let her live! I was going to let you both live while I escaped through the secret tunnel behind that shelf over there. But *noooo*, you had to go and be a stupid fucking bitch!"

He hit her with the gun across the front of her head.

She struggled to get up, but her head was swimming and stomach lurching. Hot blood streamed into her eyes, burning them, blinding her.

"You fucking cunt!" Paul yelled as he hit her again, and again, and—

Chapter 57 - Jasper Parish

JASPER EASED off the gas and swerved right in his black Mustang, into the middle lane, barely clipping a Beetle as it merged into his path without warning.

A braying honk, then a rough swerve back into the left lane.

He pressed the gas, clawing for speed, hoping they wouldn't attract any cops or Florida Highway Patrol officers on the road.

He hoped they were all too occupied with the hostage scene to notice him driving erratically as they tried to reach the house before Dodd.

Jordyn was riding passenger, dressed in her kill gear, staring out the window, eyes wide and wild, her hands playing drums on the dashboard.

"Come on, come on!"

The difference between getting inside the house before Paul did could mean the difference between life and death.

Jordyn had seen Mallory die.

She'd also seen Jasper arrive too late to save her.

And to date, Jasper had yet to prevent one of Jordyn's visions from happening. He could act on them after the fact, and he could extract revenge for the fallen. He could punish the perpetrators and prevent them from ever hurting another person. But so far Jasper couldn't prevent something once Jordyn saw it happen.

"We were too late," Jordyn had said.

"It hasn't happened yet, so we can still stop it," Jasper had said before grabbing their equipment, getting dressed, and heading out the door.

He looked at the dashboard clock: 1:55 AM.

"They got in there at 2:10 AM?"

"Yes," she said. "I saw it on the grandfather clock in her living room."

"And what time did you see us getting there?"

"Two seventeen."

They were five minutes out. They'd be cutting it *very* close, but it would put them at the house before 2:17. If they could get in before Paul, they could be waiting, and they could stop him.

Jasper was going 65 in a 45, but he didn't have time to waste.

They approached an intersection as the light turned yellow.

Jasper floored it.

Zipped through the intersection as the light turned red.

Suddenly, flashing lights in his rearview.

"Shit!"

Jasper slowed, hoping like hell that the deputy was going somewhere else. But the car behind him decelerated as well.

"Shit."

Jasper pulled to the shoulder, heart pounding.

He thought of the kill gear in the trunk, the duffel with

his break-in equipment, the guns, the knives, the rolls of tape and rope, the tarp, all the other tools of his trade.

Everything was hidden in the spare tire cavity under the trunk's carpeted false bottom. But if the deputy opened the trunk, there was no way he could avoid a thorough search. And Jasper being black only made him appear more suspicious to some deputies.

Jasper grabbed his wallet from the console and set it on the dashboard. Then he lowered his window, placed his hands at ten and two on the steering wheel, and waited. Bright beams bleached his cabin with light, making Jasper feel like any move might get him shot.

Best not to budge.

He looked over at Jordyn.

She stared straight ahead, her own hands on the dash, eyes afraid.

A second patrol car pulled behind the first.

Here we go.

Jasper waited for the deputies to meet and discuss the situation.

Jordyn whispered, "We're going to be too late."

Jasper considered telling the deputies where they were headed, maybe warn them that Mallory was in danger. But that would be pointless. Even if they believed him, they'd be too late, or they'd do something to screw things up. Maybe Paul would see them and never take Mallory to the house. Maybe he'd just drive her into the woods, kill her, and keep on going, gone forever, never held accountable for his crimes.

Jasper was the only obstacle to that happening. He might be late, but maybe he could still get inside the house and save Mallory.

But first, he had to escape a traffic stop.

"Sorry, Dad," Jordyn whispered. "We were out of this,

and I shouldn't have told you about Mallory. We should be home in bed, not out here."

"You did the right thing. We help those who are in danger. No matter what happens, we did right. *You* did the right thing. You got that?"

He wanted to squeeze her hand but didn't dare move from the steering wheel.

The first deputy approached along the driver's side.

The other officer came around on Jordyn's side, flashlights probing his car, then falling on them.

The officer was a tall white man with broad shoulders and a thick brown mustache, mid-thirties or so.

"License and registration, please," he said, his voice deep.

Jasper reached over slowly, grabbed his wallet, then handed it to the deputy, hoping he noticed the small retirement badge from his time on the job in South Florida. He met the deputy's eyes enough to show that he wasn't hiding anything, wasn't nervous, and certainly didn't have a kill bag in his trunk.

The deputy returned to his vehicle with Jasper's license and registration.

The other deputy continued to probe Jasper's car with his flashlight, searching for any reason that a more thorough search or a call to the K-9 unit might be necessary.

Jasper saw the entire night going to hell.

Please, God, let us get through this.

Please.

He stayed with his hands on the wheel, patiently waiting for the deputy. Then finally:

"Do you know why I stopped you?"

"Yes, sir. I was speeding."

"Do you know how fast you were going?"

"Too fast, and I'm sorry."

"Where are you headed at this hour?"

"Couldn't sleep, so I was going to Denny's."

"Denny's?"

Jasper shrugged and offered the officer his most relaxed smile. "Old habits die hard."

The officer smiled back. "You were on the job?"

"Yes, sir. South Florida. Fourteen years. Overnights for half of that, hence my addiction to cheese sticks and terrible coffee."

The deputy laughed, then handed Jasper his wallet. "Alright. Go enjoy your cheese sticks."

Jasper smiled. "Thank you, officer."

The deputies left.

Jasper exhaled.

He found Jordyn's hand and squeezed it. "See, everything's gonna be fine."

Chapter 58 - Paul Dodd

PAUL PACED Mallory's living room, waiting for her to wake up.

She was sitting at the dining room table where he'd left the gift, arms cuffed behind her. He also tied her ankles, to keep the bitch from kicking him in the face again.

Jessi sat across from her, also tied up, but awake.

His nose was black, blue, and aching. It also looked broken. He'd somehow gone all his life without injury to his face, until now.

He was going to make her pay.

He was going to cut her face.

Cut her all over until she begged to die.

But first, he would make her watch what he did to Jessi Price.

He wanted Mal's final moments to be filled with helpless dread, unable to stop what was coming.

Unable to stop what she'd wrought.

He was going to fuck Jessi, then kill her.

Mallory would be forced to watch the whole show.

Then, if he had anything left, he was going to fuck Mallory before finishing her for good.

Then he would flee with his go bag, stuffed with money, fake credentials, and weapons. Wes had set him up with some excellent contacts, able to sneak him out of the country. The world was large, full of black markets willing to indulge his tastes rather than punishing them.

Paul wasn't sure how long they had until the FBI agents and sheriff's deputies realized that he'd escaped the bunker. Maybe they wouldn't know for a while since the hatch door was rigged to blow the place to memory if they tried getting inside.

It would be at least a day, if not more, before they found the tunnel and realized that he'd escaped with Mallory and Jessi.

Eventually, they'd come to her house and find the bodies.

Oh, the scene he was going to make!

Paul had never been one for posing his victims, but this time he wasn't trying to stay under the radar. He wanted to give the authorities something to remember. Give those fuckers on the news something to *really* talk about!

He'd stage the scene so it looked like Mallory was violating Jessi, with something big he figured. Maybe a leg to the chair, unless Mallory had a broom lying around.

He wished he'd had time to go to the store before all of this. He thought it would fit with the holiday to replace Mallory's head with a Jack O'Lantern. Maybe he'd even get a cool name from the media like the Jack O'Lantern Slasher or something.

And to really give the crime scene investigators some-thing for their books, he could scoop the child's entrails out and put them in a Trick-or-Treat bag.

Paul laughed.

Then he remembered something about the house, an even better room to do what he planned to do.

Chapter 59 - Mallory Black

MAL WOKE up in Ashley's bed with a pounding headache, wondering how she'd gotten from the bunker to here. The room was dark, except for the dim blue light bleeding from Ashley's constellation lamp shade on the nightstand.

She started to sit up but then realized that her hands were still bound behind her, legs tied to the wooden footboard.

She squirmed, trying to break free.

"Don't make a sound," said a girl's voice from the floor.

Mal looked down. The girl sat up and came over to her.

Her heart froze as the girl's face came into focus.

No.

It can't be.

"Ashley?"

The girl reached out and touched Mal's face, putting her fingers to her lips. "Shh, he'll hear you."

"Who will hear me?"

The girl's face changed.

331

"Jessi?"

The door burst open, and the ceiling fan lights clicked on, blasting the room in sudden brightness.

Paul stood there, smiling, holding a giant blade.

"I'm so glad you've decided to join us. You're just in time."

Chapter 60 - Jasper Parish

JASPER PARKED three houses down from Mallory's, in front of a wooded lot.

He normally wouldn't park so close to a kill scene, but time was of the essence, and he was already late.

Jordyn got out of the car with him, pulling on her ski mask, slipping the hoodie up to conceal the mask from anyone who might happen to be awake at 2:15 AM and looking out their window or walking their dog.

He started to order Jordyn back, tell her not to come, but she ran out in front of him, out of reach for Jasper to call out to without raising his voice.

They reached the front door.

Jordyn touched it with a gloved hand. "They're in there. Upstairs."

"You should stay down here," he said, already picking the lock and hoping that Paul hadn't armed it.

"I'm not afraid of him. I already saw what happened. You're going to take him out."

"Yeah, but in your vision, we were too late to save Mal.

What if you staying down here changes things enough so that she's still alive?"

Jordyn stared at Jasper, considering what he said. "Okay. I'll stay in the living room."

He opened the door, bracing for an ear-piercing siren.

Silence.

Thank you.

Together they crept inside.

Chapter 61 - Mallory Black

MAL SCREAMED AND SQUIRMED, kicking and thrashing at the footboard as Dodd closed then locked the bedroom door.

"Jessi and I are gonna put on a little show for your viewing pleasure, so I advise you to shut up and stop thrashing."

Mal ignored him, screaming, "Help! Help!"

Paul yanked open Ashley's dresser and found a shirt. One of her favorites. Purple, with a unicorn barfing a rainbow. He ripped it along the bottom, wadded up the torn piece, and crammed it into Mal's mouth.

"I said shut up!" Paul grabbed her jaw and squeezed it tight. His wild eyes, dark despite their placid blue, bored straight into hers.

His nose was broken, dark, blood crusted beneath it.

She kept thrashing, refusing to stop until she managed to break her legs free. There was no way this would end well if she couldn't. She *had* to keep at it.

"Stop moving!" Paul smacked her hard across the face.

She spit the gag out, then spit at him.

Paul wiped the spit from his face, then turned, looked at Jessi, and smacked her so hard that she slumped to the ground.

Mal finally stopped thrashing.

Paul smiled. "Good. I see you get it."

He stuffed the shirt back into her mouth then grabbed a roll of duct tape from his bag on the floor and taped her mouth shut.

Mal resisted, but couldn't stop him.

Paul knelt next to Jessi, rubbed his hand over her back, and in a sickly gentle voice said, "I'm sorry, sweetie. But Miss Mallory made me do it. If she behaves herself, I won't have to do it again."

Mal glared at him.

Her voice garbled by the gag, she said, "I'm going to kill you!"

She wasn't sure if Paul understood, but he smiled just the same.

"Stand up, sweetie."

Jessi stood, crying, unable to look at him.

He walked over to Ashley's closet, opened it, revealing all of her clothes, just as she'd left them on her last day.

"Wow, this is really sad. You've kept everything exactly like it is, haven't you? Like a little museum to your dead daughter. You *do* realize she's never coming back, right?"

Mal glared, screaming, *Fuck you* in her mind.

"I had an idea downstairs. An idea that might bring this whole thing full circle for you, for me, even for little Jessi here. I think you're gonna love it."

He turned to Jessi, "Jessi, I want you to pick out a dress from the closet."

She looked confused.

He grew impatient. "I want you to pick out a dress and put it on."

"Why?"

"Don't ask me why; just fucking do it!"

Jessi swallowed back tears and did as instructed.

She walked to the closet, pulled out a blue dress, one Ashley wore to church on the rare occasions they'd gone. She looked back at Mal as if begging permission.

Paul said, "You like that one? Go ahead, put it on. Mal won't mind. Ashley *certainly* won't."

He laughed.

Mal mumbled through the gag, "What the hell is wrong with you?"

He ignored the question, looking at Jessi. "Go ahead. Put it on."

She reluctantly stripped out of her pink pajamas, then slipped into the dress.

"Oh, so beautiful. Don't you think, Mallory?"

Mal could only stare through tears, swallowing her building rage, trying to control her breath, trying not to lose her mind.

Paul ran his fingers through Jessi's hair. "Now for this next part, I'm going to call you Ashley. Okay, Ashley?"

Jessi looked at Mal.

Mal's face felt like it was going to crack.

Jessi nodded.

Paul said, "Tell me your name."

Jessi's voice, quiet and raspy: "Ashley."

"Okay, now Ashley. I wanna show your Mommy here what I did to you for your birthday. Will you help me show her?"

Jessi's entire body was shaking, tears streaming down her cheeks.

She nodded.

"Good," Paul said, his voice losing octaves. "Now I'd like you to lay on the floor."

He came over to Mal, winking as he reached over her to grab one of Ashley's pillows, then threw it to the ground for Jessi to place under her head.

Mal screamed through the gag, trying to tell Paul that he could take her instead. To *please*, just let the poor girl go.

Paul unbuttoned his pants and let them drop to the ground.

He took off his shirt.

As he threw it on the chair, Mal noticed that his entire back was covered in scars, like cigarette burns. Why hadn't his ex-wife said anything about them? Who did that? Was it Wes? Some other predator?

Or was it his mother?

She tried to scream out and get his attention, make him stop long enough to pull out the gag, so she could ask Paul who had done that to him. Maybe she could open a dialogue and convince him not to hurt Jessi further.

But right now, Dodd was a maniac who couldn't hear reason.

All traces of the pensive man in the bunker who had paused to consider his actions had been replaced by a lunatic looking to hurt the world.

Or at least the people in this room.

He dropped his underwear and turned to Mal, smiling as he stroked himself.

"Pay attention, Mallory. I want you to see exactly how Ashley's last moments felt."

He got on his knees in front of Jessi and reached out to lift her dress.

Mal screamed, thrashing and kicking at the footboard.

Chapter 62 - Jasper Parish

JASPER HEARD MUFFLED screams and the sound of banging upstairs.

Whatever Jordyn had seen Paul do in her vision, the man was doing it now. The time for sneaking quietly through the house was over.

He raced upstairs, gun in hand, following sounds to a bedroom door with vinyl letters that read *Ashley*.

He tried the knob. Locked.

He didn't bother calling out.

He backed up, then threw all of his weight at the door.

It exploded open.

Jasper saw Mallory Black tied to her daughter's bed, still alive.

And Paul Dodd, naked, kneeling in front of Jessi Price, about to rape her.

Jordyn hadn't mentioned seeing Jessi in her vision. Did that mean that things had already changed? That Jasper wasn't too late?

Paul turned around, his eyes wide in shock.

He turned to intercept Jasper, *too late*.

Jasper cocked him upside the head with his gun and sent him sprawling backward.

Jasper looked at Jessi, also wide-eyed, staring up in shock, frozen.

"Run downstairs. Now!"

She scrambled to her feet, then ran.

Paul looked up at Jasper, fists clenched at his side as he got into a squatting position, ready to charge. "Who the fuck are you?"

Jasper raised his gun and took aim. "On your stomach. Now!"

Paul ignored him, leaping toward Jasper.

The gun exploded with an ear-piercing *boom*, but it missed its mark as Paul knocked the weapon from Jasper's hands.

Jasper stumbled back.

Paul dived for the gun.

No, no, no!

He couldn't let Paul get the pistol. Mal was still alive. He could save her, change Jordyn's vision.

Jasper wondered if he'd somehow caused Mal's death. Had Jordyn left that part out when reporting what she saw?

Jasper found his footing.

Paul's fingers closed around the gun.

Jasper stomped his boot hard on Paul's fingers.

He screamed.

Jasper dug his heel in, hard, until Paul let go of the gun.

Jasper punched his already broken nose.

Paul screamed again.

Jasper stared down at the man who had inflicted so much pain on so many. The man who had violated who-knew-how-many young children, and then killed them. A man about to rape and likely murder Jessi Price in front of the restrained mother of one of his other victims, and make her watch the whole thing.

Jasper felt an odd sense of déjà vu, having suffered exactly this rage at least once before, but hell if he could remember it now.

"You sick fuck!" Jasper punched him in the face again.

Then again, and again, and again, until Paul was sprawled on the floor in a bloody mess with Jasper straddling his body.

A scream stopped him.

"Stop, Daddy!"

Jasper turned around to see Jordyn in the doorway.

"What are you doing?"

"Let *her* finish him." She pointed at Mallory.

Jasper looked at Mal, staring at him, her eyes wide and confused.

He looked down at Paul, unconscious but not dead. Certainly not getting up anytime soon.

Jasper grabbed the gun, put it in his waistband, and stood.

Mallory's eyes were dilated in fear as he approached her. Jasper pulled the tape from her mouth, then extracted the gag.

The moment it was out of her mouth, she said, "Thank you."

"You're welcome."

Mallory stared at him, likely trying to figure out who might be under the mask. "You're him, aren't you? My mystery caller."

"Yes."

"Can you get these cuffs off? I think the keys are in his pocket."

He grabbed Paul's pants, reached inside, and searched

for the key. "Can you roll over?" Jasper asked after he found it.

She did, and he unlocked her cuffs.

Then he reached for his belt, got his knife, and sawed at the ropes binding her feet.

Once they were cut, he replaced his blade and backed away from the bed before Mallory could reach him. He kept his gun in hand, ready, though not aimed at her.

There was a look in her eyes, a cop in observation, assessing a threat, and the best way to disarm it.

She didn't know that he was a good guy. Hell, she probably wondered how he knew about her daughter, or where to find her. Maybe she even assumed that he was working with Paul. It made sense. Usually in police work, the most obvious answer, the most direct connection between two unknowns, was the right one.

But this time it wasn't.

And Jasper needed her to know that.

Mallory sat up and massaged her wrists, ringed in bruises from her struggle. "Who are you?"

"Just someone sick of seeing monsters like this hurting innocent people."

"When you called me two years ago, how did you know that Ashley was in danger?"

"You wouldn't believe me if I told you."

"Try me."

Jordyn said, "Don't tell her dad."

"Sorry, I'd love to tell you, but if I do, then I'll only end up hurting someone else. Somebody who's seen enough pain already."

Paul moaned behind them.

Jasper turned around and aimed at his head.

Chapter 63 - Mallory Black

THE MYSTERY MAN looked at Mal. "So, would you like the honors?"

"Honors to do what?"

"To kill him. To stop him from ever hurting another child ever again."

Mystery Man grabbed the knife from his belt and handed it to Mal. A pocket knife with a three-inch blade, legal to carry, but would do the job in killing a man.

She held it tightly in her hand, uncertain who she would need to use it on.

Mal stared at Paul, his face broken and bloodied. He no longer looked like the menacing man who only moments ago was planning to rape and kill a child in front of her. Now he looked like a sad, broken animal. Helpless.

She did not pity him, and a part of her did want him dead. A *big* part of her. She had practiced regularly at the gun range for just this moment, him breaking into her house, and her justifiably shooting him.

But the Mystery Man had changed all of that by breaking in and beating Paul to a pulp. Shooting him was no longer about her defending herself. Killing Dodd now would be murder.

She might have been a lot of bad things, but she wasn't a murderer.

"I'm not going to kill him. Let me call the sheriff's department. They'll do it right."

Mystery Man laughed. "Yeah, *right.*"

"What?"

"They're gonna have a lengthy trial that'll cost the taxpayers millions, and it'll drag out for years. And then, if he's not found insane, and let's face it, he's pretty insane, he'll get the death penalty. But even that won't happen for another few years, and only after more money is wasted on appeals. And then the media will be hounding the families of his victims; they'll be hounding you, they'll be hounding Jessi Price and her family. It's a big fucking circus, Mallory. I don't like circuses."

Mystery Man aimed the gun at Paul and looked down at him.

Paul looked up groggy, moaning something that Mal couldn't make out.

Mallory said, "Why let him off easy? You kill him, and he never has a chance to sit in jail and pay for what he did. You said yourself that the process would take years, right? So let him sit in prison for years until he's executed."

Mystery Man looked at Mallory. "He hurt you. He raped and killed your daughter. He was about to do it again, right in front of you. Don't you *want* him to pay? Don't you *want* vengeance? I asked you before if you could go back in time and kill him to prevent him from hurting Ashley, would you? And what did you say?"

"Yes."

"And while you can't go back in time, you *can* prevent

344

him from ever hurting another child. From killing the *next* Ashley. Don't you want that?"

"It's not about what I *want*. I'm not above the law, and neither are you. The sheriff's office will arrest Dodd and put him away. Believe me; he won't *ever* hurt anyone ever again."

Mal had a new theory on who this man was. He wasn't a lawyer. He wasn't someone in Paul or Wes's inner circle who stumbled on their crimes.

For him this was personal.

Had Paul killed his child or someone close to him?

She wanted to ask, but at the same time, he held the gun and all the power. She didn't want to piss him off and have him shoot her just to safeguard his identity.

She had to play this cool if she wanted to get out of it alive.

She thought of Jessi Price downstairs, alone. Had she run out of the house? Was she banging on a neighbor's door begging them to call 9-1-1?

Or was she waiting to see who came downstairs?

Mystery Man grabbed Paul by the back of the head and sat him up against Ashley's dresser. "Tell her what you did to her daughter, *Odd Dodd.*"

Paul's eyes widened in response to that name, as much as they could in their swollen condition. "Fuck you," he said through gritted teeth.

Mystery Man knelt down, reached under Paul's neck, and squeezed. "Tell her or I choke you to death right here."

"I don't want to hear it," Mal said, standing, but not approaching.

Mystery Man looked up at her, his dark eyes wet as if he was on the verge of tears. "You *need* to hear."

He choked Paul harder. "Tell her."

Then Paul told her everything.

Her rage returned as the coward confessed his sins.

His swagger as he recounted what he'd done was replaced by something worse — detachment, as if someone else had done these terrible things. As if *he* wasn't responsible.

Mal was in tears when he finished.

Mystery Man stood there, masked face turned downward, gun aimed at the back of his skull.

"Why?" Mal asked. "Why did you do it? And not that bullshit answer from the bunker about saving kids from their horrible mothers. Why did you do it?"

Paul looked up at her with his lifeless eyes. "Because I loved them."

"You did not *love* my daughter." She took a step toward him.

Mystery Man held his distance, falling back toward the open door.

"Yes, I did love her," Paul said, staring at Mal matter-of-factly. He wasn't smiling or mocking her as he had before. Still, it only made her angrier. "And she learned to love me."

Without a thought, Mal ran to Paul, dropped down, and put the blade to his throat. She leaned in close, her nose just inches from his own broken and bloody one, her eyes boring right into his.

"She did *not* love you."

"Yes," he said, the slightest hint of a smile pulling at the corners of his mouth, "she did. And do you want to know what she said to me right before she died?"

Mal swallowed, tears burning her cheeks.

"What?"

He reached up, putting his hand on her hand with the blade.

He didn't have enough strength to get the knife from Mal. Even if he was faking weakness, there was no way she'd let it go.

But he wasn't trying to get it. He was trying to pull the blade down, toward his stomach.

She let him.

"Stick the knife in, and I'll tell you what she said."

"Do it," Mystery Man urged behind her.

Mal stared into the monster's eyes.

"Just tell me," she said, pain choking her words.

"Do it, and I'll tell you what Ashley wanted you to know."

She stood. She had to, or she would've obliged him right there.

"Do it," Mystery Man said. "Don't you want to know?"

"He's lying. He wants me to kill him, so he won't go to prison."

"Who cares?"

"I'm not lying," Paul said. "Ashley told me lots of things. She told me about how she used to have to stay after school when you were working, and how she had no friends, so she'd always read books from the library. She told me how when you quit your job you were home, but you weren't really home. She was still reading books while you did ... *whatever* it was you did when you were ignoring her. She told me about Pinky Bear."

"Shut up!"

"Or what? You *won't* kill me?" Paul laughed, then coughed blood.

Mystery Man looked at Mal. "If you don't kill him, I will. There's no way I'm letting him walk out of here."

Chapter 64 - Jasper Parish

Jasper stared at Mallory, awaiting her decision. She was still trying to balance being a cop versus being a mother and wanting to end the bastard who murdered her child.

Mallory raised the knife toward him. "I'm not letting you kill him."

Jasper stared at her. "Are you serious? You're going to threaten me to keep this piece of shit alive?"

"I'm saving you from yourself."

"What?"

"I know you believe he deserves to die, but think about what that does to you, or to me. Killing a defenseless person. You can't come back from that. Are you prepared to live with that the rest of your life?"

"Who says I haven't already killed a defenseless person?"

Something flashed across her face. "Did you kill Wes?"

Jordyn stood beside Jasper, and whispered, "Don't tell her. She'll use it to come after us."

He turned to his daughter. "Shh, I've got this."

"Come on, let's just go," Jordyn pled. "Let her have him."

"No, we're not letting him leave here. He has to pay for what he did."

"It's not worth it, Dad."

Jasper froze.

Shit. She called me Dad. That's only going to help them figure out who we are.

He didn't want to have to kill Paul *and* Mallory. But he would do anything, would kill anyone, to keep Jordyn out of jail.

He turned back to Mallory and Paul to see if they'd picked up on her slip. Mallory was looking oddly at Jasper, her brow furrowed.

So was Paul. "Who the hell are you talking to, man?"

"Who she is, who *we* are, is none of *your* business."

"I'm not asking *who* she is. I'm asking who the fuck you're talking to?"

Jasper looked at Mallory, still eyeing him with the oddest expression.

"What?"

Mallory asked, "Who are you talking to?"

"Come on, stop screwing around. Are you going to kill him, or am I?"

Mallory continued to stare, the way you stared at someone who was helpless but didn't know it. Like you stared at an Alzheimer's patient who wandered into another person's home.

"Are you saying you don't see her?" Jasper pointed to Jordyn.

Mallory shook her head.

Why were they acting like they couldn't see her?

"Come on, Dad, they're just messing with you. Let's go."

Jasper stared at Mallory. He couldn't believe that she would be playing games like this. "You *really* don't see anyone here?"

Again, she shook her head.

Paul laughed. "I think you might be even crazier than me!"

Jasper raised his weapon and shot Paul in the chest; then he turned the gun on Mallory. "Tell me the truth. Do you see anyone behind me?"

Mallory stared at him, her arms raised, pleading, "Please, don't shoot."

The gun shook in his hand. "Do you see anyone behind me?"

"Yes. Yes, I see a woman behind you."

He sighed with relief, but couldn't shake why both Paul and Mallory had lied. He could understand Paul messing with him, but not Mallory. Unless she was pretending not to see her, to prove that she hadn't heard her slip up and call Jasper "Dad." Maybe this was her way of squeaking out of this, knowing he might hurt her to keep Jordyn's secret.

But something felt *off*.

And he had that same strange sense of déjà vu from before, when he'd been pounding Paul to dough.

He looked down at Dodd, blood pooling around him, eyes half-open.

"Come on," Jordyn said. "Let's go."

Chapter 65 - Mallory Black

MAL STARED at the Mystery Man, trying to think of a way to keep him there a little longer while Paul Dodd bled out beneath her. She didn't dare try to save him, especially when Mystery Man seemed to want him dead even more than she had.

Sirens wailed in the distance.

Deputies were on the way, maybe even the FBI.

She wasn't sure if someone had figured out where she was, or if Jessi had fled the house and begged someone to call the cops.

If Mystery Man noticed the sirens, he didn't seem in a hurry to flee.

Maybe he didn't realize that she was going to tell the deputies to arrest him, that he'd shot Paul and murdered Wes.

Yes, he'd saved her life, but there was something wrong with him. He'd butchered a man and shoved his genitals into his mouth. That kind of person shouldn't be out on the streets. Plus, he was also seeing a person who wasn't there.

Mal had agreed to seeing a woman, but only because she was afraid that he'd snap — or break further — if she denied what he so clearly believed.

"You did it," she said. "You killed him. You've had your revenge."

He stared at her confused, then down at his gun.

Something was happening behind his eyes. Some realization that was confusing him.

He looked back at Mallory, then aimed the gun at her.

"Do you really see someone behind me?"

Chapter 70 - Jasper Parish

MALLORY'S EYES were brimming with tears as she met his. "Who do *you* see?"

"My daughter."

"What's your daughter's name?"

"Don't tell her, Dad. She's trying to trick you."

"Her name is Jordyn."

He continued staring down the barrel at Mallory. It shook in his hands.

"Dad," Jordyn called out, grabbing his arm, "come on. We need to go!"

Jasper ignored her.

All he could do was stare into Mallory's eyes. Again: "Do you see her?"

Mallory shook her head.

"Dad!" Jordyn shouted beside him. "Don't listen to her. She's trying to trick you."

Jordyn grabbed him by the arm, tight.

How could an apparition do that?

It couldn't.

Mallory had to be lying.

Then he realized the truth, as the approaching sirens cut through his mental cloud. "You're just trying to trick me, to keep me here so they'll arrest me."

"I'm not trying to trick you. But yes, you should stay. I can get you help."

"I don't need your help."

He started to back toward the doorway. "We're going now. Please don't make me regret saving you, saving Jessi."

Mallory called out, "Please, don't go."

He backed out of the door, then turned, and headed down the stairs.

Jessi Price was gone.

The sirens were getting closer.

He ran out the back door, clambered over a fence, charged through the neighbor's yard, and kept going, vaulting, racing as fast as he could with Jordyn by his side.

He found the car and hopped in.

Jordyn took shotgun.

He floored the gas and tore away, tires squealing.

Friday Oct. 20

Chapter 71 - Mallory Black

MAL SAT at a long table in the Creek County Sheriff's press room, with Gloria, Mike, SAIC McDaniels, Sheriff Johnson, and Public Information Officer Felicia Day as the press conference started. They'd all been up all night and were running on fumes, but they needed to let the public know that Jessi Price was safe and that Paul Dodd was in custody.

McDaniels led, thanking both sheriff's departments, the men and women of the FBI, and everyone else who helped bring Jessi Price home to her mother early this morning. He also said Jessi's father was believed to be dead, though they'd yet to find his body. He requested that the press respect the Price family as they try to heal.

He then updated the press on the broad strokes of what had happened, leaving out parts that the public didn't need to know, like how Mallory forced her way into the bunker, bypassing the FBI's crisis negotiator. He mentioned another person wanted in connection with the events, describing him as a black man in his mid to late thirties wearing a ski mask, as if that would help anyone identify him. Mike would probably circle back to Paul's ex-wife soon, get her with a sketch artist to better describe the Mystery Man vigilante.

McDaniels updated the reporters on Paul Dodd — in critical but stable condition at Creek County Memorial. Assuming he made it through, Dodd would stand trial for his crimes, including the abduction, rape, and murder of Ashley Black two years ago.

McDaniels handed it over to Gloria, who also thanked everyone involved before turning to Mal. "I'd also like to thank former homicide detective Mallory Black for helping to bring Paul Dodd to justice. Her bravery and determination have gone a long way toward returning Jessi Price to her mother."

Cameras clicked, and flashes went off as reporters snapped away.

After Gloria opened up for questions, several reporters shouted questions over each other. She pointed at one, "Alice."

"Do we know yet if there were any other victims?" Asked a woman in the front row. "Do we know if he'd done anything to any of his students?"

"We can't discuss that at the moment as this is an ongoing investigation. However, if anybody has any information about Paul Dodd, they can call our tip line."

Another reporter shouted, "How did you escape?"

Mal answered, "It's not something we can go into right now. I'm just glad to be alive, and that we could get Jessi back to her family."

Another reporter: "How does it feel to put away the man who killed your daughter?"

"I'm just glad that he can't hurt anyone else."

Reporters kept shouting, all seeking more answers than

anyone at the table were presently prepared to offer, deferring most with the words "ongoing investigation."

Following the conference, McDaniels, Gloria, and the rest of them headed into the bowels of the Sheriff's department, where McDaniels pulled Gloria, Mike and Mal into a room he'd been using as his base of operations. There she spent the next several hours being interviewed by McDaniels and Gloria, despite her being on empty.

McDaniels thanked Mal one final time, then left her, Gloria, and Mike alone in Gloria's office.

Gloria sat at her desk. "Have a seat, you two."

Mike and Mal sat opposite the sheriff.

"I want to thank you for sticking with this."

"I'm just glad that Paul Dodd will be behind bars."

"We haven't always seen eye to eye, but I've always respected you, Mal. Even when I hated you."

Mal laughed. "The feeling's mutual, boss."

Mal hadn't meant to call her boss, but old habits were stubborn bitches.

"Speaking of boss," Gloria said, reaching down into her desk drawer, then coming back up with a badge in its case. She slid it across the desk to Mal.

"I know you don't need the money. But you need to work. This is in your blood, just like it's in mine, and in Mike's. We'd love to have you back."

After a year and a half away from the job, after everything that had happened in the past few days, after thinking she would die at the hands of the monster who murdered her daughter, everything was swelling inside her.

"I don't know what to say."

Mike put a hand on her back. "Say yes."

"But," she said through tears, "you've got Skippy."

Mike laughed. "Fuck Skippy. I want Mad Dog Mal."

Mal finally broke down. But for the first time in two

years, her tears weren't born from misery. "Yes. I'd love to come back."

Gloria stood, then came around the desk and hugged Mal.

For the first time in a long while, Mal was right where she belonged.

~

AS MIKE DROVE MAL HOME, she couldn't stop thinking about swallowing a couple of pills, crawling into bed, and sleeping for at least a day, if not two.

Her head was pounding again. She was on edge, like she got after going too long without relief.

"You alright?"

"Yeah," she said. "Just ready for a nap."

"Yeah, get your naps in while you can. Man, I still can't believe you're coming back. You know when?"

Mal was starting to wonder why the hell she'd agreed to return. She needed to kick the pills before going back to work, and she wasn't sure how.

"No, she told me to let her know when I'm ready, without waiting too long. So, I don't know. Maybe next month. How long will you need to let Skippy down gently?"

"You didn't hear? Bell is putting him with you."

"Fuck you, Mike. That's not even funny."

He laughed.

Mal looked down at her phone, seeing texts from several reporters, including Presley. She wasn't anywhere near ready for the media spotlight — reporters wanting to ask how it felt to finally find the man who murdered her daughter, wanting to know all about Jessi Price, and whatever other sordid details they might be able to mine from her.

It would be a ratings coup if they could get her crying on-camera. Mal sympathized with Jessi's mother, and for Paul's ex-wife. They were about to feel the heat.

Their lives were ruined.

But at least they had their little girls.

Mal would trade it all — the media attention, the whispers from neighbors, and the dirty looks from the holier-than-thou who thought she somehow invited this monster into her life — to have her Ashley back.

She began deleting messages from all but a few of her more trusted reporter contacts. She'd talk to them when she was ready, if only to keep from burning bridges she might need once back on the job.

Mal was in the middle of texting Presley when Mike said, "Oh, boy, here we go."

He was pulling onto her street — three different news vans were camped outside.

He stopped at the end of the block. "You ready for this?"

Her heart was racing, her chest tightening.

"No. Turn around."

He did. "So, where to? Wanna crash at my place?"

"Thank you, but no. Just take me to the Hilton."

"You sure? We've got room."

"No, I'm gonna be with you all the time, I need to ease into it, slowly," she joked.

But Mal wouldn't have her pills if she went to the hotel. She'd lost them when taking her clothes off before entering Dodd's bunker. And it wasn't like she was going to ask if anyone had seen them. They were a prescription pill, but cops weren't stupid. Someone would figure out she was an addict and her return to the force would be cut unceremoniously short.

Gloria knew that Mal was a drunk, but hell, plenty of deputies were, and they managed fine. But an addiction to pills was a lot harder to be lenient with.

Mike drove her to the Hilton and pulled up front. "You need anything, let me know."

"Thanks." Mal opened her door.

"Oh, one more thing." He reached into his shirt pocket and fished out her bottle of lost pills.

He met her eyes. Mal looked away as she took them.

"Thank you," she said, eager to flee his car.

"Are these going to be a problem?"

She finally met his gaze. "No. I just take them when the migraines get bad."

"You know I've got your back, right? That you can tell me anything?"

"Yeah, I know, Mike."

"Okay, go get yourself some rest."

"Thanks," she said, and got out of the car.

MAL LAY UNDER THE COVERS, in her underwear, curtains drawn in a room that was dark, cold, and perfect for sleeping. But she couldn't let go. She was clutching the bottle of pills, trying like hell not to take one, working to ignore their siren song:

Come on; we'll help you sleep.

Just one.

You deserve it. You helped save Jessi Price.

One before bed doesn't make you an addict.

That's it. Just one.

We'll taper off tomorrow. Maybe half of one tomorrow.

But for today, one won't hurt.

She squeezed the bottle so tight it might have popped the lid if it didn't have a child-proof cap.

Just one, Mal. Come on.

One won't hurt.

One will get rid of the headache.

One will make you drift off. Nice and easy.

Just. One.

She hurled the bottle across the room, into the darkness.

She sat up, her heart racing, her chest constricted.

She had to do something, *but what?*

She could go down to the bar and get drunk, but she didn't have the energy to get dressed. Nor did she have a change of clothes. The last thing she needed was to go downstairs and get recognized with some other drunk asshole wanting to ask her about Jessi Price. Being the mother of a child killed in a high profile case was like being an unfortunate celebrity.

She *could* hire a bodyguard, but that would probably make things worse, especially now that she was going back on the job.

Mal needed to do something to move her mind from the pills.

She reached for her phone and checked her messages again.

There were several from Ray. She'd called him before going into the bunker — probably scared the hell out of him with the way she was talking.

She pressed play and listened. The first few were frantic, begging Mal not to put herself in danger. One even sounded like he was crying.

So helpless and afraid for her.

Then came today's messages. Ray sounded better, happier, more himself.

"Hi, Mal. Just wanted to see how you're doing. Saw that you got Jessi back. Congratulations. Please call me when you get this."

"Hey, Mal. Went by your house just to see if you needed anything. Saw a bunch of news vans and stuff. Let me know if you need anything, or even a place to stay."

She laughed. *What, you're going to let me stay with you and Julie? Yeah, that won't be awkward!*

Mal looked at the time and figured he was probably at work, maybe at lunch.

She wasn't sure if it was a good time to call. The conversation would surely head into serious waters. He'd want to ask questions about the man who murdered their daughter. He'd probably want to know exactly what Paul Dodd had done. It wasn't the kind of conversation you had with someone at work.

But she needed to talk to someone, and sadly had no one else. Her friends had all drifted away after Ashley's murder. Or, if she were honest, she pushed them away. In any event, the only people she had in her life any more were her partner and Ray. And if she didn't talk to one of them now, she would be giving in to the pills.

She called.

After three rings he answered. "Mal?"

"Yep," she said, awkwardly, not knowing what to say next. Sure, she wanted to talk, but after being estranged for so long, it's hard to get the conversation rolling in a way that isn't too self-conscious.

"How are you?" he asked.

"Were you serious about your offer?"

"Which one?"

Come on, don't make me say it.

"About going to the … meetings?" she whispered the last word.

"Yes."

"What are you doing now?" she asked.

"At lunch."

"I'm staying at the Hilton. Could you come over, just to talk?"

"Anything you need," he said.

"Good, because right now I need a friend."

Epilogue

ONE YEAR AGO...

JASPER WATCHED the interview with former detective Mallory Black, feeling like someone had ripped out his heart. Jordyn sat beside him on the couch, cross-legged, clutching a pillow, her eyes rimmed with tears.

The interview was part of a package which included a segment updating the audience on all the awful things that had happened to Ashley Black one year ago. The female reporter listed atrocities as the screen showed photos of the little girl during happier times, pictures with her parents, a video of her ninth birthday. Kids sang "Happy Birthday" in the background while the reporter said, "But she'd never see her tenth birthday."

The screen cut to blurred pics taken in a drainage ditch where they'd found Ashley's body, mangled and nude.

Then the reporter spent ten minutes asking Mallory about that day, what she felt after first realizing that Ashley was missing, how she felt after getting the call that her daughter's body had been found.

The reporter was obviously trying to get Mallory to cry on camera.

But to her credit, she'd thus far managed to keep her composure.

The reporter asked why Mallory left her job, but she deftly dodged the question, not assigning blame, and saying it was a mutual decision.

But Jasper could read between the lines. She'd been forced out. He'd heard rumors that she'd screwed something up a few months ago, something big. But he didn't know what. The same rumors said that Mallory was finally cracking under the stress of her crumbling life.

"If there was anything you could say to the person who killed your daughter, what would that be?"

Mallory looked at the camera, her eyes welling with tears, "I don't know. I think I'd ask why? Why would you take such a sweet girl who never hurt anyone? *Why* would you do this to her?"

The reporter tried another question, but Mallory stood and pulled the mic from her collar. "I can't do this anymore."

And the interview was over.

Jordyn wiped her eyes with her shirt sleeve. "That poor lady."

"We could've stopped all of this," Jasper said.

"What do you mean? You called her. You tried to warn her. She must not have gotten the message."

He didn't want to tell her what he meant because that would mean telling Jordyn what he did at night to the bad people she told him about. Nor did he want her to feel bad that the only reason he couldn't kill Ashley's murderer was that she didn't have a name for the man.

Jordyn seemed to pick up on his thought. "You wish we knew who the killer was?"

He nodded, meeting her eyes, to make sure she wasn't taking it the wrong way.

She didn't seem to be. Her eyes were still wet from the interview, but she wasn't freaking out or getting defensive.

Jasper said, "Sometimes I wish your gift helped out more."

"You're thinking about mom again, aren't you?"

He nodded, wiping his own eyes. "It just seems unfair. Someone or something wants you, wants *us* to know things ahead of time. So why not give us more to work with? Why not tell us Carissa had cancer?"

Jordyn scooted over and hugged her father as he fought his tears.

He hugged her tightly, and she cried into his shoulder.

Jordyn then pulled away, her eyes wide. "Maybe we can't go back in time to save the girl, but we can save her mother."

"What do you mean?"

"Well, you said we couldn't ever do this ourselves, as it would put the spotlight on us, but you never said we couldn't do it for someone else."

"What?"

She told him.

A brilliant, stupid idea.

Given Jordyn's nerves in doing anything that might out them, he was surprised she suggested it.

JASPER SAT in the bushes across the street, staring at the darkened home's front yard.

Not a single light was on. Nor was there a car in the driveway.

"Is she here?" he whispered to Jordyn.

"I think she's sleeping."

"And you're sure on the alarm code?"

"Yes. I saw it in a dream months ago."

"And you're just now telling me?"

"Well, I didn't think you planned on breaking into her house."

"Fair point."

He checked the street; nobody around.

He pulled the mask over his face, stood, then made his way across the street to the front door. Picking the lock was simple.

He went to the alarm panel and punched in Jordyn's code.

As he walked around Mallory's living room, he could almost hear ghosts haunting the halls. In the dim night lights, he could make out framed photos of the family, taken when things were good. Mom, Dad, Ashley. There was a child-sized jacket hanging on a hook in the foyer, a fridge still plastered with primitive art, two settings at the small kitchen table in the back, one with a tiny plate and cup. The house was frozen at the moment before a monster would ruin it all.

He scanned the kitchen counter searching for what Jordyn had said he'd find — Mallory's purse.

He opened it, searching for a very specific item. Fortunately, her purse was neat and orderly.

Jasper found the lottery ticket with relative ease.

She always bought her tickets at the same gas station a mile from home. And she always played the same numbers, her daughter's birthdate along with hers and a few other favorites. Sometimes she would play a random number in addition to her own set.

Jasper replaced Malory's ticket with one he'd bought at the same gas station.

It had her numbers, and another set — the one Jordyn said would win Saturday's drawing.

He closed the purse, then made his way out of the haunted house.

No amount of money could ever bring Mallory's daughter back, but it might buy her some freedom. She'd no longer have to work. Maybe she would sell her house and start over somewhere new.

Jasper knew a thing or two about starting over.

You couldn't ever completely escape your past, but you could give it some distance. Find things to distract yourself. Bury yourself in new obsessions. And, sometimes, even forget for a while.

But at night, when you were all alone, the ghosts always came back to remind you.

THE END

The Story Continues

Love *No Justice* and want to read the next book in the No Justice series? Click the link below to follow Mallory and Jasper through their next adventure.

GET NO ESCAPE TODAY

A quick favor...

If you liked *No Justice*, then *would you kindly* * consider taking a few minutes to leave a review on your favorite bookselling site. If you're a book blogger, we'd love any mentions on your blog or YouTube channel, also. Every bit of word-of-mouth helps to introduce us to new readers.

As always, thank you for reading,
    David Wright (and Nolon King)

(* *Bonus points if you got the* Bioshock *reference.*)

Acknowledgments

Thank you first to my brother-in-law, Steve [REDACTED], a former homicide detective and now a private investigator who has always helped me with the murder/death/and kidnapping-related questions I just don't want in my Google search history. Seriously, most of our conversations begin with me asking some outrageously bizarre thing, and him responding with, "Dude, what is WRONG with you?"

Steve was also an immense help in understanding how a police officer would still be motivated to catch a vigilante, EVEN if the vigilante was only going after monsters who were really, *really* guilty!

It would have been all too easy for me to have Mal and Jasper team up, which completely undermines the things that motivate Mal as a detective. Knowing WHY she would still pursue Jasper as a criminal helped us create an even more complex character in Mal going forth. A character that we've come to love.

So, thank you, Steve, for your countless hours of helping me get police and criminal things as realistic as possible. And I promise I will only use these skills for writing, not going on my own one-man vigilante spree.

Thank you also to Detective Adam Richardson, of http://www.writersdetective.com/ for taking the time to answer questions early on in *No Justice's* development process.

Thanks also to our readers who have been patient with us as we went full-on hermit mode and wrote the first three books in this series. We appreciate your patience, and we hope that *No Justice* made the wait worthwhile.

Lastly, thank you to our wives for their incredible patience and giving us the time and space necessary to dream these worlds into being. We love you.

About the Authors

Nolon King writes fast-paced psychological thrillers set in the glitzy world of entertainment's power players with a bold, insightful voice. He's not afraid to explore the darker side of human nature through stories featuring families torn apart by secrets and lies.

Nolon loves to write about big questions and moral quandaries. How far would you go to cover up an honest mistake? Would you destroy your career to protect your family? How much of your soul would you sell to get the life of your dreams? Would you cheat on your husband to keep your children safe? Would you give in to a stalker's demands to save your marriage?

David W. Wright is the co-author of edge-of-your seat thrillers including the best-selling post-apocalyptic series *Yesterday's Gone*, the paranoid sci-fi *WhiteSpace* series, and the vigilante series, *No Justice*, as well as standalone thrillers *12*, and *Crash* which was recently optioned for a movie.

David is an accomplished, though intermittent, cartoonist who lives in [LOCATION REDACTED] with his wife and son [NAMES REDACTED.]

He is not at all paranoid.

He is "the grumpy one" on the *The Story Studio Podcast* with fellow Sterling and Stone founders, Sean Platt and Johnny B. Truant.

You can email him at <u>david@sterlingandstone.net</u>

We swear, he almost never bites. Unless you feed him after midnight.

Also By Nolon King

Hidden Justice

Hidden Justice

Hidden Honor

Hidden Shame

Hidden Virtue

No Justice

No Justice

No Escape

No Hope

No Return

No Stopping

No Fear

Once Upon A Crime

Once Upon A Crime

Twice Upon A Lie

Three Times a Murder

Dead For Good

Dead For Good

Left For Dead

Dead Of Night

Wake The Dead

Dead For Life

Stand Alone Novels

Pretty Killer

12

Blown

Miserable Lies

The Target

Secrets We Keep

Close To Home

Heat To Obsession

A Simple Kill

Tell Me No Lies

Red Carpet Black

Fade To Black

Victim

Also By David W. Wright

Yesterday's Gone Season One

Yesterday's Gone Season Two

Yesterday's Gone Season Three

Yesterday's Gone Season Four

Yesterday's Gone Season Five

Yesterday's Gone Season Six

Tomorrow's Gone

Tomorrow's Gone Season One

Tomorrow's Gone Season Two

Tomorrow's Gone Season Three

Available Darkness

Darkness Itself

Available Darkness Book One

Available Darkness Book Two

Available Darkness Book Three

WhiteSpace

WhiteSpace Season One

WhiteSpace Season Two

WhiteSpace Season Three

Stand Alone Novels

12

Crash

Emily's List

Threshold